
FOREVER THEIRS

KATEE ROBERT

D1595772

Also by Katee Robert

The Hunting Grounds

The Surviving Girls

The Hot in Hollywood series

Ties that Bind

Animal Attraction

The Foolproof Love Series

A Foolproof Love

Fool Me Once

A Fool for You

Out of Uniform Series:

In Bed with Mr. Wrong

His to Keep

Falling for His Best Friend

His Lover to Protect

His to Take

Serve Series:

Mistaken by Fate

Betting on Fate

Protecting Fate

Come Undone Series:

Wrong Bed, Right Guy

Chasing Mrs. Right

Two Wrongs, One Right

Seducing Mr. Right

To Andie -
Thank you for geeking out just as hard about Galen, Theo, and Meg
as I did!

Chapter 1

"Meg, someone puked in the bathroom."

Meg Sanders closed her eyes and counted to ten very, very slowly. It didn't change Jonah's words—or their implication. By the time she turned to face him, she had her expression under control. Mostly. "You're telling me…"

"I'm clocking off." He held up his timesheet. "My shift ended thirty minutes ago and I'm about to go into overtime."

If she let that happen, cleaning up someone else's puke would be the least of Meg's worries. "Okay, go ahead." Their boss had a notorious temper when it came to overtime, and they'd all learned to avoid going over the allotted hours whenever possible. Jonah was a decent dude, and she didn't want to drop that hammer on him. "I'll take care of it." Last call had already been sounded and the lights were all up. If the last four people didn't file out soon on their own, she'd call them cabs and kick them to the curb.

Thankfully, it didn't come to that. Jonah clocked out, and she must have looked as miserable as she felt because

1

he herded the patrons out and waited for her to lock the door before he headed for his car.

Yeah, Jonah was a good dude.

He'd even blushed a little when he'd asked her out a few weeks ago, and took it well when she turned him down. She might have cited her insane work schedule that would only get more insane once school restarted in the fall, but the truth was far more pathetic.

How could anyone compare after she'd been with a prince and his bodyguard?

What was supposed to be a single night straight out of her dirtiest fantasies turned into the standard she was in danger of comparing every future relationship to. Not that she could call being picked up at a club on her twenty-third birthday and going home with two guys for the sexiest night of her life a relationship. It wasn't. The amazing sex was just that—sex.

Even if she was starting to suspect it had ruined her for life.

No use thinking about it now.

They left. They never called.

You're the one who snuck out without saying goodbye. They probably took a hint.

Meg laughed softly at the absurdity of her spiraling thoughts. She found the mop bucket and hauled it to the sink and squirted some soap into the swirling water. Easier to focus on her hurt pride than the money stress she couldn't quite escape. The deadline to pay her fall tuition was this week and she hadn't quite come to terms with the fact after all the hours and tips and even a second job she was still short.

Seriously short.

Short to the tune of two thousand dollars.

Not that much money in the grand scheme of things, but it might as well have been on the moon for all Meg could access it. She'd gone so far as to fill out a couple credit card applications, but they sat unsent on her desk at home. They were just a temporary fix. Fall tuition would turn into spring tuition, and even if she could scrape together the money this time, she wouldn't be able to do it next time. Better to just bow out gracefully now and leave her degree unfinished.

But she hadn't filled out *that* form, either.

She was stuck in place, unable to move forward or go back. If she dropped out, she was no better than what her mother had always called her: a fuck-up destined to retread the footsteps of her family for as long as living memory. Poverty. A marriage or four. Crippling debt that she'd never be able to climb out from beneath. A job that slowly sucked every bit of joy out of her life.

She couldn't do it.

She couldn't go back to that small town and that dingy trailer and face the family she'd given the middle finger to when she turned eighteen and graduated with honors. Meg had worked too damn hard to put herself in a position to make something of her life.

Look at her now.

Cleaning up someone else's puke.

She wheeled the bucket down the dim hallway to the pair of bathrooms situated near the back door. The bar could stand in for countless bars across the country. The lights a little too low, the floors a little too sticky, the alcohol a little too cheap. But it was what passed for her second home. She loved most of the people she worked with, and if her boss was kind of a dick, well, that went with the territory.

3

Meg took a slow, deep breath and pushed open the first door. The smell of vomit sent her reeling back a step, but she mastered her response. *Just get it over with and you can go home.* Home, to her tiny apartment filled with secondhand furniture. It wasn't much to look at, but it was *hers* and she loved it. There was only this filthy bathroom between her and her lumpy bed and damned if she'd let the stench permeating the air beat her.

She got to work.

It was, in short, awful.

Jonah hadn't caught the mess in time and part of it had dried. When the door swung open behind her, Meg was cursing up a storm and scrubbing with the mop at what looked like melted cotton candy and corn. *Never eating either of those things again.* She didn't even realize she was no longer alone until a masculine chuckle rolled through the bathroom.

She jumped and swung the mop around, nearly braining... Meg froze. This was it. She'd finally lost what was left of her mind, because transitioning into an exhaustion-fueled hallucination was the only explanation for *him* being *here*. She blinked and blinked again. He didn't disappear. "Theo?"

Theodore Fitzcharles III, former Crown Prince of Thalania, propped the door open with a leather shoe that was no doubt designer and gave her a pained grin. "Hey, princess."

She looked from him to the half-cleaned vomit to the mop in her hand. For one second, Meg seriously considered whacking him with it just to rumple him a little. Even when he had her pinned to a couch and was fucking her within an inch of her life, Theo never ceased to look perfectly put together. The man was downright pretty, though he was too masculine for that adjective. His face was all sharp angles and full lips and blue eyes that held stories she could only guess at. Tonight, he wore a plain white T-shirt that looked like it might have been ironed at some point, and a pair of jeans that probably cost more than Meg's monthly rent. She couldn't even hold it against him, because it was so purely *Theo*.

No, she couldn't hold that against him.

But she *could* hold the fact that he'd been MIA for *three fucking months* against him.

She considered the mop in her hands again, but ultimately decided going after him with it would just prove how angry she was. Meg dunked it into the dirty water and went back to cleaning. "Didn't expect to see you again."

"Do you normally leave your number when you don't expect to see someone again?"

He had her there, but she'd never admit it. She'd left her number when she still thought the night had passed with two strangers whose only real sin was being so rich it blew her mind. It was only when she snuck down the hall that she'd learned the truth. Theo was the exiled prince of Thalania. An exiled prince came with more baggage than she had, and that was saying something.

But she hadn't gone back for her number.

She still wasn't sure why.

Her excuse of not wanting to face them in the light of the morning didn't hold up to three months of absence. Meg scrubbed harder at the mess on the floor. "*If* it was an invitation—and it wasn't—then it was one to call me. Not stalk me to my place of business and show up after hours when I'm alone and defenseless."

He laughed. The bastard *laughed*. "Defenseless, Meg? Never. If there's anyone defenseless in this scenario, it's me."

The words proved what she'd already suspected—he

wasn't going to be any more honest with her now than he had on that night three months ago. If he'd told her who he really was in the club, she might still have gone home with them, but at least she would have done it with eyes wide open. But he hadn't been honest—neither of them had. She opened her mouth to tell him to get lost, but that wasn't what came out. "Where's Galen?"

Theo shrugged. "He had a few errands to attend to."

Another suspicion proved correct. "He doesn't know you're here, does he?" Theo might play to his own set of rules, but Galen had one priority: Theo. *He'd* made it very clear that he had no intention of continuing anything with Meg. It was the one comfort she'd had. She and Galen outvoted Theo.

At least they had until he showed up here without his shadow in tow.

Theo gave another of those shrugs that meant nothing at all. "Contrary to what you seem to believe, we're not attached at the hip."

"Could have fooled me." She waited, but he seemed content to lean against the doorframe and watch her, so Meg gave a shrug of her own and got back to work. Ultimately, his presence there changed nothing. The second she walked out of that apartment three months ago, she'd decided to leave everything—every*one*—in it behind. "We're closed."

"Meg."

She didn't want to look at him. That way lay dragons. He was too attractive, too magnetic, and he knew it. But she couldn't resist him murmuring her name in that tone of voice. She just didn't have it in her. Meg sighed and met his gaze. "It's been three months, Theo. You said you'd be gone a couple weeks, tops. Even if I was interested, and that's a big *if* at this point, the opportunity has passed."

"I'd like to take you out for dinner. Or a drink."

His ability to steamroll right over what she'd just said was a neat trick, but not one she planned on indulging. "Goodbye, Theo."

"Wait. Fuck, Meg, just … wait." He scrubbed a hand over his face and, for the first time since he appeared, she noticed the dark circles under his eyes. As if maybe he hadn't slept much since she'd seen him last. *Doesn't matter. It* can't *matter.* He let his hand drop and pinned her with a look. "Shit got complicated after we left New York, and we had to jump through some hoops until things calmed down. I wasn't going to come back here or risk contacting you until I knew it was safe."

She splashed water onto the floor and got back to scrubbing. "Theo, I had fun that night. So much fun. But that's all it was—fun. Your life is complicated. My life is complicated. There is such a disconnect between the two, it's absurd."

"Who the fuck cares about the disconnect? *We* connected. You and me and Galen."

She couldn't argue that, so she didn't try. This Theo was hard to deny, but she remembered all too well how he got when those blue eyes went calculating. He'd been raised the Crown Prince of Thalania, which meant he'd been raised to lie from birth. He wanted her, and he'd say whatever it took to claim her like some kind of trophy. She was a girl who grew up in a trailer, and he was a guy who'd grown up in a palace. There was no way he could see her as anything *other* than a trophy.

He sure as hell didn't see her as an equal.

What could she say to get through to him? "Theo, what does that apartment cost you a month?"

His gaze went shuttered. "I don't see how that matters."

"That answers my question." She laughed a little, the sound as broken and sad as the room they currently stood in. "I'm a year away from getting my master's degree and I can't even pay my tuition no matter how hard I hustle. I have no doubt that your problems are real and present and more than valid, but it's like worrying about how to fly a rocket to the moon when I can't even afford a car. We live in two different worlds."

"Princess—"

"No." Meg held up a hand, forestalling whatever argument he'd prepared. "I'm not a princess any more than you're a pauper. And that's okay, but let's be honest right now. You're standing there wearing designer right down to your skin and I'm cleaning up someone else's puke for barely more than minimum wage. We're too different, Theo. No matter how good the sex is, it would fall apart at some point, and it would fall apart ugly. I'm choosing to keep the memory of that night a happy one without all the emotional baggage three people would bring to any relationship." She shook her head, barely believing the words out of her mouth. Three people. Hot as hell in the bedroom for a single night, but in a relationship?

A recipe for disaster.

Theo sighed. "You're not going to get anywhere the way you're doing it."

She blinked. "Actually—"

He was already moving. He snagged the mop from her hands and nudged her out of the way. He curled those perfect lips at the mess on the floor and muttered something about idiot drunks, but before she could say anything, he started scrubbing the floor with a vigor she hadn't been able to muster.

Meg should stop him.

Any moment now, she'd step in, demand the mop back, and finish the job she started.

But the strange sight of Theo doing manual labor kept her rooted in place. What was he playing at? Meg didn't know, and the not knowing twisted something up inside her. No matter what his goal in coming here, she was being reasonable, damn it.

Reason always prevailed.

He finished in half the time it would have taken her. Neither of them spoke as he carried the bucket to the utility sink and washed it out. What was there to say? No matter what plans Theo held when he showed up, this was goodbye. It had to be.

He dried his hands and turned to face her. "What else do you have to do before you lock up?"

"I'm nearly done." She'd saved the worst task for last, which was just as well. The last thing Meg needed was him hovering while she tried to count out the till or something that required actual concentration. She cleared her throat. "You should leave."

"I'll walk you out."

It wasn't quite a denial of her command to get out, but it was clear he wouldn't be going anywhere until he did exactly as he intended. Meg set her jaw and went through the motions of closing up. Theo's presence shadowed her every step despite the fact he never moved from his spot near the back door. It didn't matter. She could *feel* him taking up more than his fair share of space, his energy too much for this dingy bar.

After double checking that the front door was locked and the Open sign was off, Meg headed for the back door. She nearly missed a step. God, he was so gorgeous it actually *hurt* to look at him. He wasn't as brutally large as Galen, built more like a blade meant to slice and stab than a crushing war hammer. But his white shirt still stretched across serious muscles in his shoulders and chest, and she knew from experience exactly how much strength he could bring to the table.

Stop that.

Stop thinking about that night.

Theo held the door open for her and she caught a whiff of his scent as she stepped past him. It stopped her cold. Sandalwood and spice. A combination she would associate with the best sex of her life until her dying breath. Meg closed her eyes and inhaled, taking in every bit of him she could manage, a junkie in need of the smallest fix.

She couldn't say yes to whatever he was proposing. It might start with dinner, but it wouldn't end there. And wherever it ended would only result in her plans derailed, her heart shredded, and her life in shambles.

No, Meg couldn't say yes.

She forced herself to open her eyes and keep moving. She locked the door behind her and headed for the street. Theo kept pace easily. "No car?"

Who drove in New York? Oh yeah, someone as rich as sin like Theo. "I take the subway."

"The subway." He said the words like talking about shit on the bottom of his shoe. "No. Absolutely not." Theo fished a set of keys out of his jeans and pushed a button, making a car down the street chirp. Meg didn't need to look at it to know it was expensive. Of course it was.

She clung to her patience with slippery fingers. "Goodnight, Theo." If she got into the car with him, she had no idea where she'd end up. Not because Theo was some crazy murderer, but because Meg didn't trust herself with him. Throw Galen into the mix and she was a goner.

No, her only option lay in running as far and as fast as she could.

"Meg." There it was again, that hint of growl in her name. He stepped closer, his presence overwhelming her despite there being a good foot between them. "Meg, let me walk you to the subway station." He reached out and tucked a flyaway strand behind her ear, his thumb brushing across her jaw as he withdrew. That tiny touch had lightning dancing beneath her skin. She wanted him. Good lord, she wanted him. Meg was Pavlov's dog panting for another taste.

"I don't think that's a good idea." She reached out without having any intention of moving and touched his bottom lip. Meg dropped her hand immediately, the memory of his lips on other parts of her burning through her body. What was she thinking? She had to get out of here and she had to do it now. It took every bit of will she had to step back and then step back again. "Please don't come here again."

Theo studied her with those gorgeous blue eyes. He seemed to see more than she had any intention of showing, and she held her breath as he considered. Finally, he nodded. "Okay, princess. I won't come back here again." He shifted closer and cupped her jaw. Even knowing she should shove him away, Meg couldn't help leaning in, a flower seeking his warm sunlight. His lips brushed hers, the contact so fleeting she was half sure she imagined it.

And then he was gone, releasing her from the trap of his touch and moving back. "You know where to find me should you change your mind."

"That won't happen." *It might happen.*

"I guess we'll see, won't we?" He chuckled and headed for his car.

"Arrogant ass," she muttered. Theo might be sin

personified, but he was wrong on this note. She would *not* be seeking him out.

Meg headed for the subway, every step leaching out the spark of energy being in Theo's presence had brought her. By the time she made it home, she wasn't a woman who'd caught the handsome prince's eye. She was just a graduate student with more debt than she knew what to do with and no magical solution for how to keep moving forward.

The door to her apartment was perpetually off its level, so she had to throw her shoulder into it to get it both opened and closed. The flimsy deadbolt wouldn't keep out a mouse determined to break in, but she'd never had a problem with that sort of thing in the years she'd lived here.

A quick shower and she collapsed face-down in her bed. Normally, she worked too damn hard to be anything but completely exhausted at the end of her days and sleep came with little effort, but tonight her mind wouldn't stop racing.

Impossible not to compare her shitty bed with the one in Theo and Galen's apartment, the one that had fit all three of them with ease and felt like sleeping on a cloud. Meg rolled over and cursed into her pillow. *Stop it, stop it, stop it. There are a thousand and one reasons why staying away from them is the only choice you have, and you know it. Good sex is the* only *reason why saying yes would be great.*

Good sex did not outweigh all the bad. It just didn't.

She had to remember that.

Seconds ticked into minutes into hours as Meg watched the city lights play across her ceiling. She had a meeting in the morning to explore financial options with the college, and she needed not to be totally exhausted for it, but that wasn't going to happen.

Damn Theo.

At six, she gave up and took a shower. As she got ready, she rehearsed what she'd say to the financial advisor. They saw cases like hers all the time, and unfortunately the college wasn't in the business of charity. Meg's financial aid had run dry last year, and she wasn't in a position to petition for grants at this point. She was up shit creek without a paddle, and that's exactly what the financial guy would tell her when she sat down with him.

But she had to try.

Worst case, I take a hiatus and spend a year saving money and working my ass off and complete my degree next year.

It wasn't the end of the world if she had to defer. It just felt that way.

She carefully applied her makeup—a low-key lipstick and eyeshadow meant to look like she wasn't wearing anything at all—and dressed in her one good professional outfit. A dress she'd rescued from her friend Cara's donation pile and made adjustments to, and the heels she'd worn when she graduated high school. They weren't fancy, but the black pumps completed the look better than boots or flip-flops would.

An hour later, she knocked on the door and stepped into the office. "Mr. Taneka?"

"Come in, come in." He didn't look up from his computer as she approached the faded chairs situated in front of his desk. They'd only met a few times over the course of her college career, but she was always struck by how *small* Mr. Taneka was. Physically, he could only be termed delicate, but that impression didn't last once he opened his mouth. His voice was a deep bass and his attitude, frankly, sucked. He was fewer than five years out from retirement, and his complete lack of give-a-damn was never more apparent than when she'd asked him for help.

Now, she was here to ask for it again, hopefully with a better outcome.

Meg had nowhere else to turn.

She watched the clock as he finished doing whatever he was doing on his computer. It could have been solitaire for all Meg knew. At ten minutes, she cleared her throat.

Mr. Taneka sighed. "You're still here?"

"Well… yes." She clasped her hands together and fought to keep her voice even and neutral. "We haven't had our meeting yet, Mr. Taneka. Fall tuition is due this week and I'm hoping you have a solution that will help me keep from having to take time off."

He sighed again, louder this time, and sat back. "Ms. Sanders, I don't know why you're wasting both our time."

"Excuse me?" He'd been blunt before, but this was above and beyond. She pressed her lips together to keep from screaming in his face. What did he have to worry about? He had a cushy office job and his path through retirement and beyond was all but assured.

She didn't have the luxury.

She didn't have *any* luxury.

Mr. Taneka gave her a look like she'd escaped a mental ward to storm into his office and ruin his day. "What game are you playing, Ms. Sanders? Your tuition is paid in full."

Meg blinked. "What? That's impossible."

"On the contrary, I have the information right here." He turned the screen to face her. Sure enough, the balance owed was at zero.

Impossible.

She was two grand short yesterday. Meg wasn't the type of person who just magically misplaced *two thousand dollars*. How could—

No.

No, he wouldn't dare.

She cleared her throat. "Would it be possible to see the source of that payment?"

"Ms. Sa—"

"A name, Mr. Taneka. I just need a name. Please."

Another of those long-suffering sighs. He clicked a few buttons. "A Mr. Theo Fitzcharles made the payment at five this morning."

That son of a bitch.

Chapter 2

Galen Mikos stepped off the private plane and inhaled deeply. It didn't matter that he was at a private airport, surrounded by asphalt and jet engine fumes. It smelled like honeysuckle and home. There were so many things he didn't miss about being in Thalania on a day-to-day basis —mainly the backbiting and politicking—but he missed *this*.

The country.

His country.

The country Theo would rule someday, if they managed to pull off a coup.

Galen cursed himself for his fanciful thoughts and checked his phone. There was nothing from his best friend, which shouldn't have sent his instincts clanging, but Theo tended to let his stubbornness get in the way of his good sense, and being back in New York... Yeah, Galen knew *exactly* where his friend's head was at.

Theo promised to keep his hands off Meg for all their sakes, but Galen didn't think for a second that promise would hold. Theo had a strange moral code and though he took his word seriously, he would create loopholes with that big twisty brain of his, and then it would be up to Galen to get them out of trouble.

Again.

Most days, he didn't hold it against his friend. It was just the way Theo was.

Galen owed him everything. Wading through shit-storms from time to time was a small price to pay for a tally sheet he'd never balance even if he spent the rest of his life as Theo's shadow. His friend—his fucking *Crown Prince*—would be pissed to hear him say it, but it was the truth.

And he wasn't solving a damn thing by standing here, brooding on shit he couldn't control. Theo would do what Theo would do. Galen was in Thalania for twelve hours. He'd deal with whatever situation arose when he flew back to New York.

In the meantime, he had a different kind of nightmare to deal with.

Family.

While Galen technically hadn't been exiled, he couldn't set foot in the palace without causing an international incident. The current Crown Prince was Theo's little brother, Edward, and while he wasn't a bad kid as such things went, he was seventeen and heavily under the influence of his uncle. *That* bastard, Galen would love to spend five minutes alone with. Unfortunately, it wasn't in the cards.

A matte silver Rolls Royce waited next to the hangar, and he rolled his eyes as he stalked to it and slid into the backseat. "Nice car, old man."

Dorian Mikos curled his upper lip at the sight of his son. "If I'd known you were going to dress like a peasant, I would have put down a towel."

Galen glanced down at his worn jeans and raised an

eyebrow. "Some of us don't feel the need to wave our dicks around to prove how much money we have." His father, on the other hand, was dressed in a three-piece suit that some designer had likely created specifically for him. It shone a little with every move, giving a hint of purple against the blue as the sun danced along its surface. Combined with the alligator loafers and a fucking lacy handkerchief tucked into his front pocket, he looked every inch a dandy. All he needed was a jeweled cane to swing about.

Dorian stared at him for a long moment as if deciding how best to manipulate the situation to his advantage. He was good at that shit, but Galen knew his tricks better than anyone. Just like he knew how his father reacted when his manipulations failed—with his fists. He leaned back against the door and crossed his arms over his chest, intentionally taking up more space than strictly necessary. *That's right, you asshole. Tread carefully.* "You summoned me. I'm here. Might as well stop wasting both our time and get down to business."

Another beat of silence. Dorian gave a warm smile. He was a slimmer, more metro version of Galen, dark hair groomed within an inch of its life, his carefully curated five o'clock shadow giving just enough edge that he played up his masculinity despite his clothing. An act. All of it was an act. Dorian changed personalities the way some predators changed camouflage. The end game was all that mattered to him, and if it meant staging a coup against a reigning monarch, he wouldn't blink.

He *hadn't* blinked when he'd tried and failed to take out Theo's father fifteen years ago.

Don't dwell in the past. He wants you here about the future. Pay attention.

Finally, Dorian leaned forward. "Your mother wants you home."

For fuck's sake. "Not this again." His home had never been in any of the many properties his parents owned. His father made damn sure of that. When Galen was sixteen, shit hit the fan, and the only person who offered him a safe space in the storm was Theo.

Theo was his fucking home.

Not even Thalania could compare.

And the man sitting next to him who just happened to be his sperm donor sure as fuck didn't figure into it.

"She convinced Phillip to agree to pardon you. And you know what Phillip agrees to, he'll get Edward to agree to. His hand is so far up the Crown Prince's ass, it's a wonder the Phillip's voice doesn't sound when Edward speaks."

Galen dropped his arms. "He's offering to pardon me? What the fuck does he have to pardon me for? I committed no crimes." No crime except being loyal to the only true Crown Prince. If Theo's father, the former king, was still alive, none of this shit would have happened. But a strange illness took him at the hale age of fifty-five, and hell if any of the court physicians could figure out the cause of it.

Murder by poison, most likely, though there wasn't the slightest bit of proof to uphold Galen's belief.

Even Theo didn't believe him.

"You followed Theodore Fitzcharles III into exile. You've been plotting with him to stage a coup of your own."

Galen didn't let anything show on his face. It stood to reason that rumor had flown back to Thalania on quick wings. He and Theo weren't exactly in hiding, but he didn't want to advertise their intentions—at least not until they had enough cards up their sleeves to ensure they could win. Until that point, he would deny it to his dying day. "I don't know what you've been smoking, old man, but we're just trying to pick up the pieces after the blow *you* dealt. How's Phillip these days? Do you still suck his cock morning, noon, and night?'"

Dorian's mouth went tight. "There's only one person in this car who sucks cock, and it's not me."

"If you say so." Galen shrugged. "You should have called. It would have saved you the jet fuel. I'm not coming back. I made my choice. You and Anne should learn to live with it."

"There's more."

He clenched his jaw and waited. This wouldn't be good. Dorian never stopped scheming and seeing a decade's worth of plans come to fruition wouldn't be enough to change that. His father went and proved him right with his next words. "We've arranged an advantageous match." When Galen just stared, Dorian smiled wider. "Thought that might catch your interest. Camilla Fitzcharles."

Galen laughed. He couldn't help it. The whole situation was too fucking absurd. "You want me to marry Cami? The same girl whose diapers I changed? Are you out of your fucking mind? She's a child." She was fifteen… no, it was August. She would have turned sixteen over the summer. Galen shook his head. "I don't know what you're into, but I don't fuck kids."

"She'll be of age in two years. Hardly that much time to wait in the grand scheme of things."

"Even when she's *of age*, she'll still be a kid. I'm not marrying a fucking kid." Not that Galen had any intention of marrying in the first place.

But if he ever pulled that particular trigger, it sure as hell wouldn't be for political gain.

"Next time, try a phone call and don't waste everyone's time." He climbed out of the car and headed for the plane.

It should be well on its way to being refueled, and then he'd be en route back to New York.

Back to Theo.

———

MEG SPENT the day working and stewing over the knowledge sitting like a rock in her gut. Not only was Theo back in New York, but he was meddling in her life. Not just meddling, but swinging around his giant moneyed cock like he thought he had any right to.

She poured three shots of whiskey and slid them across the bar to the waiting men. *What does Galen think of all this?* She didn't know because she hadn't seen evidence of *him* since Theo showed up.

It didn't matter.

Theo crossed the line when he paid for her tuition. She couldn't afford to repay him. If she could, then she would have paid the damn tuition herself. He wasn't stupid. He *knew* that. Which meant he was using this money to lasso her to him and hell like she was going to let that stand.

"Meg?"

She glanced over to find her best friend Cara watching her with worried dark eyes. "Yeah?"

"Honey, are you mad at that glass? You've been glaring and scrubbing for like five minutes. It's clean." Cara gently extracted the tumbler in question from her grip and set it on the shelf below the bar. "You want to talk about what's bothering you?"

She *couldn't* talk about what was bothering her. Not without admitting that she hadn't been completely honest with her friend about her financial situation. Cara knew she was broke, but there was broke and there was drowning. Meg was doing the latter. Admitting that aloud to *anyone* was as good as admitting she'd failed. Cara might not see it that way, but it was the monkey on Meg's back. Her problem and her problem alone.

Plus, if Cara knew how bad it was, she'd try to help, and Meg knew all too well how money changing hands changed a friendship. Right now, they were on equal footing. Two graduate students slumming it as bartenders to supplement their income while they pursued their respective degrees—Meg in accounting and Cara in fashion design. If Cara lent Meg money or got involved in her debt in any way, there would be no going back.

No.

She refused to let that happen.

Meg gave a tired smile. "Just stress about next semester."

"Honey, you can't start stressing about something that hasn't even happened yet." Cara propped a hand on her hip. She and Meg were roughly the same size, but her thinness was the result of model-good genetics and not of subsisting on ramen. She flipped her blond hair off one shoulder. "Do I need to stage another intervention and get you out of your head for a little bit?"

Considering it was Cara's last intervention that got Meg in this mess with Theo—and Galen, even if he hadn't showed yet—she wasn't about to agree to another one. It had seemed so damn simple at the time, a welcome relief from her reality. Cara convinced her to go dancing for her twenty-third birthday. And then she'd met Theo's gaze over a crowded dance floor and lost her damn mind. Meg forced a smile. "Thank you, but one wild night like that is enough to last me at least a couple years."

"Gah, you're twenty-three. Stop acting like you have one foot in the grave." She angled her head sideways and frowned at the patrons filtering out of the bar. "It's dead in here. Why don't you take off? If you won't let me talk you into going dancing, the least you can do is get some sleep. You look like shit."

"Jeez, Cara, don't hold back."

"The bags under your eyes have their own bags." Cara touched a gentle finger to the spot in question. She frowned. "Are you sure nothing's really wrong? Because I've seen you stressed before, and it didn't look like this." She lowered her voice. "If you were in trouble, you'd tell me, wouldn't you?"

"Cara—"

"Damn it, Meg, you aren't alone. I know it feels that way, but you're not. It's okay to ask for help."

A big guy ambled up to the bar and leered at Cara. "Hey, Blondie, how about a little extra sugar with my beer?" He licked his lips, as if the lecherous tone of voice wasn't enough to get his innuendo across.

"Hey, Big Foot, how about you let the ladies talk?" Cara snapped. "I'll bring you boys your next round shortly, but if you try to pinch my ass, I'm going to break your wrist."

His brows lowered. "You can't talk to me like that."

"Weird. I just did."

If Meg let this go on much longer, Cara would start another brawl, and then she wouldn't be getting out of here until three. She hooked her friend's arm and practically shoved her back into the kitchen. Meg couldn't quite smile at the asshole huffing and puffing himself into a tizzy, but she managed a neutral expression. "What are you boys drinking?"

"That bitch can't talk to me like that."

She cocked her head to the side. "I'm sure you were just talking about actual sugar with your beer and not sexually harassing one of the bartenders here. Our manager doesn't think too highly of that sort of thing, and he eighty-sixed the last guy who tried."

That took the wind right out of his sails. He deflated a little. "It was just a misunderstanding."

"Of course." She waited a beat, and then another. "Your beer?"

"Bud."

Naturally. The beer of the good 'ole boys. Meg got to work filling new glasses of beer for them and then brought them out to the table. She managed to get out of there without anyone slapping her ass, which was just as well. In her current mood, she was liable to pull a Cara and start a brawl of her own. She poked her head into the kitchen and found Cara pacing. "It's taken care of."

"Appreciate it. Those kinds of assholes just get under my skin." Cara gave herself a shake. "That's neither here nor there. Get the hell out of here, Meg. Go sleep or drink or do something just for you. I absolutely forbid you to run anything related to numbers until tomorrow."

That sounded great in theory, but there was on partic- ular number floating around Meg's head like her own personal demon. *Two thousand dollars. That bastard just dropped two grand without even blinking, without even asking me if that was what I wanted.* She untied her apron and fisted the fabric. Theo might have grown up playing god with the lives of the people in his country, but she hadn't asked for his help.

She didn't want his help.

And, damn it, she was going to tell him that to his face.

Meg clocked out and gave Cara a quick hug. "I don't deserve you."

"That's bullshit. I am beautiful, but I am flawed." She grinned. "By the way, that new rom-com is out this week. Want to grab snacky stuff and rent it next week on our day off?"

She opened her mouth to demure, but the truth was there wouldn't be much time for their movie nights once school started back up again. The only time they'd see each other was when they were working, exchanging snippets of life updates and gossip on the go. "Yeah, that sounds nice."

"Good. I'll see you later. Be safe."

"Always."

But she didn't feel safe.

She felt angry and reckless and ready to burn something to the ground.

AN HOUR LATER, Meg stopped on the sidewalk in front of Theo and Galen's place. It was a state-of-the-art building that backed up to Central Park, complete with an elevator requiring a key to get to the various apartments and floor-to-ceiling windows to maximize the view they'd paid an obscene amount of money for. She didn't know the kind of people who lived here, but they had to lead as lavish lifestyles as Theo and Galen did.

Not that she knew exactly what kind of lifestyle *they* lived.

Really, she didn't know shit about them that wasn't pulled straight from the tabloids—exiled prince of Thalania, party boy who shirked his duties, a player who constantly had a different beautiful woman on his arm. All of it was from when Theo was still Crown Prince, and *none* of it mentioned Galen or his relationship with Theo. More than friends but less than dating? Or maybe they *were* dating and just trolled New York clubs for girls to take home the same way they'd taken Meg home three months ago?

She didn't know.

She'd never expected to see either of them again.

Nothing was going to get solved while she stood out on the street, glaring at the front door. She squared her shoulders and marched inside. A doorman subtly stepped in front of her. "Ma'am?"

Oh right. Buildings like this operated with high-end security that included a doorman to keep the riffraff out. Meg lifted her chin and tried to look like she belonged. *Fat chance of that. I'm as out of place as a donkey at a dinner party.* "I'm here to see Theo Fitzcharles."

The doorman was an older black guy whose suit was so perfectly pressed, it made her eyes hurt a little. He studied her for a minute and stepped back. "Mr. Fitzcharles is expecting you. He's on the top floor."

That took the wind right out of her sails. "Oh. Uh. Thanks." She hadn't *really* wanted to get into it with the doorman, but a little confrontation to burn off her excess energy couldn't hurt. *Except you know better than to shit on people just doing their job. Get your head on straight, Meg.*

Easier said than done.

Her head hadn't been on straight since the last time she'd been in this building. Calling Theo and Galen's home an apartment was laughable. *Her* tiny closet of a home was an apartment. She could fit her entire place into the bathroom off the master bedroom. Calling it a suite seemed so mundane, though.

Meg didn't need confirmation on how different their lives were. Everything about Theo screamed money, even though he wasn't the kind of guy who flashed it around to get attention. He just... was. Even if she didn't know where he came from, she would have pegged him as old money.

Stop analyzing him and get up there.

The elevator ride felt like it took seven times as long as it should have, and by the time she stepped out into Theo's apartment, she was shaking. Her anger rode her so hard, it was almost enough to drown out the memories that ambushed her the second she stepped into his place. She stopped short, barely registering the doors sliding shut behind her.

There was the couch where Theo had bent her over and fucked her while Galen licked her pussy. There was the kitchen where she'd stripped out of her robe and told Galen to come and get her. If she followed that hallway back to the main bedroom, she'd find the bed where they fucked until the sun crested the sky, and then slept curled up around each other.

God, it *hurt* to face those memories.

She rubbed her hand against her sternum and tried to reclaim her anger, but the feeling slipped through her fingers like smoke. She hadn't signed up for this—for any of this.

A sound brought her around to face the hallway. Theo stood there in nothing but a pair of low-slung lounge pants, surprise written across his face. "Meg."

It was right around then that Meg realized it was well after midnight. She crossed her arms over her chest, but that made her feel too defensive so she let the stance drop. "Take it back."

To his credit, he didn't bother to play dumb. "I see you got my gift."

"It's not a gift and you damn well know it. It's financial blackmail."

Theo raised his brows. "Apparently I need a drink for this conversation." He headed for the kitchen and pulled out a bottle of whiskey that cost several hundred dollars. Theo doled it out into two tumblers with the ease of someone who had spent his life bartending. She had no idea where a prince would pick up a skill like that.

I don't care where he learned to pour like that. That's not why I'm here.

Theo slid one glass across the counter in her direction, but she didn't move from her spot by the door. To walk farther into the apartment was to run the risk of memories overriding what little good sense she had. She carefully looked around, studying the shadows lurking in the far corners of the room. Empty. Of course they were empty. She didn't know what she was thinking—that Galen would hide there and jump out at the opportune time? Even knowing the bare minimum when it came to these men, she knew that wasn't how he operated.

No, if he was in the apartment, he'd be in her face. Meg turned back to face Theo. "Where's Galen?"

The edges of his lips quirked up. "He'll be back in the morning. He doesn't like to leave me alone for long stretches of time."

"Considering the bullshit you've gotten up to since he left to run whatever errand he's on, I don't blame him." The feeling blossoming in her stomach most definitely *wasn't* disappointment that this situation would be resolved and she'd be long gone before Galen got back. He was a prickly asshole, but a perverse part of her enjoyed poking at him.

More importantly, he had the same expectations of their night together that she had. *He* would agree that Theo crossed the line, and while Meg didn't have a snowball's chance in hell of getting the former Crown Prince of Thalania to do what she wanted, *Galen* probably could convince Theo to take the money back.

Theo leaned back against the counter, the move causing the lights to catch the ripples of his muscles. They were very nice muscles. They looked even better when they flexed as he moved inside her…

Oh my god, stop.

Meg marched over to the counter and downed the whiskey. It burned her throat and warmed her stomach, leaving her with the faintly spicy aftertaste. "Take the money back, Theo. I mean it."

"Impossible. It's paid. Your semester is set. End of story." The playful edge she'd seen when he showed up in the bar was nowhere in evidence tonight. This Theo was intense enough to send her rocking back on her heels. Meg was in over her head and sinking fast, but she was determined to keep her eye on the prize.

She set the glass on the counter with a soft clink. "I'm not a whore."

"I'm aware of that." Not even a flicker of surprise or outrage. "If you were a sex worker, you would have made ten times that much for the night we spent together."

Her jaw dropped. Meg couldn't decide if he'd just complimented or insulted her, but she didn't like it one bit. A tiny voice inside her marveled at what she could do with twenty grand, but she shut it down. Having sex for money was—No. She didn't care if other people did it. It wasn't her business. But Meg had been accused of being a whore her entire life, and she'd be damned before she lived up to the slur.

Theo sipped his drink as if he had all the time in the world. "Why does it bother you so much to let someone else help?"

His words too closely mirrored Cara's from earlier. If she explained her situation to Cara, her friend would understand. She'd flirted with true poverty enough times that she'd be able to put herself in Meg's shoes and empathize. Trying to explain her realities to Theo… she might as well have tried to describe red to a blind man. His world and hers were so different, they were on different planets.

Meg straightened her spine. "I don't need your help."

"On the contrary. Unless you had a stash of money in your mattress for just this occasion, you *did* need my help." Nothing showed in those blue eyes—nothing except a heat she did everything in her power to ignore. Theo drained half his whiskey. "Your degree is important to you. I don't have to know you well to know that. Just like I know that you weren't going to be able to make the remainder of that payment. I have more money than one person can spend in a lifetime. It's nothing to donate it to a worthy cause."

She stood there and let the words wash over her. They picked at the shields she worked so hard to keep in place, burrowing deep and spreading their poison through her entire being. All of it boiled down to one word. *Charity*. She wasn't a person to Theo, not really. She was a broken thing he thought his money could fix.

If she had any whiskey left, she would have thrown it in his face.

If she was Cara, she would have thrown the glass, too.

Meg marched around the counter and into the kitchen. She grabbed the glass out of Theo's hand and downed the remainder of his whiskey. It wasn't enough to drown out the words circling, pecking, pecking, pecking. They mixed with older, harsher, words from her past. *Whore. Good for nothing. Waste of space. Failure.* She reached for the bottle blindly and nearly knocked it off the counter.

Theo caught it before she cost him even more money. Concern flickered across his face. "What's wrong?"

"What could be wrong? I'm a whore who's not even being paid her full worth." She grabbed the bottle from him and poured a double. Meg didn't drink much these days, but the current situation called for it.

Theo covered the top of the glass with one of his big hands. "Whore is a derogatory term, princess. I didn't put that word in your mouth."

"How very woke of you." She tried to slide the glass toward her, but he kept it trapped. "Theo, I am so angry, I am in danger of throwing something expensive that I can't afford to replace." Which accounted for everything in the damn apartment. "Let me drink."

"Throw something if it'll make you feel better."

His dismissive tone rubbed against her skin like sandpaper. Of course he wouldn't care if she destroyed everything in this place because he could afford to replace it without blinking or worrying about where his next meal would come from. The sheer privilege he displayed staggered her. She glared. "Put the money back, Theo. That's what I came here to say, and now that I've said it, I'm leaving."

Meg made it a grand total of one step before his voice stopped her. "No." The word fell between them, an almost physical thing that sank any chance she had of getting out of there without making a further fool of herself.

She turned. Theo wasn't leaning against the counter any longer. He'd halved the distance between them and there was a look in his blue eyes...

Something akin to possession.

Meg licked her lips, roots growing from the soles of her feet and binding her in place beneath the heat of his gaze. "You don't own me."

"I don't want to own you, princess." He took another step toward her and, this close, it was impossible to ignore the differences in their size. Meg wasn't short. Theo was just that tall. He tangled his fingers in her hair and gave it a light tug she felt all the way to her toes. "Stay."

"Oh, fuck right off." She pushed his chest, but he didn't even bother to pretend she was strong enough to move him. "You can't just lay on the smolder and expect me to drop my panties and jump on your cock. You... You..." She ran out of words to convey her fury and screeching at him like a banshee might feel good but would accomplish nothing.

Meg did the next best thing.

She kissed him.

Chapter 3

Meg had every intention of ending the contact before it began. She was proving a point, damn it. But Theo dug those big hands into her hair and tugged her close, his big body enfolding her own.

When Meg was twelve or thirteen, she'd adopted a stray cat. It was during one of the good years with her mom, and every day when she'd come home from school, no matter how shitty her day had gone or how many times she'd been humiliated by the other kids, that cat was waiting for her when she walked through the door, purring up a storm and wanting a cuddle.

Being wrapped in Theo's arms felt a whole lot like that.

It didn't make a bit of sense. He wasn't hers in any sense of the word. He was the exact *opposite* of hers. But the truth had no place here, especially the ugly truth.

Theo turned them and lifted her onto the kitchen counter. He stepped between her thighs, pressing them wide enough that her skirt fought the movement. It only made everything hotter. He used his hold on her hair to tilt her head so he could kiss down her neck. Meg arched her back, needing his mouth all over her, needing him to rip her out of the goddamn clothes that had the audacity to create a barrier between them.

Somewhere in the back of her mind a voice whispered, the words emerging from her lips. "We shouldn't."

"I know." He nuzzled her tank top lower and nipped the curve of her breast. "Galen will kill me."

Galen.

His name in Theo's rumbling voice sent a bolt of pleasure straight to her core. Last time, Galen had watched them for some time before he'd finally waded in to take the pleasure he considered his due. But Galen wasn't here tonight.

Theo skated his hands up her thighs, pushing her skirt higher until she had to lift her hips to allow it to bunch around her waist. His thumbs feathered along the edges of her panties. "Black lace." He cursed low enough that she had to strain to hear him.

If he didn't rip off her fucking panties, she might expire on the spot.

But this was Theo, and Theo never seemed to do anything unless he damn well wanted to. He traced her clit through the fabric. "Fuck, Meg, I missed you."

"No." She grabbed the back of his neck and dug her nails in a little until he met her gaze. His blue eyes were fire, bright enough to make her whole world glow. If she let him, he'd sweep her away and ensure she enjoyed every second. Meg couldn't let him. She couldn't be swept away. Not again. "No, Theo."

He stopped the torturous slide of his thumb. "No?"

She used her free hand to cover his where he cupped her pussy. "Don't stop *that*." Still he didn't move, searching her face for answers she didn't have. She drew in a shuddering breath. "I am furious at you. My wanting to fuck you doesn't change that. It doesn't change *anything*."

"Doesn't it?" He raised a single eyebrow. "You think you can keep it separate."

"I know I can. The question is—can you?"

Theo's smile sent her stomach into a dizzying flip. "Naughty princess. You want to use me for my cock and then walk away. Your own personal sex toy."

She dragged her gaze over him, from his dark hair to those wicked blue eyes to his sinful mouth, down his broad shoulders, his clearly defined chest, to the jeans clearly sporting a hard-on for the ages. "I have a sex toy. In fact, I have several. None of them look a thing like you."

His laughter rolled through her. "Fine, princess. I'll play your game. No more telling you I miss you." He hooked his fingers through her panties and dragged them down her legs, stepping back so she could kick them off. Theo went to his knees between her spread thighs, looking at her pussy so intensely she could feel it like his touch. "I definitely won't tell you that I jacked myself to the memory of you countless times in the last three months."

"Theo…"

He pressed a painfully gentle kiss to each thigh and then his breath ghosted over her clit. "I sure as hell won't tell you that when I fucked Galen, I imagined you were there with us. I came so fucking hard, princess, just from thinking about you while I was buried in him to the hilt."

She stared down at him, mesmerized despite herself. "Fantasizing about me while you're having sex with Galen…" She had to stop because the image unfurled in her mind and stole her breath. Of Theo moving behind Galen's big body, kissing the back of his neck as he drove into Galen, reaching around and stroking Galen's cock so they could reach their pleasure together… "Fuck," she breathed. What was she saying? Meg swallowed hard. "It's rude."

"Is it?" He dragged his tongue over her pussy in a long lick as if savoring her taste. "I wasn't fantasizing about fucking you while I was fucking him, princess."

She tried to focus past the pleasure of his mouth, his big hands holding her thighs wide as he devoured her. "I... What were you fantasizing about?"

"Him." He sucked on her clit hard enough to make her back bow. "Fucking." Another long lick. "You."

And just like that, the image in her mind shifted. Theo drove into Galen, and Galen drove into *her*.

She whimpered, her pleasure building as much from the fantasy as from Theo's mouth. He rolled his tongue over her clit, working her in just the way she needed. How the hell did he remember that after all this time? She tried to put on the brakes, to slow her pleasure, to make it last, but Theo drove her before him like lightning before thunder. She couldn't resist him.

She never should have tried.

Meg came with a cry that filled the room around them. Theo didn't give her a chance to recover, though. He stood and stepped back between her thighs to take her mouth. She tasted herself on his tongue and hell if it didn't make her toes curl. Meg wrapped her legs around his waist and he lifted her off the counter and walked them down the hallway, still kissing her, never missing a step. "You've done this before," she murmured.

"Not like this. Never this." He kept her pinned to him with one arm around the small of her back and used his other hand to pull her tank top off. Meg ran her hands down his muscled chest. He really was too beautiful. It almost hurt to look at him and touching him only magnified the sensation.

He spun and pinned her between his body and the wall next to the door, thrusting against her. The seam of his pants pressed against her clit and Meg cried out. "More."

Theo dragged his mouth up her neck and set his teeth against the sensitive spot below her ear. "Impatient, wanton girl. If I pressed you against those windows for the world to watch me fuck you, would you let me?"

She twisted to look at the windows in question, massive panes stretching from floor to ceiling and offering a view of Central Park below. With the lights on in the bedroom, anyone close enough to look would be able to see everything Theo did to her in startling detail.

It would be so wrong.

Her body tightened at the thought. Theo bit her again, harder this time, making her breasts ache and her nipples tighten in response. His low laugh vibrated against her skin. "We both know you would."

"Yes," she whispered.

"No." He released her, letting her slide down his body until her feet found purchase on the hardwood floor. Only then did he step back and stalk to yank the curtains closed. Closing off her view of the world gave the room an intimate feeling, as if they were the last two people alone in the world. *Except Galen. Galen's out there somewhere.* No amount of distance would erase *that* man.

Theo turned to face her. "Strip."

There wasn't much left to take off. She shimmied out of her skirt and tossed her bra away. Even from across the room, she could hear his breath hitch and hell if that didn't make her feel like the sexiest woman in existence. Theo rubbed the back of his hand across his mouth. "There's only one person I'd put on a show for and unfortunately he's not here. Next time."

"There's no next time, Theo." She meant it to come

out firm, but the words lifted at the end, as if she was asking him to confirm that truth.

His lips quirked. "Then, yeah, Galen is most definitely going to kick the shit out of me when he gets back in town."

She started for him and then stopped. "Is... You talked about it, but..." Meg pressed her lips together. "If you two are an item..."

"We're not. Not in the way you mean." Theo stalked toward her, the light dancing along his muscles as if it couldn't resist him any more than she could. "What Galen and I are is complicated and not exclusive when it comes to what's happening tonight."

She tried to pick apart that statement. Realization washed over her. "You can have sex with women, but not other men."

"Something like that." Theo stopped in front of her and shifted his fingers through her hair. "He won't kick my ass because I fuck you, princess. He'll do it because he's jealous he wasn't here with us." He lowered his voice. "He should be here with us."

"Another time." She had no intention of saying it, of promising him anything. She was still furious that he'd pulled that stunt with the money and Meg didn't make a habit of spending time with people who made her furious —her bar patrons excepted. But the thought of completely closing the door on another night with both Theo and Galen hurt too much.

His grin made her heart stutter. "On the bed."

She obeyed, crawling on the mattress and reclining among the pillows. Theo rewarded her by stripping out of his lounge pants, shoving the denim down his strong thighs and kicking free of it, leaving him naked. The sight of his cock straining against his stomach had her biting her bottom lip. She knew what came next. She *craved* what came next. "Don't make me wait."

"One condition."

"Damn it, Theo." Of course there were conditions. The man wouldn't know uncomplicated if it slapped him in the face. "What condition?"

He pulled a string of condoms from the nightstand and tossed them on the bed next to her. She counted six and raised her eyebrows. Theo gave an unrepentant grin. "Stay the night. If this is the end, then let's end it with fireworks."

He's playing me. Theo had no intention of letting this go. If it was the end, he wouldn't have all but promised her another night with both him and Galen. She wouldn't have all but agreed.

It was a terrible idea.

She couldn't deny the temptation his words brought. Nothing would change if she spent the night riding Theo's cock. She would still manage to convince him to take the money back. This would still be a period at the end of their encounters, rather than a semi-colon. Why not take the pleasure he offered?

He doesn't have to play you—you're playing yourself.

It's only one night.

That's what you said last time.

She met those intoxicating blue eyes and nodded. "Yes."

"Thank fuck." He was on her in seconds, shoving her legs wide and he ground the base of his cock against her clit. He tangled his fingers in her hair and took her mouth like a she was the sweetest kind of candy and he'd never get enough.

Like he'd devour her whole.

She reached blindly over and snagged the condoms,

ripping one free. Seconds later the foil was gone and she rolled it over his cock. He allowed it, shifting back to give her the room to work. *Hurry, hurry, hurry*, her body cried. She needed him inside her and she needed it now. Meg guided him into her and he thrust hard, sheathing himself completely.

Oh god.

Theo broke free of her mouth and pressed his forehead against hers, their breath mingling between them. Each of her exhales came out as, "Oh god. Oh god. Oh god."

He gentled his touch, stroking her hair as if she was a wild animal he had every intention of taming. "Stay with me, princess. I've got you."

As if this was something she submitted to, rather than chased down and tackled to the ground because she wanted it so badly. Meg laughed. She couldn't help it. "Fuck me, Theo." She hitched her leg around his hip so she could take him deeper. "I need it hard." She leaned up until her lips brushed his ear. "Take me like Galen is watching and you want to give him a show."

Fuck me until he can't hold back any longer and joins us in the bed.

An ache started in her chest, a longing for a man she barely knew. She wanted Galen here with them. Theo must have felt it, too. He withdrew and flipped her onto her stomach, urging her hips up even as he impaled her again. "You want me to fuck you like Galen's watching."

"Yes," she moaned.

"Knees wider, princess. Let's give him a show."

———

GALEN BREATHED a sigh of relief when he hit the button to take the elevator up to the apartment. The entire flight back to New York, he couldn't shake the feeling that something terrible was going to happen. He didn't put stock in *feelings* over facts, but Galen trusted his instincts. As much as he would have liked to chalk up his unease to dealing with his father, it didn't explain away things as neatly as he wanted them to.

Theo hadn't answered his calls or texts in hours.

They had a policy since their exile; when they weren't together, they checked in at regular intervals. Too much shit could go wrong. Too many people were gunning for them. Phillip might not be willing to brave the potential political storm to send an assassin after Theo, but as soon as he installed Edward as king, all bets were off.

Even if Phillip wouldn't take that step, there were half a dozen other countries who *would*. The fact they hadn't yet amazed Galen a little bit. In their position, he would have ensured Theo didn't survive the flight to the States. Easy enough to bring their plane down if someone had pockets deep enough.

Every one of their enemies had pockets deep enough.

The elevator doors opened and he stepped into the apartment. He hadn't been back here in months. He and Theo had wasted precious time pursuing a lead that took them nowhere, and Galen could admit he was glad to spend time in New York again. He loved the shit out of his country, but there was something about the mad pulse of NYC that drew him in despite himself. So many strangers packed into such a tight space, all living their lives on top of each other and steadily ignoring anything they didn't feel like dealing with. Here, people didn't care what his past was. They didn't give a fuck about his future, either.

It was freeing.

He stopped short. His memories of the last time he was in this apartment had to be playing with his mind. For a second, he could have sworn he caught a strain of the same floral perfume Meg Sanders had worn the night they brought her home. Galen closed his eyes and inhaled again, slower this time. Yeah, that *was* Meg's perfume, which didn't make a damn bit of sense because three months was more than long enough…

A flash of something out of place from the corner of his eye brought him around to face the kitchen. The black lace thong on the floor hadn't been there when they left New York. Meg had worn red that night and Theo ripped the fucking thing off her.

Goddamn it, Theo, you promised.

He should have known better. He should have sent Theo to Europe or Australia to follow some imaginary errand while he was occupied in Thalania. Anything but letting his friend come back here to start shit neither one of them were capable of following through on. Galen stalked down the hallway, the sliver of morning light shining from behind the bedroom door confirming his worst fears. He used a single finger to push open the door.

They were in bed together.

He watched Theo move over Meg. *In* Meg. She had her legs locked around his waist, her heels digging into the dip at the bottom of Theo's spine. Galen had tongued that dip more times than he cared to count. He should stop them. Should clear his throat or let loose the curses rattling around in his head at their recklessness.

But, fuck, they were beautiful together.

Theo rolled, taking Meg with him, and ended up on his back with her astride him. That's when Galen realized his friend had spotted him. Theo knew he liked a show and the bastard thought he could entice Galen to join them. Meg didn't have the same training—the same awareness. Or maybe she was too far gone. She braced her hands on

Theo's chest and rode him as if paradise lay just on the other side of her next stroke. Her ass bounced every time she slammed down onto Theo's cock, and fuck if that didn't make Galen want to climb onto the bed and take a bite out of her. He leaned against the door jamb and crossed his arms over his chest. Waiting.

Her rhythm went choppy as she chased her pleasure. Theo cupped her jaw with a hand and leaned up to kiss her. He grinned, the bastard, and said, "Look who's home, princess."

Her hazel eyes met Galen's and that was it. She came with a cry to bring the roof down on them all. If Galen wasn't already rock hard from the show they'd just put on, any blood left in his body would have rushed to his cock in that breath of a moment. *Fuck.*

He managed to hold it together as Theo rolled them again and drove into her, chasing his own pleasure. Even as part of Galen was already planning how he'd get them out of this mess, he appreciated the view. Theo came with a curse and rolled off Meg to give him a cocky grin.

Galen legitimately couldn't decide if he wanted to walk over there and kiss Theo or punch him in his pretty face. Meg, at least, didn't look happy to see him. She shoved the covers back and jumped to her feet. He saw the exact second her knees buckled and was there to catch her before she landed on her ass on the hardwood floors. "Hey, Meg. Long time."

"You don't say." She stared up him as if searching his face for answers. He had none, and whatever she was looking for, she didn't find. Meg shook her head and jerked her arms out of his grip. "Tell Theo to take his money back."

On the bed, Theo growled. "I thought we were past this."

"You thought wrong. It's morning, which means it's over." She pointed a finger at him like she was a teacher lecturing a troublesome student. Galen had never wanted to see any of his teachers naked, but if Meg had been one of them, maybe he would have made an exception. Meg spun to face him. "Did you approve of this bullshit?"

He'd had a clear view of what he thought was happening when he walked through the door of the bedroom. It appeared Galen was half right. They might have been fucking seconds ago, but she wasn't lust-drunk.

No, Meg was fucking pissed.

Galen retreated back to the doorway and resumed his position. "I don't have the slightest fucking idea what you're going on about."

"Going on. *Going on.*" Meg dragged her fingers through her long dark hair. She didn't seem to notice she was still naked and flushed from the fucking Theo had laid on her, and hell if that didn't make Galen like her a little bit more. She'd lost weight since he'd seen her last—weight she couldn't afford to lose. He couldn't quite count her ribs, but another few pounds and he might be able to. There were faint hickeys on her breasts and thighs, which confirmed his suspicion that Theo hadn't waited a damn hour after Galen boarded his plane to move on Meg.

He really should have known this was going to happen.

She snapped her fingers in front of his face. "Stop staring at my tits and focus."

"They're nice tits." He mostly said it to be an asshole, and she flushed a deep red that he kind of liked.

"You're a pig. You're both pigs. Overbearing asshole pigs."

He'd suspected Meg had a temper, though to be fair, Theo had the ability to drive a saint to a screaming fit in

44

less than an hour if he put his mind to it. Galen looked over her shoulder to his friend. "What did you do?"

"You don't have to sound so accusing. She needed help. I provided said help. Now she's acting like I snuck into her room and pissed on her foot."

Meg's lips moved as she silently echoed what he'd just said. She shut her eyes and Galen knew without a shadow of doubt that she was counting to ten. Maybe twenty. As much as he enjoyed Theo under most circumstances, this situation was half a breath from exploding in all their faces. He needed to get it defused and get Meg the fuck out of here before someone realized she was the same woman who'd been in their apartment last time they were in town.

It might already be too late.

Chapter 4

Sleeping with Theo wasn't a mistake. It was a goddamn catastrophe. Meg didn't even know how it happened. One second she was trying to keep from kicking him in the shin and the next she was riding his cock and crying out his name as she came. The man had some kind of seduction magic and, as enjoyable as the last few hours had been, she was *not* here for it.

Worse in so many ways, now Galen was blocking the exit with his big sexy body, and she couldn't help but remember the way he'd growled filthy words in her ear that branded her right down to her soul. The only thing saving her from doing something truly regrettable was the fact that he looked just as pissed as she was.

Thankfully, the thunderous expression in his dark eyes was aimed squarely at Theo. "What did you do?"

Theo seemed to tire of lounging in bed and climbed to his feet. It was everything Meg could do not to drink in the sight of him. There were people who were handsome or pretty or beautiful… and then there was Theo. His features should have been too sharp, his eyes too blue, his hair a little too mundane color of dark brown. Apparently whatever god created him hadn't gotten the memo. In addition to being the most beautiful person in the room, he moved with a confidence that only someone born into it could pull off.

He grabbed another pair of lounge pants from the dresser. "She was short on tuition. Now she's not."

So few words to encompass the level of betrayal Meg couldn't quite shake. *She was short on tuition. Now she's not.* As if it really was no big deal, this bomb he'd dropped into her life. She turned to Galen, needing him to understand just how many ways Theo had crossed the line, but his dark brows lowered and he glanced at her. "That's it?"

That's it. *That's it.*

If she hadn't already suspected Galen came from money, that would have confirmed it. No one who had ever been poor would need to ask that question, because they'd instantly know exactly how Theo had crossed the line. Meg pointed at him. "Get out of my way."

He studied her as if debating the wisest course of action, but something must have shown on her face because he slid out of the doorway. She turned to look at Theo. "If that night—if *last* night—meant anything to you at all, you'll take the money back." Meg grabbed her bra and skirt on the floor next to the door and yanked it on. She found her shirt in the hallway and her panties in the kitchen.

If there was anything quite as humiliating as having to grab up the clothes Theo had stripped from her like she was following some kind of sex breadcrumb trail, she didn't know what it was. Neither of the men came out to see her off, which was just as well. She had nothing more to say to them.

Are you sure about that?

Yes, damn it, she was sure about that.

Meg dressed quickly and walked to the elevator. She stared at the doors, willing herself to push the button and get the hell out of there. From the first moment she met those two, she knew they were nothing but complicated. Her bartender instincts had been right—they usually were—and now she was in up to her neck and sinking fast.

My tuition is paid. I can go to school this semester. I am that much closer to graduating.

But at what price?

Nothing came for free in this world. Even if she couldn't see the strings, this gift had them attached. *All* gifts had them attached. Meg worked too hard to get this far, only to be derailed now. She didn't know if she could force the college to refund the money without dropping out— not when she didn't have the funds to replace that amount.

Two choices; Drop out, or take the money.

Her head pounded and her stomach twisted itself in knots. All of the stress she hadn't been able to escape for months doubled between one breath and the next. Meg was well and truly trapped. No easy path lay before her, and there was no convenient right answer.

She knew what Cara would say. Take the money and give both the men her middle finger as she walked out of their life. If they were stupid enough to drop that kind of money on her, it was their problem, not hers. But Cara moved through the world in a way that defied Meg's comprehension. She loved her friend, but she didn't under- stand how she could reason her way into anything.

Sometimes, she wished she could do the same.

"Meg."

She'd hesitated too long, and now here was Galen, stalking down the hallway toward her. She held up a hand. "I'm leaving."

"Not alone."

Meg blinked. "I'm sorry, what?"

"You heard me." Galen reached around her, his big arm brushing her back, and pressed the elevator button. "You're playing in a game where you don't know the rules and you don't know the stakes. So, yeah, I'm not letting you walk out of here alone."

If she squinted and tilted her head a little to the left, she could almost pretend he cared. "You can't honestly think that someone is going to snatch me off the street in this neighborhood."

Galen gave her a long look. "I get that you're pissed about the money, but you shouldn't have come back here."

Wow, Galen, tell me how you really feel.

The worst part was that she couldn't even be mad at him over it. He was right. She shouldn't have come back here. Theo was like some giant sun moving through her life, and he drew her in despite herself. The elevator doors opened and she stepped inside, the metal box feeling ten sizes too small once Galen moved in behind her. Theo was big, but Galen was *huge*. He had the kind of body that would have been right at home on a Viking ship, pillaging villages and throwing a helpless maiden over each shoulder without breaking a sweat. His dark hair was a little longer than when she'd seen him last—not quite military short anymore—and his dark eyes seemed to take in everything about every room he walked into.

The elevator shuddered into motion, but it barely had a chance to drop before Galen pushed the emergency stop button. He turned to her as if he trapped people in elevators every day. "We need to have a conversation."

Meg slid back a step even as part of her buzzed at the thrill being this close to this man. What the hell was wrong with her? First Theo, and now Galen? Before, she could chalk the whole thing up to being intoxicated by the idea of both of them together. Now? Now, she didn't have that luxury.

The sad truth? She wanted them. Both of them. Together *and* separately.

If one thing hasn't changed over the years, your taste in men is still shit.

Just like your mama.

She shoved the thought away and tried to focus on Galen. "Hurry it up, then. I have places to be."

His lips quirked, and if he was anyone else, she would have accused him of being amused at her pissy attitude. But he wasn't anyone else. He was Galen. "I'll keep it brief." He glanced up and she followed his gaze to a tiny camera situated in the corner of the elevator. Meg hadn't even noticed it before. Galen growled and grabbed her shoulders, turning her so that his back was to the camera and his big body blocked out the sight of it—and its sight of her, she'd bet.

She should have slapped his hands away. Anything was better than feeling the heat of his palms against her bare shoulders. If Theo was the sun, then Galen was the tide. He was just as liable to drown her as Theo was to burn her up, but hell if she didn't want to give it a try. *Stop it, Meg.*

He released her before she could do something stupid, but he didn't step back. "You can't come back here. Ever."

"Tell Theo—"

"I am not Theo's errand boy, Meg. I'm not telling Theo shit." He glared. "I am telling *you* that you can't come back here. I don't give a fuck if you've got a chip in your shoulder bigger than England or that you're pissed about a measly two grand. Get over it."

"Get over it," she repeated. "That's really easy for you to say. You—"

He covered her mouth with his hand and stepped closer. "Don't waste both our time with that bullshit. I don't give a fuck about your pride or Theo's impulsiveness or any of that other bullshit. What I *do* give a fuck about is keeping him alive and safe." He hesitated for the briefest of seconds. "And, damn it, I'll feel bad if something happens to you because you're seen associating with us."

"Can't have that," she mumbled against his palm.

"Theo is untouchable right now. I'm a pain in people's asses, but between not wanting to piss Theo off into doing something like staging a coup, and not wanting to piss my family off in case I might come back into the fold, I'm as close to untouchable as a person can get, too. *You* are not. *You* can be hurt. *You* can be used as a pawn, with or without your consent. Go back to your safe life, Meg. Take the money. You need it more than Theo does, and if you stopped letting your pride have the wheel, you'd realize that."

Slowly, his words penetrated the fury rattling around in her brain. Meg grabbed his wrist and pulled his hand away from her mouth. This wasn't about the money at all. This was Galen... protecting her? "You can't seriously think that someone in Thalania would consider my fucking you means I'm important enough to use as a weapon against you."

Something like concern flickered through his dark gaze. No, that was *definitely* concern. Holy crap, Galen actually cared. She didn't know what to do with that information. It shouldn't matter. This was the end, for better or worse, no matter what door she'd let herself believe she left open with Theo last night. They were too different and it would never work. *Galen*, at least, seemed to understand that. "Galen—"

"It doesn't matter what I think. It matters what our

enemies think. If you know who Theo is, then you know why you can't be with him."

She threw up her hands, her frustration needing a physical outlet. "No shit I can't be with him. I don't even *want* to be with him."

"That's not what it looked like when I walked in fifteen minutes ago. It looked like you were more than happy to be in his bed, and being in his bed means being in his life."

It was like they were playing two very different board games and trying to explain the rules, and then getting more and more irritated when the other person didn't understand what the hell they were talking about. Meg shook her head. "I don't know how many times I have to say this to get through to you and him or anyone else paying attention at this point: I don't *want* anything. Theo is the one who showed up at my bar asking for dinner. I turned him down. Then the bastard went behind my back and paid my tuition. I came here to get him to take the money back. The sex just happened."

"Just happened," he echoed. His expression iced over, snuffing out what little concern he'd let through. "Well, you had better make damn sure it never *just happens* again. I mean it, Meg. This has to be the end of it. This isn't about wants or any of that bullshit right now. This is about reality. And the reality is that Theo is meant for a future that doesn't include you."

The way her stomach dropped had nothing to do with feeling rejected, and everything to do with being fed up dancing to a tune set by others. Or that's what Meg told herself as she leaned around Galen and punched the button to get the elevator moving again. "Don't worry, asshole. I'm more than capable of protecting myself. I've been doing it all my life."

THEO STEPPED out of the shower to find Galen glaring at him. "I know."

"Do you? Because sometimes I think you need the goddamn sense knocked into you." Galen yanked his shirt off and fuck if it didn't take Theo's breath away even after all these years. He watched his friend strip and step into the still steaming shower to turn on the water, visually tracing the scars creating a path down his back and over his ass to his thighs. Galen hated those scars, but Theo saw them for what they were—evidence that all the bullshit back home hadn't beaten him. That his father hadn't beaten him.

That nothing would beat him.

Theo would make sure of it.

He wrapped his towel around his waist and leaned against the bathroom counter. He could try to distract his friend with fucking, but the reality was they needed to have this conversation. Ugly truths were more the rule than the exception these days, and he had no doubt Galen's recent visit home fell into that category. "What did you father want?"

"The usual. Me, home, dancing to whatever tune he sets." He said it so calmly, as if seeing his father didn't bother him in the least, as if facing down the man who made the first sixteen years of his life a living hell was just a normal occurrence.

Theo knew better than to push through the hard exterior to the pain beneath. If Galen wanted to get into it, he would. If he didn't, then Theo wouldn't push. No matter how much he wanted to.

Galen ducked under the water and rinsed his hair. "And he wants me to marry Cami."

Pain lanced through Theo, a draft horse kick to the chest. "Cami is sixteen-fucking-years-old." His baby sister should be protected and coddled until she hit eighteen, and even then, marrying her off to *anyone* not of her choosing was out of the goddamn question. "What the hell is Phillip thinking?"

Galen finished washing himself, rinsed, and turned off the water. He'd always been like that—showering in under five minutes. Every move he made was efficient to the extreme.

Even when he fucked.

When they were teenagers, after all the shit had gone down and Galen was living in the palace with him, Theo used to watch him when he thought Galen wasn't looking. But then, Galen was always looking. Nearly two decades as friends who were often more and the mutual attraction had nowhere near burnt itself out.

Galen dragged the towel over his body and tossed it aside. "You've got that look about you, Theo." He shook his head, his short dark hair standing on end from the rough toweling. "Should have known fucking Meg all night wouldn't be enough to take the edge off."

"It wasn't the last time." That was the crux of it. One night with Meg wasn't enough. *Two* nights with Meg hadn't even begun to scratch the itch. He wanted more. Galen and Meg wanted more, too, though both were determined to ignore that for their own reasons. Theo had no problem being the one to get them all in a room together, no matter how much the other two dragged their feet, because once they were alone, chemistry would do the rest. Every touch lay another piece of foundation he had every intention of capitalizing on.

Galen disappeared into the bedroom and came back wearing nothing but a pair of shorts. "It will be this time.

You know better than to pull this shit, Theo. You're not some horny teenager who can't keep it in his pants. The stakes are real."

They were, but Galen didn't make a habit of lecturing Theo like he was a wayward child. The truth dawned. Galen was *jealous*. He would have noticed it sooner, but it was a foreign state for his friend. When nothing else was sure in their life, they were sure of each other. It didn't matter if they dated other people, they always circled back to each other, a connection that went deeper than all the surface shit of fucking and infatuation.

Theo crossed his arms over his chest and watched Galen brush his teeth. "Are you more pissed that she fucked me or that I fucked her?"

Galen rinsed his mouth and set his toothbrush carefully back in the holder. He didn't look over, bracing his hands on the counter as if he would rip it off the cabinet and throw it across the room. It might be marble, but Theo had no doubt he could do it. Galen sighed and straightened. "Both, you asshole. I'm jealous of both of you." He ran his hand over his face. "You're not going to leave her alone."

"You wouldn't if you allowed yourself to be the slightest bit selfish."

"Why bother when you're being selfish enough for all three of us?" Galen stalked closer, until they were nearly chest to chest, and grabbed Theo's chin. "She doesn't want Prince Charming and she sure as fuck doesn't want the baggage we bring to the table. Leave her alone, Theo, or I swear to your dead father that I'll knock you the fuck out, toss you on a plane, and dump you as far from New York as possible."

He'd do it, too.

Galen saw them as unequal—as himself forever in Theo's debt. He'd repaid the imaginary debt a thousand times over, but it still drove him in a way Theo couldn't talk him out of. If he thought he could protect Theo from himself, he'd do it in a heartbeat.

Theo leaned forward, and Galen allowed it. He kissed his friend softly on the lips. "I'll leave her alone, Galen. She made her opinion of me pretty damn clear."

Galen released his chin and gripped the back of his neck, bringing them forehead to forehead. "You stupid son of a bitch. Why the fuck did you pay her tuition?"

"It seemed like a good idea at the time." Theo ran his hands up his friend's chest. "I missed you."

"I've been gone less than forty-eight hours."

"What's your point?" Theo took his mouth and wrapped a hand around Galen's cock through his shorts, giving Galen a rough stroke. Being with Meg had been great, but this was something else altogether. He and Galen moved together as easily as breathing. They'd been fucking since before they could legally drive. Theo turned them around and shoved Galen against the bathroom counter hard enough to make the drawers rattle. "I'm sorry."

Galen watched him go to his knees through dark eyes. "No, you're not."

"No, I'm not," Theo agreed as he yanked Galen's shorts off. He looked up his friend's body and, fuck, he was something else. Powerful and brutal and sexier than he had any right to be.

He was also wrong about this.

They were good together. They were fucking great together.

But they'd be better with Meg.

He had no desire to make his pitch at the moment. They had time, and the desire dancing between them like a live wire was too strong to hold off. Theo had never been much good at reining himself in. Not when what he wanted was so damn close.

He sucked Galen down hard, using just a hint of teeth that drove his friend wild. Theo loved this moment right before Galen lost control, loved sucking him off, loved the feeling of submission and power, all wrapped up in a tangled bow.

Galen cursed. He gripped Theo's hair and started moving, fucking his mouth with quick, rough thrusts. Words spilled from his lips just like they always did when he let himself off his leash. "You think you can suck me into submission, into forgetting who was riding your cock all night long? How many times did she make you come, Theo? How many ways did you fuck her?" He picked up his pace, hammering the back of Theo's throat. "You selfish bastard, you had *better* suck my cock like you mean it. And when you're through, I'm taking your ass right there in the sheets where you can still smell your fucking."

Galen used his grip on Theo's hair to yank him off his cock. "On second thought, I'm not interested in waiting. The bed, Theo. Now."

———

DORIAN MIKOS STUDIED the information laid out on his desk. Many years ago, he'd thought that the best way forward was to rule Thalania, and he'd paid the price for his mistake through years of exile. He wouldn't make the same mistake twice. The Mikos family would never sit on the throne, but if he played his cards right, they would be the power behind it.

He gathered the photos and papers and left his office. Though Phillip Fitzcharles played a careful game with the public to keep them from turning on him, he'd allowed himself free rein in this part of the palace. Gone were the understated decorations, replaced by the paintings he favored, a mishmash with no regard for theme or period.

Dorian very carefully didn't let his disgust show on his face. Phillip was a tool, and tools had their uses. The man controlled the future king of Thalania, and as a result, he had to be handled carefully. Dorian would *not* see exile again. Not while he breathed.

He knocked on the door to Phillip's office and let himself in. "We have a problem."

Phillip didn't look up from his desk. "There's always a problem."

Dorian came to stand before the desk and strove for patience. These petty power games were beyond both of them, but Phillip still insisted on the formalities. He studied the other man as Phillip finished up. The Fitzcharles family's line ran unbroken back to the origin of Thalania, and despite plenty of intermixing with various bloodlines, it ran true. They were all dark haired, tall, and attractive. The attraction just varied from person to person. Phillip looked like a whittled down version of his late brother—too thin, too pinched, too dull. He knew it, and the comparison never failed to provoke a response.

That wasn't what Dorian was here for today, though.

Finally, Phillip pushed his paperwork aside and focused his watery blue eyes on Dorian. "Yes?"

Dorian pulled the top photo out of the file and held it up. "There's a girl."

The interest died in Phillip's eyes. "I don't care about a girl. They're both men in their prime. Of course there are women."

The fool. He should know by now that Dorian wouldn't bring him information that wasn't confirmed several times over and important. Dorian bit back his impatience and pulled the next photo. "You misunderstand me, Phillip. She's not just a girl one of them fucked. They *both* did."

Phillip froze. "Let me see that." He grabbed the picture out of Dorian's hand. The picture was slightly fuzzy since it had been pulled from a security camera, but there was no mistaking Galen and Theo, or that they were both entangled with the woman sitting between them. The next photo showed them leaving together, and the final one was them getting into a cab together.

"I also have footage from the elevator confirming she went into their apartment and didn't come out until morning." The state she'd been in confirmed everything he needed to know.

Galen would do anything for Theodore Fitzcharles III. That fool had turned his boy into a slavering guard dog who jumped when he said jump. His son, a fucking *Mikos*, catering to every whim. And his boy didn't even have the ambition to use it to his advantage.

Phillip flipped through the file, his thin lips moving as he read. Finally he closed it and set it down. "This could mean nothing."

Again, he smothered his irritation, giving Phillip a practiced smile. "Or it could mean everything. The girl is a weak link, and with the right leverage, we can use her to guide them onto the path we want them to take." No one thought for a moment that Theodore would take his exile laying down. Dorian certainly hadn't. He knew for a fact that Phillip intended to have him quietly killed once Edward was on the throne.

They may not have that kind of time.

Beyond that, if there was a way to salvage Galen's status and bring him back into the fold, Dorian would ensure it happened. The boy had had his fun. It was time for him to stop fucking around and start dancing to the tune that made sense.

If he cares about this girl, we can use her.

Phillip finally nodded. "Get me confirmation."

Dorian never let his triumph show. "Of course, Phillip. That's a brilliant plan."

Chapter 5

Three days passed in a fog. Meg couldn't seem to focus. No matter how hard she tried, her thoughts skated away from whatever she was working on and back to that apartment. To Theo. To Galen. Every shift she pulled at the bar, she half expected to turn around and find Theo lounging against a wall, heat in his blue eyes.

But he never showed.

It was *good* that he never showed.

She was still furious about the money, her embarrassment and pride and relief all tangled up into a mess inside her. He might think he was doing her a favor, but all he'd done was keep the wolf from the door for one semester. In a few months, she'd be right back in the same place, laying sleepless in her bed and staring at her ceiling as she tried to make the numbers add up.

They never did.

She had to cut some of her hours once school started back up, which meant a cut in money that she couldn't afford. There was never enough hours, never enough money, never *enough*.

One problem at a time.

If only life worked that way.

Meg cleared a table, going through the motions while her mind was a million miles away. There was another thirty minutes before she could kick the stragglers out of the bar and close down. Cara was supposed to be here with her tonight, but her friend had come down with a nasty bug and spent the last six hours hugging her toilet. Since no one else could—or was willing to—cover for her, that meant Meg was closing alone. Again.

She deposited the empty glasses in the back and went to check on the pair of guys in the corner booth. They'd been drinking for a couple hours, and if she was the fanciful sort, she would think they were mobsters or something. They both wore black jeans and shirts, and one had a leather jacket draped over the seat next to him despite how warm and sticky the night was outside the pub's air conditioning. They looked normal enough in a blah kind of way, but something about them had her fighting not to avoid their table.

Meg pasted a smile on her face as she neared. "Can I get you two another drink?"

"The check." His words were flavored with a faint accent she couldn't quite place.

Thank God. She nodded, making sure none of her relief showed through her expression. "Sure thing." Meg walked back to the computer and printed out their tab. She looked up and went still. The men were no longer in their booth. One had moved to stand just inside the door, and the other approached her with the kind of intent that sent alarm bells blaring through her head.

She trusted her instincts. She couldn't afford not to, not as a bartender, and not as a woman living alone. Meg glanced at the phone farther down the bar and decided that going for it might incite the kind of response in this man that she desperately wanted to avoid. She kept her smile firmly in place and slid the receipt across the bar to him. Where he couldn't see, she palmed her phone and used her thumb to unlock it. If it was a damn flip phone, she could have texted without looking. She fumbled for the right app. Jonah didn't live that far away. If she could text him for help, he'd come and sit with her until she was able to lock the doors.

The man dropped cash on the bar but didn't move away. "Your name's Meg."

"That's what it says on my name tag, so it must be true."

His lips quirked into a smile that didn't come close to reaching his brown eyes. "Meg Sanders."

Ice dripped down her spine. He knew her last name. There was no way he could know her last name. "Who's asking?"

"I'm not asking. I'm telling you." His smile grew. "It's important you know who you're dealing with before we go further in this conversation. I would hate for you to do something foolish and force me to hurt you."

Oh god.

This wasn't a robbery. Thieves didn't bother to learn the names of the people they stole from. It also wasn't some druggie wanting to get his jollies off with the bartender and refusing to take no for an answer. This was something else altogether. Galen's warning flashed through her head. She hadn't really taken him seriously. There were plenty of dangers for a single woman living alone. It was hard to fathom the kind of threat he'd worried would come for her.

She should have paid better attention.

"What do you want?" She tried to keep her voice even and uninterested, tried to prevent the panic crawling up her throat from bleeding into the rest of her body. Tried and failed.

"I would think it's obvious by now. We're here for you." He glanced over his shoulder and his partner flipped the lock on the front door. She knew that tone, knew that look. There would be no reasoning, no rational conversation. He wanted to hurt her, and he would enjoy doing it. Several of her mother's boyfriends over the years had similar expressions right before things went very, very bad.

Meg didn't hesitate.

She bolted, sprinting through the doorway and into the kitchen. Twin curses sounded behind her, but the bar slowed her would-be attackers down. She flew through the back hallway and out the door. Meg made it three steps into freedom before a rough hand closed around the back of her dress. Ripping fabric had never sounded so ominous.

Her attacker grabbed her arm and slammed her into the wall next to the door. He didn't seem disinterested now. No, with the fire in his eyes and breath hissing from his mouth, he looked downright demonic. "That was a stupid thing to do."

She tried to knee him in the balls, but he easily turned his hips to avoid the blow. He shook her hard enough that her head smacked the wall behind her. "Fool woman."

"We're too open out here," his partner said softly. "Get her back inside."

She fought. She kicked and screamed and punched. It didn't matter. He hauled her around like a child throwing a tantrum, dragging her through the door and back into the bar. They hauled her to a chair in the middle of the room, where they zip-tied her wrists behind her back. The chair was icy against her bare back, her dress hanging from her in shreds.

He grabbed her throat, rough fingers digging into the fragile skin there. "Be a good girl or we'll zip-tie your ankles, too."

It would leave her completely helpless, far more so than she was now. She nodded as much as she was able to, cursing herself for not being faster. She could have made it if she hadn't hesitated to run.

He released her and fear gave her words flight. "I don't have anything to steal. Take what's in the till if you want, but it's not much. Just take what you want and go." Maybe she was wrong. Maybe this really was a mundane robbery.

Liar. This is anything but mundane.

He crouched in front of her, and he was tall enough that it brought his face almost even with hers. "We came here for you."

The one truth she didn't want to face. *Galen was right. I should have listened. Why didn't I listen?* Her mind went fuzzy with the screams she wouldn't allow herself to voice. Meg pressed her lips together, fighting to think. There had to be a way out of this. There *had* to be.

But the zip ties were tight enough that her fingertips tingled, a sure sign that she'd lose feeling in them before too long. The doors were locked. If she couldn't get away from them with a head start, how was she going to do it while tied to a chair?

Don't panic.

If only it was that easy to command her body's response. She lifted her chin, forcing herself to look at first one of them and then the other. "What do you want?"

"You know Theodore Fitzcharles III."

She stared. This couldn't be happening. Oh god, this

could *not* be happening. She hadn't taken Galen all that seriously when he said being close to them was dangerous. Of course it was dangerous—to her head and her heart and her foolhardy body. She never actually thought it would be *dangerous*. Even if, rationally, she understood that Theo was the former Crown Prince of Thalania, he was so... Normal wasn't the word, but it was the only one she had. He was just a rich man who made her crazy. She'd let herself believe that is all he was, because it was all she could handle.

But if that was the truth, then she wouldn't be tied to a chair right now.

Apparently, he didn't need a response, because he continued. "And Galen Mikos."

Meg tried and failed to swallow past her dry throat. "I wouldn't say I know anything about them."

He ignored that. "You matter to them."

She shook her head. "I don't know if you understand how the hookup culture works, but we just had sex. That's it. I'm not dating either one of them. I'm never planning on seeing either one of them again."

"If that was true, Theodore wouldn't be paying you. We wouldn't have been sent here in the first place."

If I get out of this alive, I'm going to strangle you, Theo.

Movement over the shoulder of the second man caught her eye. Meg barely had a chance to register that they weren't alone when the man hit the floor, his eyes rolling back in his head. Galen stepped out of the darkness like some kind of avenging angel. "Get away from her."

The man shifted behind her and his hand came down to grip her bare shoulder. "Your father would like a word, Lord Mikos."

Galen stalked closer, seeming to grow with every step, the menace radiating from him sending panicked thoughts bleating through Meg's head. It didn't matter that his rage was focused squarely over her head. In that moment, she had no doubt that he was capable of killing someone—that maybe he already had—and that he wouldn't lose sleep about it afterward.

The man's hand tightened on her shoulder and Meg couldn't hold in a whimper of pain. Galen's dark eyes flicked to her face and then to the source of her pain. He'd been pissed before. Now he looked downright lethal. "Get your hand off her."

"Lord Mikos—"

"If you don't stop touching her right fucking now, I'll start by taking your hand, and that won't be where I stop."

The man's hand spasmed on her shoulder, but none of that emotion leaked into his voice. "Threats don't become you."

Galen kept coming, his measured steps telegraphing the kind of violence Meg had only ever seen from a distance. If she thought for a second he was coming at her, she might have died on the spot out of sheer terror. The man behind her stepped back, dragging her and the chair with him, but he was too slow. Galen grabbed his wrist and twisted, the sick sound of bone breaking echoing through the quiet of the room. He planted a foot on the side of the chair and sent her skidding out of the way and then he was on her attacker.

Meg tried to fling her hair from her face so she could see, but she only got glimpses of Galen's fist rising and falling, of the fury coming off him in waves, of the meaty sound of contact as he punched the man over and over again. He wasn't lost in a rage, though. There was only icy anger written across his face as he delivered each blow, a punishment for the offense of touching her.

Oh my god.

He lifted the man by the front of his shirt and shook him. "Feel free to deliver this message in detail to my father: no one touches Meg. You come for her again and a beating will be the least you'll suffer." He disappeared down the hallway, dragging first one man and then the other after him.

Meg focused on drawing in air from a room that seemed to have none. She just... He just...

What the hell was going on?

Galen reappeared and moved quickly to her side. She couldn't stop a flinch as he knelt next to her, couldn't stop a sob from working its way through her chest, though she'd be damned before she let it past her lips. He went still, his dark eyes thawing. "I'm going to cut the zip ties, Meg." When she didn't immediately respond, he kept speaking in that soft, measured tone. "You're safe, okay? They won't be back."

He didn't sound like he believed it any more than she did.

Galen pulled a knife from somewhere and a second later she was free. She should have run. Should have screamed for help again. Should have done anything but sit there like an idiot as he examined her hands, massaging the feeling back into her fingertips. The gentleness was so at odds with the scrapes across his knuckles from the beating he'd just delivered that it made her head spin.

He just kept rubbing her hands as if his touch would make everything better, would send her an hour back in time before... She still didn't know what those men wanted. Not really. Her pain, a message to Theo, something. She opened her mouth, but what was there to say? This changed nothing. It couldn't.

"Come on." He stood and tugged on her hand, pulling her effortlessly to her feet.

It would be so easy to go with him, to let him stand between her and whatever new threat arose. Because there would be a new threat. If Galen's father sent those men, then... God, she didn't know. She just didn't know.

Shock.

Meg was in shock.

She dug in her heels, forcing him to stop moving. "What just happened?"

He looked around the bar as if seeing it for the first time. "You're safe," Galen repeated.

"I think we both know that's a lie."

He gave a short nod, ceding the point. "You need to come with me, Meg. You're not safe alone right now."

But she couldn't just let herself be towed along by the current that was Galen and Theo. Meg pulled against his grip, narrowing her eyes when he didn't immediately release her. "How did you know to be here tonight?"

Another hesitation, this one more pronounced. "I'll explain once we're somewhere safe."

That sounded a whole lot like he'd find a way to distract her from her questions once they were somewhere "safe." Or hand her off to Theo, who would no doubt dodge her questions with the ease of a career politician because that's exactly what he was. Meg twisted her hand in Galen's grip and grabbed his wrist. "Galen, I need answers. Now."

"No, you don't. What you need is to get out of here before the adrenaline crash knocks you on your ass."

"Don't tell me what I do or don't need like you know what's best and I'm a stupid kid. I said I need answers, and I mean it."

He cursed long and hard. Galen shot another look toward the back of the bar, obviously weighing his chances of just hauling her out of here so he didn't have to bother with her questions. He finally turned to face her, speaking in short, clipped sentences. "My father found out about you. That means Theo's uncle knows about you. This was a test, putting out feelers for more information. I stepped in, which means they know you fucking matter. Now they won't stop coming for you until they have the answers they want."

"You tipped your hand when you stepped in. Why?"

His dark brows lowered and he stared at her for a long moment. "You know damn well why."

It finally hit her that Galen's *father* had sent those men. She ran her free hand over her face, trying to think past the fear coursing through her in time with her heartbeat. "Your father *and* Theo's uncle are behind this?"

"For the last fucking time, we will talk about this when we get to the apartment." He gave wrist another tug that nearly sent her off her feet and towed her out of the bar, barely pausing to let her lock up behind her. "You can't come back here."

"Oh, fuck right off with that noise." She pocketed the keys and looked around. "You didn't kill them and throw their bodies in the dumpster, did you?"

He blinked. "Give me a little credit. If I was going to pull off a double murder, I'd at least stash the bodies somewhere that wouldn't link back to you."

Meg couldn't decide if that was actually comforting or just downright scary. In the end, it didn't matter. She let him drag her along to the street. "I need to go home."

"Wrong. If they sent someone to your work, there's no doubt someone at your place." He flagged down a cab and all but shoved her inside, following her in and crowding her across the seat with his massive body. He took up too much space, and her body tightened in response to his thigh pressed hard against hers.

She could say it was the adrenaline messing with her mind, but Meg tried not to make a habit of lying to herself. There was no one to blame for her riding Theo's cock all night a mere three days ago except herself, just like there was no one else to blame for her wanting to crawl into Galen's lap and have him reassure her that everything would be okay.

You know better.

You can't afford to let someone else handle your problems. You know how that ends.

She cleared her throat as he gave the address to the driver. "I'm assuming that you're going to make a call and assure your father that I have nothing to do with either you or Theo, and then I'm going to go home."

He didn't say anything, didn't look at her. The only response was a slight tightening in his jaw.

Fear curled through her stomach and slithered outward. "Right?" The strength bled out of her voice, leaving her sounding weak and scared. "Right, Galen?"

"I don't have an answer you're going to like."

"Then give me the one I won't like."

Silence reigned for several blocks. "My father has certain goals in place, and bringing me back under his influence is one of those goals. He'll use whatever—whoever—he can in order to make it happen." He turned a dark look on her. "Right now, he's likely decided that he can use you."

Why?

But then, Meg knew why. Galen had warned her, after all, and she'd ignored that warning just like she'd ignored the little voice inside her that said she would regret giving in to her desires. Lust and logic never went hand in hand, and after a lifetime of clinging to logic, she'd let lust take the wheel.

Now she would pay the price.

She should have kept pressing him, but the events of the last however-long bled through her, sapping what was left of her argument. What if she demanded he take her home and then someone broke in during the night? She had a deadbolt on her door, but that wouldn't keep out someone determined to get in.

To get to her.

The man had said he wanted to have a conversation about Theo, but that didn't make sense if Galen's father had sent him... did it?

She didn't know enough. Meg might as well have wandered through a magic mirror all she understood the rules here. In her world, men did not send muscle after women their sons fucked once or twice. They did not hurt people the way the man had seemed to insinuate they would hurt her if she didn't give them the answers they sought.

She didn't sign up for this.

She didn't *want* this.

But Meg couldn't help feeling like whatever mirror or wardrobe or method of travel she'd wandered into, the return path to reality was now closed to her. There was no going back, no matter how desperately she wanted to.

It took too long and nowhere near long enough to reach the apartment where Theo waited. Galen didn't speak again and she had nothing to say. His answers were not answers, and if there was one person who would know how to fix this, it was Theo.

She hoped.

What if Theo doesn't want *to fix this? You're a fly trapped in a web. Does it matter if it's of Theo's making or someone else's?*

You'll be devoured either way.

GALEN STEPPED out of the cab and pulled Meg after him. At this time of night, there was still plenty of street traffic—plenty of opportunity for his father's men to blend in until they were close enough to attack.

They already *had* attacked.

He hustled her off the sidewalk, half carrying her in his rush. She cursed at him, but she could be pissed. At least she was still alive. He didn't believe for a second that Dorian would order her killed, not when he would see her as a tool just waiting to be used. But he *would* attempt to take her, and that Galen couldn't allow.

He didn't relax until the elevator doors opened into their apartment and he caught sight of Theo pacing back and forth through the living room. *He's okay. Meg's okay. They're safe.*

Except they weren't.

Shit had hit the fan in the most fucked up way possible, and there was no cleaning up this mess.

Galen released Meg's arm and ensured the security system was booted up and the door was locked. "Trouble?"

"Not here." Theo rounded the couch and stopped just out of reach. He devoured Meg with his gaze, no doubt taking in her tangled hair, her torn dress, and the way she shook like a junkie in need of a fix. *Adrenaline letdown.* Theo cursed. "I'm sorry, princess."

Meg crossed her arms over her chest and slid back a step, shying away from him—from them both. "I… I need a minute. A shower. Something."

Theo gave a short nod. "Take what you need."

She headed for the bedroom and spun at the last second. "*Alone.*"

"No shit," Galen growled. "Go. Take your time." He

considered her too-wide eyes and the way she wrapped her arms around herself. She wouldn't take comfort from them, not when they were the reason she was in this mess to begin with, but he'd be damned before he let her curl into a ball. He just needed to hit the right button. He made a show of looking her up and down. "We don't touch walking wounded anyways."

Her spine went rigid and her hazel eyes icy. "Fuck you."

There you are. Better she be angry than terrified. He could work with angry. The scared woman in the back of the cab, looking for reassurances that he couldn't give her —that kind of comfort wasn't in Galen's skill set. He preferred the harsh truth to silken lies, and there was no truth he could give Meg that wouldn't result in her terror.

He stared until she squirmed. "Already did."

Meg raised a shaking finger. "I swear to god—"

"Children." Theo's voice snapped through the room, a sharp tone that a person ignored to their peril. Meg made a sound perilously close to a snarl, but Theo ignored it. "Go shower or do whatever you need to get your head on straight. You're fucking terrified and you're snapping at the biggest dick in the room just to prove that you're not help-less. It's wasting time we don't have."

"His dick isn't the biggest," she muttered.

Galen almost laughed. Even scared out of her damn mind, Meg still had a mouth on her, and hell if he didn't respect her more for it. "Go shower. The adults are talking."

She made a sound like an angry teakettle and stalked down the hallway. He waited for the sound of the door slamming, but a soft click was all he got. "Damn."

Theo stalked into the kitchen and snagged the whiskey

bottle. He took a long pull and then passed it over. "Tell me."

"Two men. I didn't recognize them, but they claimed Dorian sent them." Galen drank from the bottle, letting the whiskey burn away the awful feeling in his chest when he'd walked through that door and found Meg tied to a chair with two men standing over her. He'd thought— It didn't matter what he'd thought. He got there in time. They hadn't done any lasting damage.

At least not the physical kind.

"She can't go back."

Galen stared at the bottle. He tightened his grip and put serious consideration into bashing Theo a few times with it. "You just couldn't leave her alone, could you? It took them a grand total of three days to figure out she might matter and come after her. Fuck, Theo, this shit is on your head."

"I know." Theo watched him. Those blue eyes saw too much, just like always. "And yet I'm not the one who was skulking outside her work. You told me you were meeting a contact."

Caught.

He opened his mouth, and then abandoned the lie before he gave it voice. "You put her in danger. I was ensuring she stayed safe."

Theo's lips quirked, but his eyes went hard. "Lie to yourself if you need to, but don't you dare lie to me. I know why you were there—the same reason I was a week ago. You couldn't stay away from her any more than I could." He bracketed Galen's throat with his hand, his thumb caressing Galen's pulse point. Theo leaned in. "I shouldn't have paid the tuition with my own name, and I'll be the first to admit it. But we are both moths to her fucking flame, and you don't get to play the beleaguered bodyguard—not right now, and not with me. You want her."

"Yes." The word felt ripped from him, taken despite his best efforts to stay silent.

Theo's grip tightened and his gaze dropped to Galen's mouth. "We can't stay in New York. They'll have eyes on her place."

"They wanted to take her, Theo. There was a van illegally parked near the back door. They might have set her up to answer questions, but they were going to take her." If they had, Dorian would use her for whatever purpose he had in mind, a lever to get Galen to dance to his tune, and then he'd discard her like yesterday's trash. Even if he didn't kill her, there would be scars, and she wouldn't be Meg anymore.

Theo pressed his forehead to Galen's, grounding them both. One breath. Two. Three. On the fourth, he stepped back and released him. "You were there in time."

"I might not have been." If he'd managed to resist the siren call of Meg's presence, if he'd had more control, if he'd really gone to meet his local contact instead of doing the skulking Theo accused him of.

"You were there in time," Theo repeated. He glanced down the hallway to the master bedroom where they could still hear the shower going. "Make the call. I know for a fact you have a passport with her name already set up."

Caught again. They'd survived this long because they anticipated and played out more scenarios than their enemies did. A month ago Galen had a passport for Meg created. He'd called himself a fool ten times over for doing it, but now it would save them all kinds of trouble with red tape.

"She's never going to forgive us for this." For dropping

a bomb on her life and leaving destruction in their wake. The two grand was nothing compared to what came next.

Theo sighed. "I know. But better she's pissed and alive than the alternative. Make the call, Galen. We need to be out of New York before dawn."

Chapter 6

Meg sat wrapped in one of Theo's T-shirts and tried to make sense of the words coming out of Galen and Theo's mouths. She shook her head. "I'm sorry, but you're going to need to repeat that."

They exchanged a look, one of those flashes of dark eyes meeting blue that telegraphed an entire conversation she wasn't privy to. Theo rubbed the back of his hand over his mouth. "You aren't safe here."

"Then I'm going home."

He crouched next to the bed, putting himself even with her. "Meg, I'm not talking about the apartment. You're not safe in New York. If Dorian has people after you, he's not going to stop just because Galen intervened once. Hell, if anything, that will only confirm his suspicions. He will send more, and they will be worse. And once they're done *talking* to you, they will shove you into a car, take you to the airport, and deliver you to Dorian wrapped up like a Christmas present." He didn't look away, didn't smile to lessen his words, didn't soften his tone. "If he gets you in Thalania, we can't help you, and no one there will."

It's not fair. The cry of a child faced with circumstances beyond her control. She wanted to kick and scream and throw things until the helpless feeling in her chest dissipated. She wanted to punish both of these beautiful men for bringing this awfulness into her life, for making her a pawn in a game so far beyond her that she wasn't even a piece on the board. It didn't matter if neither of them intended for this to happen—they'd known the stakes so much better than she had. How could she make an informed decision when she didn't know everything at stake?

In the end, none of it mattered.

"How long?"

Another of those loaded looks between the two of them. "We're not sure."

Her throat burned and she closed her eyes against the moisture gathering there. She'd had hard times before, and they hadn't broken her. This wouldn't, either. But, damn it, she was *so close* to reaching the cumulation of her plan and to have it snatched when it was only a finger's breath away... It hurt. It fucking hurt and she was entitled to be upset. "I need time to process."

"You don't have much." This from Galen where he leaned against the doorframe. "We have to move and we have to do it soon to get ahead of this."

Meg took a deep breath and then another. "You have a plan." They'd probably talked about it while she broke down in the shower. With the water cascading over her head, she could convince herself that it was responsible for wetting her face and not her tears. There could be no breaking down now, not when apparently the danger hadn't subsided. If anything, it sounded like Galen helping her had only made things worse.

You should have just taken the money and let them walk out of your life.

If you had, this wouldn't be happening.

Theo pushed to his feet and moved to stand next to Galen. They were so damn different, though they were both tall, dark, and gorgeous. Theo was the very essence of aristocracy—refined and sharp and changeable. Galen looked like he brawled in back alleys when he was looking for a good time. And they were both watching her with identical expressions on their faces, as if they expected her to dissolve into a puddle of tears and throw a tantrum that her life had just been shattered to pieces.

"I'm furious and scared, but I'm not going to shatter. Stop worrying about handling me and just tell me the damn plan."

Theo nodded, almost to himself. "You'll have to withdraw from college or push back to next year. For better or worse, this will be finished within the next nine months."

"Nine months." The words tasted of dust on her tongue. Deferring for a year wouldn't ruin her life, but it *would* ruin her timeline. She could already picture the triumphant cruelty on her mother's face when she heard the news, the croon in her voice as she whispered, *I always knew you'd fail. Thought you were better than us, but you're exactly the same. A failure. A fuckup. Blood always outs.*

No, I can't think like that.

It wasn't the end. She wouldn't let it be.

"I'm sorry, Meg. I really am. This wasn't part of the plan." Theo checked his phone. "Galen, can you meet the courier in the lobby. He should be here shortly."

Galen nodded and disappeared down the hallway. Seconds later, the sound of the door closing permeated the apartment. She looked at Theo. "A year from now your brother reaches his majority."

"Half-brother." He said it with the distracted air of someone who had to correct people constantly. "And yes, my uncle can't move directly against me in the meantime, but he won't hesitate to remove anyone who gets too close. They still think they can draw Galen back into the fold." He shook his head. "If they took you to Thalania, it might even work."

"We had sex twice. How does that translate to manipulating Galen or hurting you by taking me? It doesn't make any sense." People had sex all the time. Emotions didn't come into it. She couldn't claim that rule applied to this situation. How could she be in bed with them and *not* be affected? But there was no reason for Galen's father or Theo's uncle to realize that. Not so quickly with so little evidence.

What evidence could he even have? *She* didn't even have evidence that this went beyond an intense physical attraction and what appeared to be Theo's perverse desire to drop large sums of money on her.

"He must have found out that we shared you." Something like guilt flared over Theo's face. "We weren't as discreet as we should have been in the club."

Despite everything, her body flared hot at the memory of being caged by Galen's big body while Theo slipped a hand up her dress. "No, we weren't very discreet." She stared. "But that still doesn't answer my question —why me?"

"That moment in the club was the first time we've slipped up since I was exiled. Neither of us has been a saint, exactly, but we've been careful."

She blinked. "So he was going to... what? Send his guys to tune me up a little and see if that pulled you out of the woodwork?" Beat her and leave her to see what she did, who she called. If Galen hadn't arrived in time, or at all, would Meg have called Theo to warn him?

Yes.

She couldn't even pretend she wouldn't have.

Theo would have come to her immediately. She might not know him well in the grand scheme of things, but she knew that without a shadow of a doubt. He would have rushed to her—they both would have. And the end result would be the same.

Thank god Galen was there.

Theo shook his head. "It doesn't matter now. Galen stepped in and so they know hurting you will draw us out. That puts you at risk, and there's not a single thing we can do to stop it at this point." He watched her closely. "We could set you up somewhere for the time being, but I'd prefer you come with us."

"Come with you," she repeated. "Where?"

"Overseas. There is a… discrepancy that led to my being removed from my position as Crown Prince after my father died, and Galen and I intend to rectify it."

That meant absolutely nothing, but she filed it away to deal with later. Right now she cared less about Theo's exile than she did about her life tumbling into shambles around her. Selfish? Without a doubt. Meg couldn't bring herself to feel bad about it. "I don't have a passport, Theo. How am I supposed to come with you out of the country?" As much as she'd always dreamed of traveling, at the current junction in her life, a passport was a luxury expense. Even if Theo threw money at this problem, there will still a waiting period.

"Galen's taken care of it."

She blinked. "That seems convenient." How the hell had he pulled that off? *Why* had he pulled that off? Passports took time and securing one inside of three days had to be impossible, which meant Galen had done it earlier. Perhaps much earlier. *What the hell is going on?*

"He likes to plan for every eventuality." An answer that meant nothing at all.

Yet another thing to file away to deal with later. The weight of all the things she didn't know pressed down on her, threatening to flatten her to the floor and never let her up. "I'm going to lose everything."

"No. Never that." He hesitated, but then his eyes went hard. "We've paid your apartment through the next twelve months, as well as the remainder of your tuition." He held up a hand as she shoved to her feet. "Do *not* argue with me, Meg. I don't give a fuck about your pride right now. You're in danger because of me—because of us—and you should damn well be compensated for us fucking with your life. If everything has to be on hold until I sort out my country's issues, then I'm going to make damn well sure you don't suffer more than necessary."

This wasn't a fight she could win.

It didn't seem like she could win *any* fights when it came to this situation.

The front door thumped open and Galen appeared in the bedroom a moment later, a handful of garment bags dangling from his hand. He laid them on the bed and glanced at Theo. "We leave in ten."

"Got it." Theo motioned at the garment bags. "Pick something to wear and pack the rest in the bag in the closet. No arguing, Meg. We don't have time for it. You can file your deferment paperwork online once we get to our destination." He followed Galen out of the room and shut the door softly behind him.

"You son of a bitch," she snarled under her breath.

No, he might not have intentionally put her in this position, but he sure as hell was enjoying playing god with her life. Turning her into a kept woman, a plaything for him to cart around with them as they pursued this *discrepancy*. She marched over to the three garment bags and unzipped them one after another. Two sundresses that flirted between innocent and sex appeal. A maxi dress with a deep diving neckline. And a pair of designer jeans with a plain white T-shirt. All in her size. She looked at the price tag on the white shirt and cursed. Of course it was designer, too. Why not? He wasn't exactly the kind of guy to pop into Walmart and buy something on clearance.

Sending them back was the smart thing to do. If he was telling the truth about paying her rent and tuition, then she was already in a hole of owing him that she'd never climb out of. Adding clothing she never would have paid this kind of money for on top of it?

She should demand they stop by her place.

Meg stopped short and closed her eyes. Galen thought there were men watching her apartment, which meant going back there put them in danger they wouldn't be in otherwise. All for the sake of her pride.

It's not pride when he's the one in the wrong.

It didn't matter. She'd find a way to pay him back or convince him to let her stop somewhere that was more in her price range, like a Salvation Army. Meg cursed again and yanked Theo's shirt off. The dress she wore to bartend was ruined, otherwise she'd have put it back on.

As she lifted the jeans and shirt from the bag, she caught sight of a lingerie bag tucked behind it. Meg shot a glare at the door and dug into it. Lace panties in nude and red and bright pink—enough to last her a week without laundry. Bras to match, as if a matching set was really a priority right now.

They were nice though…

No, Meg. Use only what you have to and stash the rest so he can return it.

She grabbed her old bra and a pair of pink panties and pulled on the new clothes. Since they didn't have time to fight about it, she stashed the rest of the clothing in the bag Theo had indicated, pausing to ensure that all the tags were still attached. She hooked the bag over her shoulder and headed out of the room.

Exhaustion weighed her down, but Meg kept her spine straight and her chin high. Life kicked her in the face all the time. There was no reason to be surprised it'd delivered a particularly devastating blow just when she was so close to achieving her goals.

So close that you were never going to be able to make that tuition payment on your own.

So close that deferring was already in the plans even before shit hit the fan.

A year would not make a bit of difference. She wouldn't let it.

Just like she wouldn't let herself think too closely about what it would be like to spend time in close quarters with Theo and Galen in the intervening time.

Oh god, what am I doing to do?

———

THEO DIDN'T DRAW a full breath until the plane touched down in Germany. It seemed counterintuitive to fly closer to Thalania and his uncle's reach, but the next step in their investigation lay in the area. They couldn't afford to put it off, especially now that Meg's safety hung in the balance.

The woman in question hadn't said two words to either of them the entire twelve-hour flight. She curled up in her first-class seat, wrapped the provided blanket around herself, and from all appearances, she passed out cold.

Now, she stepped into the cloudy German morning and blinked. "Frankfurt," Meg said as if tasting the idea.

Galen rented them a car and then they were off, driving out of the city and into the country. Meg sat in the passenger seat, eyes straight ahead as if she didn't trust herself not to stare at everything like a tourist. So prideful, his princess. She would start a fight before she'd admit that she'd never been out of the country, or that she'd desperately wanted to travel growing up. He'd bet good money on both being true.

Theo leaned up between the front seats and pointed at rows of vines growing up an absurdly steep incline just off the Autobahn. "Grapes for wine. I would think white, since that's what this region is known for."

Tension kept Meg's shoulders so tight, it was a wonder she didn't shatter. "I didn't ask."

"Come now, princess. I know you're furious at me, and rightly so. I fucked up. But what's to say you can't enjoy this opportunity?"

"I can think of a few things," she muttered.

She wasn't ready. He couldn't push this, no matter how viciously the guilt ate away at him. Theo made people happy. It was what he was good at, and it had the added bonus of bringing them around to his way of thinking and accomplishing his goals. He charmed and joked and occasionally threatened, and the path paved itself before his feet.

Until last year, when everything he thought he knew turned out to be false. Until he was stripped of his rank, his very identity, the only home he'd ever known.

It was a lie. It had to be.

But he'd seen the paperwork, all presented with a little

smirk from his uncle Phillip while Dorian lurked in the background. The dates didn't line up. Theo knew his mother was married to someone else before she married his father. Everyone knew it, and half the country had been scandalized by the whole thing, but eventually the love match won over even the most traditional citizens. How could it not when Theo's parents looked at each other like the sun rose and set in their spouse's eyes?

Ten years together was nowhere long enough.

"Theo." Galen spoke softly, as if he knew the direction Theo's thoughts had taken. "We're here."

They'd left the Autobahn while Theo was thinking dark thoughts, and now they wound through narrow roads encroached by a forest that felt the same way the ones in Thalania did. Old, full of magic and other fanciful things he'd long since outgrown. They weren't that far from the Black Forest, and it was all too easy to imagine the thick tangle of trees held all sorts of monsters just out of sight.

They were more likely to be monsters of a human variety than witches and curses.

Galen took a turn onto a road so narrow, if another car appeared they'd have to careen off the road to avoid a head-on collision. Deeper and deeper into the trees they went, until yet another turn brought them to a giant iron gate. It was old and rusted in some places, a plant that looked like ivy climbing over part of it, giving the impression of a location forgotten by time. Theo took it in and then looked at his friend. "Atmospheric."

Meg leaned forward and peered out the windshield at it. "Are you about to tell me that this is owned by a reclusive billionaire who happens to suck people's blood and has an aversion to the sun?"

"Everyone knows vampires populate Wall Street, not mansions hidden away in the foothills of Germany."

Theo swallowed a laugh, but his chuckle escaped at the flabbergasted look on Meg's face. She pointed at Galen. "You made a joke."

"It's been known to happen."

She twisted to meet Theo's gaze for the first time since they left New York. "He makes jokes?"

"Sometimes." He leaned forward and lowered his voice to a mock whisper. "Don't let Galen fool you. He's an asshole and a badass, but he gets off on surprising people."

She gave a half smile. "And here I thought he got off on watching."

Heat shot through him, but Theo had enough control not to let it show on his face. The fact Meg was making even the smallest joke was progress that he refused to endanger. He hadn't bargained on Galen's father finding out about her existence so quickly, but ultimately it changed nothing.

He wanted Meg.

They both did.

And, damn it, she wanted them.

If they could all get out of their own way long enough to let it happen. She was a perfect fit for him and Galen, and time would only prove that.

He just needed to give them both time to come to terms with it. Galen was too stubborn by half and he'd spent so long denying himself the things he wanted, it was pure habit at this point. He wanted Meg, and so he refused to go after her. If Theo didn't love the bastard so much, he'd kick his ass until the truth penetrated that thick skull. Galen deserved everything, and if he wouldn't take it for himself, then Theo would just have to take it for both of them.

Meg...

Meg was a surprise. Every time he thought he knew

how she would react, she did a one-eighty on him. Her reaction to the money was expected. She had more pride than anyone he'd ever seen, and Theo hadn't thought she'd take his strong-arming money on her gracefully.

He just hadn't expected her to kiss him in the midst of their argument. To take her pleasure even while denying him the possibility of a future.

Their Meg had a mean streak that he couldn't help but admire. She was no wilting flower in need of protection, at least not when the obstacles she faced were of the more mundane variety. No one could stand against Phillip and Dorian, though. Not without a whole lot of help and some big guns to back them up.

Theo climbed out and unlocked the gate, waited for Galen to pull the car through, and then relocked it behind them. He barely got the door of the car closed behind him when Meg turned fully around in her seat to face him. "This isn't some contact's house. This is yours."

"Not mine." He had to fight to keep the sorrow from his voice, even after all these years. "It belonged to my mother a long time ago, passed down in an unbroken line from when her people first settled in the area." One of the few remnants he had of her, though she hadn't come back to this house after she reached adulthood, so it held no memories for him to cling to even if he were so inclined. "She grew up here."

Meg turned back to stare at the house emerging from the trees. The area had long since overgrown, giving the whole property the feel of a place forgotten by time itself. What was once a pristine white building was now a peeling, faded mess. Meg cleared her throat. "It looks like it's going to come down on the head of the first person to walk through the door."

"Nonsense. I commissioned someone to restore the inside six months ago."

"The inside."

Galen chose to answer that almost-question. "We brought someone in from out of country who had no ties to Thalania or the Mortimore family. It's in everyone's best interest if this house continues to appear abandoned."

Phillip might suspect they were up to something, but if he thought for a second Theo had a chance of unraveling the lies he'd spun to secure his place as regent, no promises made to Edward would hold him back from trying to destroy both Theo and Galen. "This house technically passed to a cousin of mine, but they've agreed to give me use of the house for a tidy sum and the renovations."

"I see."

Galen shot him a look of warning and pulled the car around to the old garage. It had been built much more recently than the house, constructed of wood instead of stone, though time hadn't been any kinder. They climbed out of the car and Galen opened the trunk, revealing their bags and a pair of handguns. He passed one to Theo and checked the clip on his before turning to the house. "Stay in the car, Meg."

"Like hell I will."

Theo let Galen take point on this. He was the security expert, the one who had the training for this particular circumstance. They were equal in every way that mattered, but Theo's strengths lay in politics and people and manipulation. Galen could kill a man half a dozen ways with his bare hands and specialized in a variety of methods to protect someone. Before their lives had gone to hell, he'd been Theo's head of security, and he'd developed the skill set to support that role.

He *would* be Theo's head of security again.

This wasn't over. Far from it.

Galen made a sound suspiciously close to a growl. "We have to clear the house. We can't do that with you plodding along behind us, because we'll be worried about you. Sit you ass in the car and wait for us to give the all-clear."

If looks could kill, Galen would be a steaming puddle at Meg's feet. "I'm not an idiot. I realize that you need to secure the house. If I stay out here, what's to stop someone from snatching me while you're occupied in there?"

Galen stepped closer and lowered his voice. "You've got a smart mouth, Meg."

"Don't try to intimidate me with your size just because I'm right and you don't want to admit it." She crossed her arms over her chest and somehow managed to look down her nose at Galen despite his having a good ten inches on her. "I'll be quiet and follow orders, but I'm not sitting out here."

Galen glanced at Theo, but Theo gave a slight shrug. It wasn't his rodeo, and he'd support whatever decision Galen made when it came to this. Finally, Galen cursed. "You're with me. You act too much a pain in the ass and I'll shove you in a closet to wait until we're done."

"Sir, yes, sir."

Galen turned away from her, hiding a faint smile. Oh yeah, he liked Meg's smart mouth just as much as Theo did.

Theo set aside his plotting for the time being. He wasn't as good with a gun as Galen was—no one could match Galen's skill—but he was more than decent, and distraction was unacceptable for the task ahead of them. The house wasn't tiny so it would take time to get through. The upstairs consisted of six bedrooms, each with their own bathroom and walk-in closet. Downstairs was a massive kitchen, another three bathrooms, living room, and a smattering of other rooms for a variety of purposes. Clearing it would be a bitch.

He fell into the old pattern of things, moving several steps behind Galen, keeping Meg between them. He didn't need instructions to know that if shit hit the fan, he was to take Meg and get the hell out of there while Galen dealt with the threat. "Ready?"

Galen nodded. "Let's do this."

Chapter 7

If Meg wasn't hip to how fucked her situation was, accompanying Galen and Theo while they cleared the house would have brought the whole thing home. They moved as a unit that barely accounted for her presence, as if they had done this kind of thing countless times before. She kept up with them, and in her heart of hearts, she knew that if they came across someone who wanted to hurt them —to hurt her—they would dispatch that person without mercy.

It should have scared her.

It did, in a way.

But it also wrapped around her like the strangest safety net she'd ever experienced.

Knowing that anyone who wanted to get to her had to go through *both* of these men... Yeah, no one was getting to her. It wasn't enough to make her forgive them for putting her in this situation to begin with, but it softened something brittle inside her that had spent the last twelve hours on the verge of breaking. She might be on a path she never could have anticipated, but at least she wasn't alone.

It took longer than she could have anticipated to clear the house, but finally Galen pronounced himself satisfied. He led the way back to the kitchen, and Meg allowed herself to take in the place without the threat of someone being there hanging over their heads. Even knowing Theo had commissioned a renovation inside, she'd still expected to find the place in shambles based on the appearance of the outside.

She was wrong.

It was downright homey. The floors beneath her boots were hardwood that shone in the low light coming from the windows clouded with age. The walls were a strange mix of exposed stone and a soothing off-white color that she couldn't quite call eggshell. All the accents were a rustic wrought iron that served as a reminder that they were in a modern-day fairytale mansion. The only way it could get more fantastical was if there were turrets and it was an honest-to-god castle.

They congregated in the kitchen. Galen combed through the pantry and then the fridge, and cursed. "I thought he would have been here by now."

"We didn't give him much notice." Theo checked his phone. "Speak of the devil. He'll be here in ten." He lifted his gaze and focused on Meg. "Why don't you go make use of that monster of a tub I paid through the nose for? We won't be long."

She tilted her head to the side. "I didn't invite you up." Though, damn it, her body tingled with the possibilities to be had in the oversized tub. It could easily fit all three of them and—*No, I am not here to let them bang away what little brains I have left.*

Theo raised his brows with a knowing smile, as if he knew the direction of her thoughts. "Another time, then."

"Keep your head in the game, asshole," Galen muttered.

Cute, but Meg wasn't about to let them sidetrack her. "Why don't you want this person to know I'm here?"

They exchanged a look. Galen turned away, obviously lobbing that grenade to Theo, who gave her the charming smile that had her throwing her panties at him three months ago. "Meg—"

"No." She held up a hand, hating that she had to fight not to clench her thighs together. God, he was good. The man turned on his switch and she had to fight every instinct to keep from panting at his feet. "Answer the question." She paused, decided being a dick wasn't going to get her far, and tried a smile of her own. "Please."

"Alaric is a cousin. While I trust him enough not to betray family, I can't guarantee that umbrella of protection will encompass your presence."

Galen gave a harsh laugh. "What Theo's dancing around saying is that Alaric might not fuck with family, but he'd sell his best friend for the right price. He'd use the knowledge that you're here with us as a bargaining chip without a second thought."

She opened her mouth to argue, reconsidered, and closed it. As much as she hated being shuttled to the side, she wasn't stupid enough to think she understood the rules in this game they played. They were in deep water and sinking fast, and Meg only had these two men to act as her guides.

It didn't mean she had to trust them implicitly, but fighting them every step of the way just for the sake of her pride was a stupid waste of time and energy. "Okay."

Theo leaned against the counter and crossed his arms over his chest. "You gave in too easily."

"Fuck, Theo, know when to quit while you're ahead."

Galen jerked his thumb as the doorway leading deeper into the house. "Go take a bath or take a nap or count the speckles on the ceiling for all I care. Just get out of here."

"You have such a way with words, Galen." She left the room with a measured pace, heading in the direction of the nearest of the two staircases in the house. Meg casually glanced over her shoulder, but neither of the men had followed to ensure she obeyed. *Amateur mistake.*

Growing up, her mother had initially tried to hide exactly how bad their situation was. The debt, the repeated loss of jobs, the drinking. When Meg was small, the only way she could figure out what was going on was to eavesdrop. Maybe she should have felt guilty for doing it, but it gave her back a sliver of control in a situation in danger of drowning her. Just like it had when she was a child.

She circled around to the formal dining room with a table large enough to feed twelve on the other side of the kitchen and pressed herself against the wall near the doorway. Theo and Galen spoke in voices so low, she couldn't quite pick up their words. She inched closer to the opening.

Someone knocked on the back door.

———

GALEN SET himself up just inside the door as Alaric strode into the kitchen. Theo had a truly obscene number of cousins spread across Europe—the Mortimore family seemed to have taken it upon themselves to spread their seed far and wide—but Alaric pissed him off just by breathing. Today that feeling was a thousand times worse.

Meg was in the house.

Alaric paused inside the doorway and took in the room

with his sharp blue eyes. "Love what you've done with the place."

Theo gave his politician's grin. "You know I couldn't stay here without it being up to my exacting standards."

"Of course not, Prince Theo." Alaric smirked. "I got your stuff in the car."

Galen had watched him pull up and back as close to the kitchen door as possible, so it was unlikely that he had any nasty surprises waiting. Still, it never hurt to assume the worst. He nodded at Theo. "I'll help him."

"Galen Mikos." If anything, Alaric's grin widened. "What are they feeding you Greek boys? You're positively huge."

He knew better than to let this little shit get under his skin. Alaric was a spoiled bastard who'd had everything handed to him from birth, the pampered youngest son of one of Theo's aunts. And he still turned out to be an asshole who fucked over everyone who crossed his path. Theo thought because family didn't number among his victims that it meant he could be an asset.

Galen knew better.

If the price was high enough, Alaric would turn over his own goddamn mother.

He shouldered past the blond man and walked to the car to pop the trunk. It was filled to the brim with groceries. Galen grabbed as many as he could and hauled them back into the kitchen. Three trips and the counter disappeared beneath reusable grocery bags. Theo handed Alaric a wad of cash that would have made Meg shit bricks. "Thanks, cousin."

Alaric, the piece of shit, flipped through the bills. Counting. He pocketed the stack, apparently satisfied that they hadn't tried to get one over on him. "Lot of groceries for the two of you."

Galen went still, but nothing showed on Theo's face—not even a flicker in his charming smile. "Galen eats enough for four men. As you said, he's… massive." He sank enough innuendo into the last word to make his cousin blush a deep red. Theo kept talking, every inch of his filled with a studied casualness. "And the other thing I asked you to look into?"

"I went to the village. It's old school, so they only have electronic records from '01 forward." Alaric hesitated. "It's like *he* claimed—it burned down last year. Whole thing. They lost a couple decades worth of birth certificates, including hers."

Galen crossed his arms over his chest and leaned against the counter. Watching. The truth was there in Alaric's restless hands and the tension in his back. He couldn't see the kid's face, but he'd bet his last dollar that he was having a hard time meeting Theo's gaze. He lifted his hands and let them drop. "Sorry, cousin."

"It's no matter." Theo pulled him into a quick hug. "If I need anything further, I'll call."

Alaric took a touch too long to walk out of the room, and seemed to have some trouble with his car. Theo joined Galen at the window, watching until the man finally drove away—peering out at the house the entire time. "Trouble."

Galen nodded. "He's lying. There was a fire—the papers confirmed Phillip's story—but he's holding something back."

"I know." Theo sighed and rubbed a hand over his face, suddenly looking years older. "We'll drive down there tomorrow and see what we can find. Even if the clinic burned down, there should have been backup records stored in a secondary location. We just have to find them."

"Lot of trouble for someone to go through."

"That's what I'm thinking." Theo gave himself a shake. "Looks like we're on the right track."

A floorboard creaked just outside the kitchen and every instinct Galen had went on red alert. He held up a hand and motioned for Theo to keep talking.

Theo's brows drew together but he nodded. "We'll get the groceries unloaded and figure out the next step tonight." He kept going, rattling off menu ideas and other nonsense.

Galen crept around the kitchen island. He touched his gun, but he didn't think for a second that it was an enemy on the other side of the wall. No, it was a nosey little woman who didn't know how to follow orders. Sure enough, when he burst into the formal dining room, he was greeted with a startled yip and the sight of Meg landing on her ass.

Amusement crept through him as she climbed to her feet, as dignified as a queen, and brushed imaginary dust from her jeans. Meg lifted her chin. "Galen."

"Meg." He raised his eyebrows at her audacity. She was just going to brazen through this, and hell if that didn't have him fighting a smile. "I could have sworn you were ordered to go upstairs."

She raised her eyebrows in response, a perfect mirroring of his expression. "How am I supposed to know what's going on if you send me away every time you're about to have an important conversation?"

"You could ask."

She opened her mouth, seemed to reconsider, and shut it. Those witchy hazel eyes flashed. "You wouldn't tell me."

"Too late to find out now." He grabbed her and tossed her over his shoulder, enjoying the way she yipped again and immediately started cursing him out. He walked back into the kitchen to find Theo had made good use of his time. Half the groceries were unloaded. Galen gave Meg the tiniest of shakes. "We have an eavesdropper."

"So I gathered."

Meg finally managed to finish sputtering. She smacked his back. "Put me down, asshole. You can't just manhandle me whenever you feel like it. I didn't sign up for this. I didn't sign up for any of this."

He couldn't argue that, but she seemed to be forgetting one crucial fact. Galen readjusted his grip on her, sliding her more securely onto his shoulder. "Funny, but I could have sworn Theo offered to get you set up somewhere while we dealt with this problem. You chose to come with us, just like you chose to ignore my order to keep yourself out of this. So tell me again how you didn't sign up for any of it."

She just cursed more viciously.

Galen met Theo's gaze, his friend weighing her response. Theo finally grinned, the first real grin Galen had seen on him in months. "I'd say this infraction deserves a punishment, wouldn't you, Galen?"

"If you try to spank me, *I will fucking gut you*."

Galen tilted his head in question, but Theo was focused entirely on Meg. He motioned for Galen to set her on the counter, which he was only too happy to do. They might be tempted to play this game out, but the truth was that Meg *hadn't* signed up for the mess she was on the receiving end of. She was a civilian. No matter how he'd warned her, she couldn't be expected to know the stakes.

Before.

She knew them now.

Theo moved to stand opposite her, just out of reach. "Spanking, princess? Don't be so pedestrian."

She looked at him for a second like she might actually try to follow through on her threat, and Galen tensed in response. But just like that, the rage melted away, replaced some irritation. She pointed at Galen. "Don't pick me up again."

"Don't eavesdrop on conversations you're not invited into."

She glared, turning that accusatory finger on Theo. "And you—no punishing. What the hell is wrong with you?"

Theo gave a slow smile that had Galen's pulse picking up. He knew what that expression meant. Meg was playing right into his hands, and he had her exactly where he wanted her. "There's a reward at the end, so I think you'll find the punishment is more than worthwhile."

She blinked. The moment spun out between the three of them, ripe with possibility. Galen should have said something, done something, to put an end to it, but when it came right down to it, he was a selfish bastard. He'd always been one. In the months since the exile, he'd only seen Theo put down his weight of responsibility twice—both times when he was inside Meg. She did something for Theo that Galen was incapable of. Theo looked at Galen, and he saw endless reminders of home. Of what they'd lost. Of the price he'd paid for being caught flat-footed.

Meg was outside it all.

Or at least she had been.

Theo let the silence spin on and on, and then he stepped forward and patted Meg's knee. "Later, princess. No need to make a decision now. Let's eat."

━━━

MEG'S BODY WAS A TRAITOR. Or maybe Theo was a sorcerer. Or perhaps it was that Galen infected her with lust with just his touch. More likely, it was a combination of all three.

Her eavesdropping hadn't netted her any worthwhile information. Theo's cousin seemed untrustworthy, and there was something about a clinic being burned down and records lost, but without context clues, it might as well have been in Latin for all she understood it. And then Galen tossing her over his shoulder and Theo talking of punishment...

Meg prized herself as a smart woman. She wouldn't have made it to where she was in life without brains and drive and being too stubborn to back down even when the going got hard. The going *started* hard. It was just life, and she didn't know when to quit—or at least that was what her mother accused when she got a good drunk going. *Girl, you don't know when to quit. One of these days, life is going to kick you right good in the teeth and then you'll be sitting where I am now, drinking away your pain.*

No.

Never.

Meg stared at her glass of wine. Falling into bed—*back* into bed—with Theo and Galen was a mistake. It had to be. Their strings had already entangled her and tipped everything she knew as truth on its head. They might feel a little bad that she was paying the consequences of their mutual pleasure, but she didn't get the feeling that either of them would do anything different.

Would you?

That wasn't fair.

But then, life wasn't fair. She knew that all too intimately.

She was here. They were here. The danger lurked in the shadows around them and showed no signs of dissipating anytime soon. She'd refused their offer to set her up somewhere until this all blew over, refused to sit on her hands while important things in her life were decided without her presence.

What more could she possibly lose by throwing sex back into the mix?

More than you can possibly imagine.

"Meg?"

She blinked and realized that the conversation had gone on without her. Dinner was long gone, the plates cleared and only the wine left behind. Meg picked up her glass to cover her embarrassment, hoping like hell they thought her blush was about zoning out and not picturing them all naked together. "Sorry, I was thinking of something else."

Theo lounged in his chair on the other side of the table, a small smile pulling at the edges of his lips. "You've been distracted ever since we sat down to eat. Something weighing on your mind?"

You ass, you know exactly what's weighing on my mind. This so-called punishment. She sipped her wine. "Should there be?"

"You've been going over all the possibilities for punishment Theo could have possibly cooked up in that big brain of his." Galen stared her down with those dark, dark eyes, daring her to deny it.

Conversations with him were a game of chicken. Even when she knew she should back down or swerve, she couldn't stop herself from rising to the bait. "I'm a grown ass woman. I will not be *punished* just because I happened to overhear part of your conversation."

"Hmmm." Theo contemplated his wine glass as if it held all the mysteries of the universe. "It's a game, princess. We all know how well you like to play when you're inspired." There was that smile again, the one that promised to fulfill all her darkest, filthiest fantasies. And, damn it, she knew he could do it, too. Theo pushed his chair back. "But never let it be said that we coerced you." He finished off his wine and glanced at Galen, which was all the other man needed to push to his feet and follow Theo toward the doorway.

Meg stared. "What are you doing?"

Galen disappeared through the doorway, but his shadow darkened the wall just out of sight. Theo turned to face her. "You know what lies on the other side of punishment. If that's something you want, we'll be in the last bedroom at the end of the hallway." He paused, blue eyes stripping her bare, laying all her sins on the table between them. Theo shrugged. "If that's not something you want, then this ends here."

"Ends?" She swallowed past her suddenly dry throat. Surely, he wasn't saying what she thought he was saying.

"We'll keep you safe, Meg. The money stays where it's at, no strings attached. This?" He motioned to encompass both of them and Galen. "This is a separate thing. If you want it—us—then you have to make that call. No coercion. No seducing you out of your senses. You come into this with eyes wide open."

"Theo…" She didn't know what to say. It had been so easy before, when she didn't know the extent of who he and Galen were, and later when she was so furious she told herself it didn't matter anyways. Choosing this now meant something, and she couldn't lie to herself and say it didn't. "What if I change my mind?"

He didn't look away. "Then you change your mind. I'm not demanding you sign a lifetime contract, princess. I couldn't even if I wanted to. My life isn't my own."

It belonged to Thalania.

That right there should be enough to warn her off. She couldn't have Theo in any permanent way, and Meg knew beyond a shadow of a doubt that she couldn't have Galen without Theo. He offered her something temporary, and if she couldn't accept that, then she had no business going up to that room.

"Think about it. Be sure." He turned without another word and walked away, Galen falling in half a step behind him.

Meg should clean the wine glasses and go up to the room where they'd left her bags. Not the one at the end of the hallway, though she remembered *that* room well enough from their quick rush to clear the house. The obvious master bedroom in a mansion full of suites, the walk-in closet bigger than her entire apartment back home, the massive jacuzzi tub and even larger tiled shower with no fewer than five shower heads.

And the bed.

That bed was large enough to fit five people, situated on a massive wrought iron frame, each corner spiraling up as if attempting to kiss the arched ceiling. That bed was made for fucking.

There is the punishment to consider…

The warning lacked any weight, though. Meg drank her wine slowly, letting the truth settle over her. There had never been any decision to be made. Her destination was decided the second she chose to come with Theo and Galen. Facing that, acknowledging that, burned. If she had nothing else, she had her pride, and her pride demanded she ignore Theo's offer and go to bed alone. Better to lay there and imagine all the dirty things they could be doing than submit to a punishment like she was a naughty child.

But was it really better?

No.

Last spring, she'd thought she'd only have one night with Galen and Theo and so she'd soaked up every minute with them, a starving woman at a feast she'd never be able to consume in a lifetime. This truth they chased—the one both were so sure would set Theo back on the throne—might have a conclusion in a day, a week, a month. Or it might stretch out for the next nine months as the clock ticked down to Edward Fitzcharles's coronation.

Either way, was she really prepared to deprive them all of something they wanted for the sake of her pride?

Meg finished her wine. She washed all three of their glasses and set them in the drying rack. She walked upstairs and into her room and took the quickest shower of her life, not even pausing to enjoy the mosaic art tiled into the shower walls. After the briefest of considerations, she pulled on a short silk robe hanging on the back of the door. She might be doing this, but she wasn't willing to show up naked as an offering.

Taking a deep breath, she padded down the hallway to the door Theo had indicated. She raised her hand to knock and then reconsidered. Meg twisted the handle and walked in.

Galen sat propped against the headboard, a tablet in his hand, wearing nothing but a pair of faded jeans. She spent a precious second visually tracing the scars that criss-crossed his chest. He glanced up and went still. "Theo." Theo stepped out of the bathroom, a towel wrapped around his waist. He didn't say anything, both of them seemed to be waiting for something.

Waiting for *her*.

This was her last chance to bolt.

She straightened her shoulders and met each of their gazes in turn. "I'm ready for my punishment."

Chapter 8

Meg couldn't breathe. She was here. She was doing this. The implications stretched out before her, tangling over each other and leaving only a mess in their wake. Nothing good would come of this in the long term. But she'd been focused on the long term for so damn long. The next step, the end game, the path that would lead her out of the trap she'd been born into. That would help her realize the American Dream.

She almost laughed at the thought. If that dream existed anymore, it came attached with crippling student debt and a Xanax prescription to battle existential dread. None of that mattered, because it was hers and hers alone. It paved the way for her independence and her freedom, and for that she'd make sacrifices too innumerable to count.

None of that mattered in this moment. The future didn't matter, either, because it didn't exist for them. If Theo somehow reclaimed his birthright, he would be King of Thalania, and no matter what the stories said, kings didn't marry poor girls from Michigan who wanted to be accountants.

Strangely enough, that realization freed her up to take the first step and then another, to close the door softly behind her. Both men stared at her as if weighing her declaration against the truth, so she waited. She'd made her choice. She came. She damn well wouldn't repeat herself.

Theo moved first. He didn't ask her if she was sure. He'd made the lines pretty damn clear before she ever walked into this room. He walked to circle her, trailing a single finger along the line of her shoulders, lifting her dark hair to sift his hands through it. "Very nice, princess." He stopped behind her and pressed himself to her back. "Don't you think she looks nice, Galen?"

Galen typed something on his tablet and set it aside. "She looks like trouble."

"Because that's exactly what she is."

They talked about her as if she wasn't even there. She hated it. She loved it. Meg licked her lips, unable to contain a shiver at the feeling of Theo's breath ghosting down her neck. She heard his grin in his voice. "You know the rules, Meg."

No point in pretending otherwise. "I say stop, it all stops."

"Yes." He kissed her just under her ear, a spot he seemed to gravitate toward. Theo maneuvered her until she stood at the foot of the bed, framed by those massive iron spirals. He snapped his fingers at Galen. "The ties."

"The *ties?*"

Galen reached into the nightstand and tossed two sets of cuffs to the foot of the bed. Meg stared at them, at what they represented, something hot and ugly squeezing her chest. "You have bondage gear in your nightstand."

"Galen likes to be prepared." Theo reached around her to pick up one, his big hands moving over it with the ease of long familiarity.

They'd done this before.

Of course they'd done this before.

She didn't think they were coming to her virgins—she certainly was no innocent before they met—but somehow being faced with bondage gear that they must have used on some other woman, maybe in this very room. The ugly feeling inside her gained teeth and claws.

And then Galen was in front of her, clasping her chin tight enough that little sparks of pain flickered along her skin. "Where did you go?"

"I'm right here." The words came out wrong, sharp and cutting. He looked over her shoulder and she smacked his wrist. "Stop that. I'm not some wild thing to be handled, and talking about me like I'm not there, like I'm just some toy that's interchangeable with any other—"

"*Interchangeable?*" Theo murmured in her ear. "Do you really think that?"

Galen's frown cleared, leaving something almost smug in its wake. "Your princess is jealous, Theo." He sat back on his heels on the mattress, towering over both of them. "For all your eavesdropping, you don't listen very well. We've never been in this house before today." He watched her look at the cuffs again and gave a cutting smile. "Theo is very particular about what goes into his bedroom."

"I—"

He grabbed the other cuff and held it in front of her face. Soft fabric lined the inside of her where it would clasp a wrist or ankle, shielding sensitive skin from the bite of leather. Galen turned it so she could see the leather itself. It was so new, it shone in the low light, not a single crease marking it as used.

Oh.

Shame withered her jealousy, and she couldn't quite make herself hold his gaze. Theo tucked a single finger under her chin, lifting her face to Galen. He murmured against her ear. "No one has been in this house since it was renovated." He snapped one cuff around her wrist and Galen tightened it. "No one has slept in these rooms." They repeated the process with her other wrist. "No one has fucked on this bed, or in the shower, or in the tub." Galen reached up and snagged a metal tether she hadn't seen woven in with the iron bedpost. He adjusted the length and attached her left cuff to it, and then did the same with the right.

It left her spread, her arms held up and away from her body. Helpless.

Theo traced the edge of her robe, parting the fabric easily. Giving Galen a show. He nipped her neck, his voice low and almost dangerous. "We'll fuck you here, princess. We'll fuck you in every bedroom, and then we'll take you downstairs and fuck across this entire goddamn house." He cupped her breasts, rolling her nipples between his fingers until she arched back against him. "On every surface. Against every wall. Until none of us can ever walk into this place without seeing it overlaid with those memories."

She wouldn't be walking into this house again once this was over.

He and Galen would.

Warmth spread through her, killing the last of the ugly feeling. She gave the tethers an experimental tug. "Okay."

The heat of Theo's body against her back disappeared. He circled around to study the picture she made and nodded to himself. "Part the robe a bit more. I want to see her."

Galen obeyed, untangling the tie at her waist and

pushing the robe until it was only the angle of her bondage that kept it on her shoulders. He moved away without touching her further, crawling to the edge of the bed and sitting there as Theo came to stand between his big thighs. He seemed to consider something and nodded to himself. "Jeans off, Galen. Lay on the bed with your head at the foot."

She watched helplessly as Galen obeyed, stripping with a casual grace that had heat licking at her skin. They were so fucking beautiful it took her breath away. Handsome on their own, but together they somehow become *more*. Theo's refined control played off Galen's rough and tumble meanness. Galen looked like some ancient gladiator who'd charged into their midst, big and brutal and scarred. Theo would have been at home in any aristocracy in Europe, almost pretty and playing at games she could only guess at.

And yet it worked. *They* worked.

Galen climbed back onto the bed and took the position Theo had indicated, his head inches from where Meg stood. The mattress was tall enough that they were even with her hips and she shivered at the sight of Galen laid out like the best kind of feast. His cock was already hard, laying thick and heavy against his stomach, and he watched her with dark eyes that promised things she could only guess at.

Theo tossed his towel to the side and joined Galen on the bed. He pushed the bigger man's legs wide and knelt between them. Theo gripped Galen's thighs and held perfectly still, his gaze dragging over the man before him and up to where Meg stood. He was a king surveying his kingdom of two, and she had no doubt in her mind that he'd just planned out the remainder of the night down to the finest detail.

"Are you ready for your punishment, princess?"

"Yes." The word burst out of her as if summoned, an agreement to something she needed more than she needed air. Her very own deal with the devil, though he didn't want her soul—he wanted her body.

He gave her a smile with a hint of cruelty. "Good. Be very quiet, and very still, and you'll get your reward at the end." He leaned down and took Galen's cock into his mouth.

Holy shit.

The truth sank into her. She'd been prepared for spankings, a punishment interwoven with pain. She hadn't been prepared for *this*.

Galen reached over his head to grip the edge of the mattress as Theo sucked his cock, both of them watching *her*. If she arched her hips, she might—*might*—be able to brush against his fingers, but Meg knew without a shadow of a doubt that he'd remove his touch if she tried.

They wanted her strung up like some kind of decoration at the end of the bed, still and silent, while she watched them fuck.

Theo couldn't have devised a more ingenious punishment. She was going to kill him... as soon as he uncuffed her.

Galen cursed long and hard, and half sat up. Theo met him there, claiming Galen's mouth the same way he'd claimed his cock. Once upon a time, she'd compared them to two opposing forces of nature, and that was never more true than in that moment. They clashed, their big bodies moving together in a dance older than time. Galen gripped Theo's hair and wrenched his head back, kissing his way down his neck. There was nothing cold and calculated in this. They'd stopped concentrating on putting on a show for her the second they kissed.

They touched each other like they'd forgotten she was there.

Meg watched, so mesmerized, she forgot this was supposed to be a punishment. Galen fisted Theo's cock, earning a low curse as he pumped, slowing their pace. Theo nipped his bottom lip and then tongued the spot as if soothing the pain away.

God, they were beautiful and catastrophic and she would never recover.

Theo twisted Galen to face her and moved to kneel behind him, his legs on either side of Galen's. He paused as if checking her view, and gave her that dangerous grin. "We're forgetting about our Meg's punishment."'

"Can't have that," Galen murmured, his eyes gone so dark they were almost black.

In this current position, she realized Theo was actually taller than Galen, though Galen was wider through the shoulders and chest. Theo reached around and stroked Galen's cock. "Look how hard he is, princess. You remember how good it feels to have his cock inside you."

Galen leaned back against Theo and gave her a look that was pure challenge. Demanding she… What? She didn't even know what she was supposed to do. Meg could barely breathe, let alone pull her thoughts together into some semblance of sanity. She was need, boiled down to her animal urges, her body aching under their attention. Her breasts felt unnaturally heavy and her pussy was so fucking wet, it was a wonder they couldn't see it.

Maybe they could.

Theo gave Galen's cock another stroke. "Do you remember what we talked about when I was eating your pussy in the kitchen last week?"

She swayed forward, making her chains clink. Oh

yeah, she remembered. Meg licked her lips, trying to focus. "You said you pictured Galen fucking me while you fucked him." She shivered and pressed her thighs together. It did nothing to help the way her clit throbbed as if begging for them to touch her.

Beg.

Now the challenge in Galen's gaze made sense. This wasn't just about giving her a show she had no way to take part in. This was about humiliation and desire and leaving it all on the table. She'd been holding back from day one, and they knew it.

Fuck that, I'm not begging.

Theo must have seen her decision on her face. He nodded as if to himself and released Galen. "On your back, my friend." While Galen obeyed, he grabbed lube from the nightstand and squirted some into his hand. He stroked his cock, covering himself slowly, making a show of it, and Meg couldn't help jerking on the chains again.

This time, neither of them looked at her.

Theo covered Galen with his body and took his mouth again, but it was slower now, a searching kiss that made *her* whimper just from watching. He propped himself up on one elbow and reached between them. They lay perpendicular to Meg, and Galen's leg blocked the sight of Theo's cock sliding into him. She rattled the chains again in frustration. "Theo…" Meg hesitated too long and he started moving, fucking into Galen in slow, steady thrusts. "Theo, let me see."

He clasped the back of Galen's neck and reached between them to fist Galen's cock, pumping him in time with his thrusts. Galen gripped Theo's hips, moving in perfect rhythm even as he arched up to kiss Theo again.

She might as well have not been in the room.

And hell if that didn't make the whole thing hotter.

She arched forward, but they'd cuffed her too far from the mattress to be able to rub herself against it. Meg writhed, a wild thing in a trap, so close to paradise and yet the gates were closed to her. She was so busy fighting the restraints, sure that if she could just reach them, it would all be okay, that she almost missed Theo's tempo picking up. He thrust harder, drawing growling curses from Galen's lips as he fucked him with both hand and cock, taking and giving in equal measure. Galen's heels dug into the mattress, every muscle in his body standing out in stark relief, and then he came in great jetting ribbons across his stomach. Theo gave him one more pump and then leveraged himself back, gripping Galen's hips as he started driving into him in earnest.

She held her breath, watching his strokes become less even, watching his blue eyes slide shut as he swore long and hard, watching for the exact moment where he lost control and came deep inside Galen.

Time stood still.

Meg couldn't think, couldn't speak, couldn't do anything but watch as Theo pulled out of Galen and slumped next to him, pausing to drop a quick kiss on his mouth before he rolled onto his back.

This...

She wanted this. All of it. The reservations that clung to her like cobwebs from the moment she decided on this path went up in flames. Who the fuck cared what the future brought? They had right now, and right now Meg needed these two men. She needed to be with them together and separate and to be able to watch at her leisure just like she was now.

Except the feeling pounding through her blood wasn't *leisure*.

It was desperation.

"Theo." Her voice came out hoarse and broke in the middle of his name so she swallowed and tried again. "Theo, please."

He rolled onto his side and ran a hand down Galen's chest. Galen arched into the touch, a giant wolf of a man. "She said please."

"It was such a nice please, too." Theo grinned, his blue eyes hot on her. "Apparently she liked the show."

"Apparently."

Theo gave a stretch of his own and rolled off the bed. He offered Galen a hand and hauled him to his feet. "You've held on this long, princess. Hold on a bit longer." And then the bastard walked into the bathroom. Seconds later, the shower turned on.

Galen stared after him and then spun on his heel and stalked toward her. She lost sight of him as he moved behind her, and Meg forced herself not to try to twist to follow his movement. It wouldn't work and she'd look like an idiot. She couldn't stop the shivers of need racking her body, though.

"Desperate little thing, aren't you?" And then his voice was in her ear, its vibrations drawing her nipples to hard peaks. He ducked under her arm and sat on the edge of the bed. "Spread."

Meg nearly sagged in relief and then scrambled to obey. She spread her legs wide, fighting to keep from cursing him for taking so long to touch her.

He saw it, though. Of course he did. He reached down and pushed his middle finger into her, cupping her pussy with his big hand. "Do. Not. Move."

She bit her bottom lip, half sure she'd taste blood. Her need pulsed through her like a live thing, demanding she take this pleasure and grind against his palm until she orgasmed. She was so turned on, it would take a grand total of five seconds and it would all be over.

Galen's lips twitched. "Good girl." He withdrew slowly and pumped his finger back into her. "You like this."

"Yes." She vibrated with the need to move, pleasure dancing closer with each drag of the pad of his finger over the spot deep inside her. "Galen, I'm—"

"Don't you dare come," his voice lashed her, sharp enough to fight back the budding orgasm. "You take what we give you. And I didn't give you permission to come."

It took her three tries to find her words. "I don't think I'm into BDSM."

"BDSM?" He smirked. "Baby, this isn't even close. You broke the rules, and that deserves a punishment." He kept fucking her slowly with his finger, his forbidding gaze daring her to break his command. "Do you feel contrite?"

"Yes," she sobbed. "Galen, please, I'm so close, *please.*"

His expression softened and, for one eternal heartbeat, she thought he would be merciful. "No." He gave her one last pump and withdrew. Holding her gaze, he lifted his hand and sucked his middle finger into his mouth, tasting her. She moaned, a desperate animal sound that Meg couldn't have controlled if she'd tried... and she didn't even think to try.

"Mmmm." He looked down his body, and she followed his gaze to where his cock was hard once more. "How close are you to coming?"

"Close," she whispered.

He stood and pressed a devastatingly soft kiss to her mouth. "Good." Galen sifted gentle fingers through her hair, his dark eyes unforgiving. "Next time you get off to the idea of me watching you while you fuck Theo, you better make damn sure I'm in the room." He brushed his lips against her forehead, the tender touch completely at odds with his rough words. "I'm going into that shower and I'm going to brace Theo against the wall, and then I'm going take his ass. He always loses his mind when I hit the right spot, and you'll hear him moaning though you won't get the same show you did just now."

Her throat tried to close and her eyes burned. "Galen, I'm sorry."

There it was again, that softening that hit her like a sucker punch. This time, he didn't smother the expression. He smoothed her hair back. "I'm not. I'm just as much of a selfish bastard as Theo is, and I'm not sorry that he reeled you back in. I'm sure as fuck not sorry that you're stuck with us for the time being." He gave her a slow smile that held a hint of meanness despite looking at her like he wanted to devour her whole. "But I'm a spiteful asshole and so, fuck yeah, I'm going to punish your pretty pussy until you're begging for mercy, and we're all three of us going to enjoy every minute of it." He laughed, low and sinful. "Well, I'm going to enjoy every minute of it. You're going to stand here and suffer a little bit longer before you earn that reward of yours."

He dropped to his knees, hitched her right leg over his shoulder and then his mouth was on her, fucking her pussy the same way he'd fucked her with his finger. Warm and wet and wanton, moving up to tongue her clit in deliciously slow circles designed to make her loose her mind.

He told her not to come.

Meg bit her bottom lip again, harder this time, fighting against that slow slide toward oblivion. She couldn't help it. It was too good and on the heels of his harsh words, too damn forbidden. Her hands flailing in the cuffs, grasping at air as her knees went out, and then Galen was holding her weight, lifting her to his mouth to get better access.

Oh god, she was going to orgasm.

She writhed, planting her free foot against his shoulder and kicked, wrenching him away from her. He hit the bed and the bastard had a shit-eating grin on his face. He swiped a thumb across his bottom lip. "Good girl."

He ducked back under her arm and gave her ass a stinging slap. And then he was gone, disappearing after Theo into the bathroom. Several long minutes later, low moans echoed through the space, proof that Galen was as good as his word.

Meg sagged in her cuffs. She closed her eyes, her pussy pulsing in time with her racing heart, her body crying from averted pleasure. She should hate them. She should scream and fight and curse until they let her down so she could suffer the rest of her humiliation in peace.

And yet…

She shivered, the faint sound of flesh meeting flesh coming from the bathroom. Of Galen fucking Theo. She could see it perfectly in her mind, exactly as he'd described. Theo's hands braced on the wall, Galen's on Theo. His big cock disappearing into Theo's ass with each savage thrust. Meg moaned and her hips moved of their own volition, seeking friction, practically humping the air with her need.

The shower turned off.

She opened her eyes as, seconds later, Theo and Galen strode back into the room. Galen took up a nearly identical position as he'd been in when she walked into the room, against the head of the bed, one hand tucked casually behind his head. The only difference was that he was gloriously naked now. Theo moved behind her, a presence she felt even before he stroked his hands over her body, along her sides up to cup her breasts and then back down to her hips, one dipping to explore her pussy. "Poor Meg. Aching and empty and teased until pleasure becomes pain. You've suffered admirably, and you followed our Galen's orders so sweetly." His thumb brushed her clit and he pressed his body against her back. "Are you ready for your reward, princess?"

Chapter 9

Theo uncuffed Meg and let the chains dangle back against the bedposts, a visual reminder of where she'd been and where she may be again. Seeing her cuffed there, her body flushed with lust, her eyes on them as he moved in Galen… It had taken every ounce of Theo's not-inconsiderate willpower not to call the whole thing off and drag her into bed with them. He loved Galen. He enjoyed the hell out of Meg. But the three of them together?

Fucking perfection.

He lifted her hair from her neck and twisted it around his fist. "You didn't answer me, princess."

"Yes," she whispered, her voice hoarse. "I'm ready for my reward."

He couldn't keep himself from touching her, running his hands over her tight little body, exploring her in a way he hadn't been able to since that first night. When they were together in his apartment last week, it had been fast and furious fucking with short periods of exhausted rest in between.

This was different. This was *more*.

Theo cupped her breasts, enjoying their weight as much as he enjoyed her sharp inhale. "You were so very, very good. I'm prepared to let you choose how you want your reward delivered."

"Both. I want both of you."

He grinned at Galen over her shoulder, but his friend had too much control to let his intense expression flicker. He tightened his grip on her hair, pulling her head to the side so he could taste the sensitive spot on her skin. Meg smelled like summer, bright and sunny with a hint of floral.

Like home.

He tamped down on the sorrow the thought brought. In the six months since he'd last been in his country, he'd traveled the world. Nowhere else brought about the same complicated mess of responsibility and love and anger that Thalania created in him. He missed it.

He'd get it back, but that was a fight for tomorrow. Tonight was about Meg and Galen and finally getting them to where he wanted them to be.

Together.

Theo lifted her into his arms. "Okay, princess. You can have both of us." He moved around the bed and set her on the edge. "Lay against the headboard."

She scrambled to obey, taking up a spot just off the center, putting herself right next to Galen. Galen responded by rolling onto his side and dragging his big hand down the center of her body, stopping just over her belly button.

Theo drank in the sight of them. She was so tiny next to Galen, a breakable thing to be protected at all costs compared to the modern-day warrior who would go to battle for Theo in a heartbeat. Her pale unmarked body almost perfectly complimented the scars on Galen's darker skin. Beauty and the Beast.

And they were his.

"Give her a kiss, Galen. I'd say she's earned it."

Galen leaned down and claimed her mouth. She whimpered and tried to turn toward him, but he easily held her flat on her back with his hand over her stomach. Giving Theo a view.

Watching wasn't usually Theo's preference—he liked to be right in the middle of things—but they created such a captivating sight that he was content to crawl onto the bed and sit just out of reach near their feet.

The punishment had thrown Meg off. It was the only explanation for her taking a full minute to realize she didn't want to lay passively and take whatever Galen gave her. His princess wasn't the passive type, which was why he enjoyed fucking with her so much. She reached down and fisted her small hand around Galen's cock, the sight sending all of Theo's blood rushing south.

Galen was having none of it, of course. He liked things the way he wanted them and to hell with anyone else. He grabbed her wrist and pinned both arms over her head, barely breaking the kiss before he took her mouth again. If left to his own devices, he'd tease her until she lost the ability to do more than beg.

Another night.

Theo moved, shifting to settle near their hips. He parted Meg's legs, guiding one over Galen's thighs and the other over Theo's shoulder. She tried to break the kiss, but Galen used his free hand to cup her jaw, keeping her mouth on his. *Good boy.*

Theo ran his thumbs down either side of her, parting her folds. Her pussy glistened with desire and he could no more deny himself a taste than he could deny his next breath. He licked her slowly, taking his time and enjoying the way her hips jerked beneath his grip. She was so wound up, if he didn't let her come soon, she might shatter. Galen had teased her too long, and they were bordering on cruel.

He loved it.

Theo sucked on her clit, working her with lips and tongue as he pushed two fingers into her. He kept his pace consistent, driving her breath by breath to the edge. Her thighs went tense and clamped around his head and then her fingers were in his hair, holding him to her. As if he wanted to be anywhere else. Theo loosened his grip on her hips, letting her ride his face as she took her pleasure. Her pussy clamped around his fingers as she came, and Theo looked up her body to watch Galen eat her cries.

Beautiful.

He kept fucking her with his fingers as he brought her down. One orgasm was nowhere near enough after how long they'd teased her, but he had other plans for the next. Theo lifted his head and withdrew his fingers to trace down the seam of her body to her ass and press against her lightly. As expected, she froze. "Tell me something, princess."

Galen released her mouth and moved down her body to cup her breasts. She stared at Theo with wild hazel eyes. "What?"

He pressed against her again, more firmly this time. "You said you wanted both of us."

"Yes." She dug her heels into the mattress, though whether it was because of Galen's mouth on her breasts or Theo's finger pressed against her ass was anyone's guess. Meg seemed to realize she was on the verge of struggling and took a slow breath that morphed into a moan when Galen set his teeth against the underside of her breast. "I can't think when you do that."

"Good," Galen murmured.

"Galen." Theo put enough steel in his tone that his friend growled and moved back a little. They couldn't afford to push her too hard, and muddling her ability to say yes was out of the question. No one would wake up tomorrow with regrets. He'd make damn sure of it. Theo waited for Meg to meet his gaze again, keeping up the steady pressure against her without actually penetrating. "Is this what you want?"

She propped herself up on her elbows. "I... Yes. I want both of you. I just..." Trepidation flared in her hazel eyes. "This is new territory for me."

A virgin ass.

His cock jumped at the thought, even as Theo called himself a Neanderthal for giving a fuck if someone else had been there before. He glanced at Galen, and he didn't need to hear his friend's words to know his thoughts. *Careful*. This would require handling to ensure everyone had an equally good time. "You'll have what you want, princess." He nodded at Galen and moved back to grab the lube from the nightstand.

Galen snagged a pillow and then flipped Meg onto her stomach over the top of it. It left her ass a little in the air and she tensed as if expecting him to jump on her and ravish her like some kind of animal. Galen, that glorious bastard, knew it. He resumed his position next to her and kissed her as he wedged his arm beneath her body. Theo didn't need to see it perfectly to know Galen was playing with her pussy. The way her body jerked told him everything. Galen murmured in her ear, just loud enough for it to carry to Theo. "This time I won't hold back your orgasm, baby. While he's pushing that big cock into your tight little ass, you're going to ride my hand."

"Galen—"

"That's right. Rub that wet pussy all over me. You only

get one finger right now, but that's all you need." He nipped her shoulder. "Theo's watching and he's so fucking hard for you."

Theo climbed back onto the bed and knelt between her spread thighs. "For both of you." He held up the lube until Galen grabbed it with his free hand, and then Theo parted her ass cheeks. She was so wet from their mouths and her earlier orgasm that it had wet her here, too, but it wouldn't be enough for what came next. He nodded and Galen squirted some lube down her crease. She jerked, but Theo wasn't in a rush. He ran his fingers over her and pressed the first knuckle of his middle finger into her, letting her get adjusted to the penetration. "Relax, princess. We've got you."

Galen nipped her shoulder again. "Feels dirty to take your pleasure like this, doesn't it? Grind on me, baby. Let us give you what you need."

Theo spread more lube, pushing deeper into her, ensuring she was as ready as possible. His cock ached with need, his balls heavy and his body tight with the knowledge of what came next. Long minutes passed, broken only by Meg's ragged breathing and Galen's low filthy whispers about how good it felt to have her pussy riding his hand. How good it would feel when it was his cock.

Soon. Soon.

Satisfied he'd prepped her, Theo slipped his fingers out of her and slathered lube over his cock. He met Galen's dark gaze, the desire there making it hard to breathe. This was what they'd both wanted since that first night—since far longer than that. They'd shared women before, but simple, dirty fun, with limited trust involved.

This? This required a whole hell of a lot of trust.

And Meg gave it to them.

Theo braced one hand on the side of her head and

guided his cock to her ass. He bore down, but paused when she froze. Galen understood and immediately rubbed her back, soothing her. "Relax, Meg. Breathe. Just breathe and let him do the work."

Slowly, oh so slowly, she obeyed.

Theo guided his cock into her another inch, and then another, slowly and surely filling her completely. He shifted her hair to the side and pressed an open-mouth kiss to her neck that had her shifting restlessly against him—against Galen's clever fingers. "Let me tell you a secret, princess."

"What?" she gasped.

"We've never shared a woman like this—like we're about to."

She went still, as if the implications had just settled over her. "Never?"

"Never," Galen confirmed.

Theo slid his free hand beneath her hips and rolled them. He ended up on his back, with Meg sprawled against his chest, his cock still buried in her ass. Theo carefully hooked his legs under hers and spread her wide. Galen moved to kneel in the space he'd created. He ran his hands up Meg's thighs and then down again, repeating the move with Theo's thighs.

A wicked grin pulled at his lips and he cupped Theo's balls, rolling them over his palm. "She's tight, isn't she? Clenched around your cock, trusting you to treat her gently and not fuck her ass like you want to." One final squeeze and he released Theo, which was just as well. He was hanging on by a fucking thread.

Galen looked at them both, and Theo knew him well enough to see beyond the mask, to recognize the possessiveness beneath. Galen might as well have growled, *mine.* He ran his hand up Meg's body to bracket her throat. "He's nice. I'm not. When I take your ass, and I will, I'm going to ride you hard, baby. Theo can have your pussy that time, or maybe your mouth." He dragged his thumb over her bottom lip. "Play nice and we'll even let you choose."

She shivered over Theo like a live wire. "Galen, I—"

"Not tonight." His hand disappeared down her body and Theo didn't have to see to know he was playing with her pussy again. Galen frowned. "Are you on birth control?"

What?

"Yes," she murmured.

Galen, what are you doing?

Galen didn't look at Theo, blatantly refusing to answer his unspoken question. He just kept working Meg with his fingers. "We're clean. We haven't fucked anyone but each other, and we were tested less than six months ago."

Fuck, Galen. Theo held his breath. The audacity to broach this conversation *now*, in their current position... "Galen—"

"I'm clean." Meg gave another shiver, clenching around his cock. "I... I got tested after we were together."

Galen didn't look away from her face. "Do you want me to get a condom?"

Theo started to sit up, but froze when Meg moaned. He soothed a hand down her body and glared at his best friend. "You can't just—"

"You didn't put on a condom, Theo."

He cursed. Fuck, but Galen was right. "I'm clean."

"I know that. Now she does, too." Galen leaned down over them both and pressed a soft kiss to Meg's mouth. "Do you want me to get a condom, Meg?" he repeated.

"No." She reached one hand behind her head to hook around Theo's neck, and the other around Galen's. "No, it's okay. I trust you. Both of you."

Theo had to close his eyes to smother the guilt her words brought. She shouldn't trust them. In this, yes. Always. He would never put her in a position where she would be harmed by fucking them. But it was his selfishness that had put her in literal danger, and he didn't fucking deserve her trust as a result.

Galen stared at her for another long moment, as if gauging her sincerity, and then he reached between them. "Remember to breathe."

———

"I—" Whatever Meg had been about to say disappeared in a whimper as Galen started working his cock into her. She was already full of Theo, and Galen wasn't small by any definition of the word. She gripped his hair, holding him close even as she writhed between them.

"Breathe," Theo murmured in her ear. He pressed a hand flat against her stomach, holding her still as Galen thrust deeper, wedging himself inside her until he was sheathed to the hilt. His dark eyes held a storm of desire and a ruthlessness she was growing to appreciate even as she dreaded it. His gaze flicked up to Theo's and he dipped down to take Theo's mouth even as he began moving in her.

She'd half expected the rough fucking he'd promised her, but Galen went slowly. It was still almost too much. She couldn't move, could barely breathe through the fullness. Being pinned between them, her legs spread wide, her body filled in a way she never could have dreamed.

Meg shifted, but once again, Theo's hand on her stomach stopped her. This time, when he spoke, his strain was evident in his tone. "We're hanging on by a thread, princess. Don't want to hurt you." He skated his hand down to stroke her clit, timing the small circles with each of Galen's thrusts.

Each muscle flexed on Galen's body as he buried himself to the hilt. "Hang on." He moved them onto their sides and hitched Meg's leg high on his hip. The new position made her whimper. Galen hesitated. "Okay?"

"Don't you dare stop." She reached behind her to tangle her fingers in Theo's hair. "You're both just... so deep."

"Mmmm." He held her clenched to him and kissed her, his tongue conquering her mouth even as his cock had conquered her body. Or maybe it wasn't a war. She didn't know anything anymore, except that she might die right here in this bed from the pleasure they dealt her, and Meg couldn't bring herself to care. She was so busy tangling with Galen's mouth that it took her precious seconds to realize Theo had begun to move behind her.

He held her hips perfectly still and dragged his cock nearly all the way out of her before starting an equally slow thrust back into her. She shivered like a live wire, her body sending her conflicting messages. *Too much. Not enough. Stop stop ohmygod stop. Don't stop. Oh fuck, don't you dare stop.*

Through it all, Theo never ceased his tantalizing circling of her clit with his clever fingers. And Galen never stopped kissing her. Meg arched back toward Theo and broke away from Galen's mouth for half a second. "More. I want more."

Theo froze. "You're sure."

"Yes."

Galen laughed harshly. "Give the lady what she wants, Theo." He lifted her leg up and out, opening her completely for them.

They'd been careful before. Too careful.

They weren't now.

They began fucking her in earnest. Each stroke timed to perfection. They thrust and withdrew as one man, leaving her alternately achingly empty and almost too full. All the while, Theo played with her clit as if he had all the time in the world to coax her to orgasm.

Meg couldn't move. Couldn't do more than take what they gave her, pleasure with a hint of pain, their bigger bodies overwhelming her smaller one. She felt used, dirty in the best way possible. They took their pleasure from her body, and through it all one truth vibrated through her.

I'm the first.

The thought tipped her over the edge. Meg's body went tight, white exploding across her vision as her orgasm sucked her under. They didn't stop, didn't slow down, just kept fucking her as her orgasm went on and on, her toes curling so hard they hurt.

Theo's strokes broke. He cursed and Galen hooked the back of his neck and kissed him as Theo pulled out and came on her back in searing streams of cum. Galen pushed him, and then Meg was half tossed face-down onto Theo's chest as Galen moved between her legs. He urged her hips up squeezed her ass, parting her cheeks just like Theo had done earlier. "Soon, baby. Soon." He spoke so low, he might have been talking to himself.

And then he guided his cock into her pussy with enough force that she slid several inches up Theo's chest. Theo was there, tangling his fingers in her hair and claiming her mouth even as Galen braced one arm over her shoulder to keep her in place and fucked her in short, brutal thrusts. She felt him swell inside her. He cursed and pulled out, shooting across her back, mixing his cum with Theo's. She melted onto Theo's chest, boneless.

Meg blinked slowly, staring at the tastefully colored wall on the other side of the bed. "I think I found religion."

Galen huffed a laugh and dropped down next to them. He kissed Meg and then Theo, and then rolled onto his back and stretched like a giant cat. "That so?"

"Mmhmm." She had to clear her throat. "There was a second in there where baby angels sang and I'm pretty sure I saw the face of god." Meg reached out with a shaking hand and dragged her finger over the scar that ran perpendicular to Galen's collarbone. "I think we're going to have to do this again, though. Just to be sure."

Theo's laugh filled the room. "Not tonight, princess. The only thing left on the agenda tonight is another shower and a long soak."

She shifted experimentally. Her whole body ached as if she'd run a marathon—or ridden two sexy as fuck men to completion—and she was decidedly…sticky. "That sounds doable."

"So glad you approve."

Galen huffed out another of his chuckles and rolled to his feet. "I'll get the shower going."

Meg smiled against Theo's chest as she listened to him stalk into the bathroom. Several long moments passed before her body formed back into muscles and bones and let her lift her head. Instead of a goofy smile on his face, Theo's dark brows were drawn together in a frown. She frowned back at him. "What?"

"I don't want you to have regrets."

She started to make a pithy answer, but stopped and shook her head. "I thought things couldn't get better after that first night with you two. I was wrong. This was so much better."

He smoothed her hair back from her face. "All the same, a conversation about being tested and whether or not to use condoms shouldn't be done in the middle of fucking. It skews the outcome."

Ah.

Meg took a slow breath, trying to get her sluggish thoughts into an order that made sense. "Do *you* have regrets?"

"When it comes to you and Galen? No. Never."

She had a feeling he wasn't solely talking about the condom conversation, but she let that go. "I meant what I said. I trust you two. I have an IUD. I'm not getting pregnant without someone yanking that thing out, or I wouldn't have agreed to go bare." When he just stared at her, waiting, she huffed out a breath. "No, Theo, I don't have regrets. Did the fact it felt a little wrong get me off all the harder? Fuck yes, it did. But I still wouldn't have said yes unless I was willing to do it."

He searched her face as if debating whether she was going to change her mind and yell at them for coercing her later. Meg could have told him it wasn't even in the realm of possibilities. She owned her choices, for better or worse.

At least she did when she made them with eyes wide open.

Finally, Theo nodded. "If you change your mind, no one will hold it against you."

"I know." She pressed a quick kiss to his lips. "Come on. Galen's getting lonely in that big shower all by himself."

Chapter 10

"They took her to Germany."

Phillip Fitzcharles pinched the bridge of his nose. He should have killed that bastard nephew of his months ago, a quiet accident that was very tragic and convenient. It would have saved him the epic headache the boy had become. If he was in Germany, he was searching for evidence that Phillip's claims about Mary were lies. As if he could fake something of that proportion without the paperwork to back it up.

He had, but that was beside the point.

Theodore couldn't know. It was impossible.

Phillip turned to face Dorian. Such a small-minded man, mean and ambitious. There was nothing wrong with ambition, but Dorian always reached too high, too fast, and he failed because of it. It was his ambition that resulted in his exile nearly twenty years ago—an order reversed by the current Crown Prince.

He checked his watch. The Crown Prince who would be there shortly. "They're in Mary's old house?"

"Yes. It's owned by one of the many Mortimore sisters, but Theo is there with Galen and the girl."

Dorian might be a monumental pain in his ass, but the man's contacts were without parallel. Phillip paced to one side of the room and back. "You burned the clinic."

"I saw to it personally. The records no longer exist."

It wasn't enough. Despite heavy bribes, the information was scattered and unreliable. There could be other copies of the records filed elsewhere. Dorian had his men do a cursory search, but just because they hadn't found something didn't mean it didn't exist.

And if it existed, then Theodore *would* find it. He was too desperate not to.

Phillip glanced at the doorway Edward would be coming through at any moment. They had to wrap this up quickly. The boy was already suspicious, and the only way Phillip had placated him was to promise that Theodore and Galen could come home after he was crowned— stripped of their respective titles, of course.

He couldn't let it happen.

As long as Theodore was in Thalania, he was a threat to the crown. The people loved him, and he'd been raised to rule. He couldn't stand next to the throne without over-shadowing it.

Without overshadowing Phillip's influence.

He moved closer to Dorian. "This can't go on any longer. Do you understand me?"

Dorian's brows drew together. "My son might still be useful."

The only person who could successfully harness Galen was Theodore, but telling the man that accomplished nothing. Dorian's ambition lay in convincing his only son to wed Camilla Fitzcharles. Despite the offer, it would never happen

—something Phillip knew when he proposed it—but it kept Dorian from getting any untoward ideas. "That's fine. If you can find a way to separate them, do it. But my nephew and the girl need to be dealt with, Dorian." If she was sleeping with Theo, there might be a chance she was pregnant and *that* was a nightmare Phillip had no intention of dealing with.

"Consider it done."

"Good." The door opened and Phillip turned with a practiced smile as Edward Fitzcharles walked into the room. "Good morning, Edward." The boy took more after his mother than his father, lean and pale with a face that hadn't quite lost the softness of childhood. Theodore had radiated personality from a very young age, sure of his place in the world, but his younger brother didn't have quite the same presence.

The difference served Phillip well.

"Good afternoon, Uncle." Edward dropped into the chair across from him. "What's on the agenda today?"

Murder.

Phillip kept his smile in place as Dorian slipped from the room. If things went well, in a few days his little problem with Theodore and his woman would be nothing more than a tragic news story.

▭

GALEN WOKE as Meg climbed out of bed. He kept his eyes closed and his breathing even, curious about what she intended. Last night had been intense, to say the least, and most women would need some space after it. Or that's what he told himself as he listened to her pad to the doorway and down the hallway.

It sure as fuck wasn't rejection.

He rolled over and laced his fingers behind his head. It

was early—barely five—but he'd get dressed and go for a run soon. As intense as the fucking was last night, Galen needed to burn off some energy. They hadn't dodged any bullets by coming here. Theo took precautions to cover their trail, but ultimately, he was the exiled prince of Thalania. People paid attention to him, especially in Europe.

If he thought for a second it would have worked, Galen would have tossed both Theo and Meg on a plane and sent them somewhere safe while he hunted down these leads. It shouldn't have been this difficult to get the evidence they needed, especially in this age of technology where everything was on the internet.

But try as they might, they couldn't get concrete answers about Theo's mother—about who she'd been before marrying his father.

About her first marriage.

It should have been as easy as a Google search and, failing that, contacting her family to obtain records. But both her parents were long dead and while one of her legion of sisters had maintained control of the family property in Germany, the rest of them had scattered to the four corners of the earth. It didn't make sense, and their caginess when it came to talking about Mary set Galen's teeth on edge.

There was a secret there—a big one.

And he didn't think for a second it was the same one Phillip had used to oust Theo—that Mary was still married to her first husband when she ran off with Theodore Fitzcharles II, got married, and got pregnant. Not necessarily in that order. Phillip might have the paperwork to prove it, but something wasn't quite right.

Galen and Theo fully intended to find out the full story.

It would have been a whole lot easier to do if any of Mary's sisters were actually interested in talking to their nephew.

Footsteps in the hallway brought him back to the present. Meg slipped through the door and froze when she met his gaze. "You're awake."

"So are you." He glanced at the thing she held in her hand. A book. "Bored?"

She tilted her head to the side and made a show of raking her eyes over him and then Theo where he still slept on the other side of the mattress. "I have two gorgeous men in bed. How could I possibly be bored?" When he gave her a look, she sighed. "Yes, I'm bored. We dodged jet lag for the most part, but I'm usually up and moving by this time."

"Me, too." He patted the mattress. "Show me your book."

Still, she hesitated. "I should probably just read in my own room. I don't know why I even came back in here."

Galen didn't navigate bullshit easily. It wasted everyone's time to spin comfortable lies when the truth was right there glaring in a person's face. Meg came back in here because she wasn't ready to leave last night behind, because she craved intimacy to go with the fucking. She might not be willing to admit it to herself, but he knew it for fact.

He should send her to her room. A sharp comment would be all it took to get her back up. She was too prickly and prideful to stand and take it if he spelled out her vulnerability in the space between them.

"Get your ass back in this bed."

She glared, but she marched back to the bed. Instead of crawling up from the foot of the mattress in the same way she'd exited, Meg walked around to his side and climbed over *him*. He almost let her, too, but if she was going to be a brat, he'd be a fucking brat right back. Galen looped an arm over the small of her back, plastering her against his chest. "If you wanted sex, you should have just said so."

"If I wanted sex, I'd be sucking your dick." She smacked his chest. "Let me up, Galen."

"Tell me about your book."

She gave him a look like he was crazy. Maybe he was. "Here? Like this?" She wriggled and his body responded. It would be the easiest thing in the world right now to kiss her, to shift his grip to cup her ass and guide her to grind against his cock until she was begging for it. And, fuck, he wanted to. Something must have shown on his face, because Meg shivered. "It's five o'clock in the morning."

"Mmmm." He loosened his hold on her and stroked his hand up her spine and back down again.

She licked her lips. "I hate when you do that. That sound doesn't mean anything." Meg shifted so her arms were on either side of his head, bringing them flush together. Yeah, this was nice. She rolled her hips a little, seeking his cock.

"Sure it does." He reached for the lube they'd left on the nightstand and squirted some of it onto his palm. Galen urged Meg up on her hands and knees and palmed her pussy. He slid a finger in, two, and then one again, until she was ready for him. Last night had been a lot of abuse on her sweet little pussy, and he wanted her here with him right now, hot and needy and not the slightest bit uncomfortable. Galen spread the lube up to her clit, playing with her for a few seconds before impatience got the best of him. "Now."

"Yes." She didn't wait for him. She grabbed his cock and guided it into her. Meg sank onto him in a smooth move, her eyes drifting shut for half a breath before she opened them, as if she didn't want to miss this any more than he did. She planted her hands on his chest and rolled her body, fucking him slowly. "Forgive me."

He watched the point of their joining, watched the slow slide of his cock into her pussy, the sight so good, it was almost unbearable. "There's nothing to forgive."

"Liar," she breathed. Meg lifted herself until only the head of his cock was inside her and rolled her body again, fucking just that part of him. He went to reach for her hips, to stop this goddamn teasing, but she grabbed his hands, laced her fingers with his, and pushed them down to the mattress on either side of his head. He could have broken her hold without even trying, but Galen didn't. He let her hold him down, let her tease him, let her put on a show that was only for him.

And Meg, sexy, infuriating, too-smart Meg, knew it.

She sank onto him suddenly, sheathing him completely and grinding hard. "It's just us right now, Galen."

Fuck, the way she said his name.

He could have pointed out that it *wasn't* just them. That it never would be. That Theo lay right there next to them while she rode Galen's cock and whispered dark things to him.

He didn't.

He let Meg play out the dirty fantasy, and he embraced the tiniest hint of wrong. Theo wouldn't give a fuck about Galen and Meg having sex without him any more than Galen gave a fuck about *them* having sex. There was jealousy, sure, but it was a small jealousy that would never fester.

In that moment, the truth didn't matter.

This thing between them all might be complicated, but it didn't carry the potential of dire consequences the same way everything else in his life did right now. A bruised heart was the worst he had to worry about if things went sideways with Meg.

And fuck if that wasn't just as seductive as the way she rode his cock.

He angled his hips so she could grind her clit against his pelvic bone, and Meg wasted no time doing just that. This wasn't the fast, angry fucking he'd walked in on between her and Theo that day back in the apartment. She was fucking Galen like they might not get another moment and she wanted to wring an orgasm out of him before the timer went off. It was sexy as fuck. Her grip spasmed on his wrists, and it took every ounce of control he had not to flip her and drive into her like an animal.

"Your cock feels so good, baby. It fills me up. I could keep riding you all day like this, riding your cock while you watch me just like that." She leaned down and licked his bottom lip. "Sometimes the way you watch me is almost as good as fucking, Galen. Did you know that?"

Her words seduced him just as much as the tight clamp of her pussy around his cock. He wouldn't last much longer, not with this new version of Meg whispering filthy things in his ear while she fucked him. God, this woman. Every time he thought he had her figured out, she revealed a new facet and he was intrigued all over again.

Truth be told, he never *stopped* being intrigued.

"I'm close, baby." Her strokes hitched, little shudders working through her body. "I'm going to let you flip me." Her lips brushed his again. "And then you better cover my mouth while you make me come. Theo needs his sleep."

Fuuuuuuck.

Galen didn't wait for permission. He rolled them. He hooked one of her thighs over his arm to spread her nice and wide for him, and then he covered her mouth with his hand. He knew what she expected—for him to drive into her—but she'd had her fun. It was time for his. Galen fucked her slowly, thoroughly, keeping up the exact same pace she'd set when she was on top. He set his teeth against her neck, against the marks left there by Theo's mouth. "Dirty girl. You get off on doing things you think you shouldn't."

The slightest nod was her only response. He could feel her breath coming faster as her orgasm bore down on her. Galen shifted his angle so he dragged along her clit with every stroke. *Yes. There.* "I'll tell you a secret, baby." He caught her moan in the palm of his hand and kept going. She was almost there. Galen nipped her again. "Theo's been watching us from the moment you slid that tight little pussy onto my cock."

Meg came with a cry, and Galen couldn't hold out any longer. He thrust into her again and again, chasing his pleasure as her pussy milked him. Finally, a small eternity later, he shifted back to her side and pressed a soft kiss to her lips.

"You…" She twisted to confirm what he already knew. Theo lay on his side, his head propped on his hand, watching them with a small smile on his face. "Theo."

He leaned over and kissed her, and then kissed Galen. "Morning."

Meg blushed a bright crimson, as if caught in the middle of something she'd be in trouble for. She still didn't get it. Galen tucked her against him, her back to his front and pulled Theo closer to her other side. Theo had told her the truth. This wasn't forever. It couldn't be with the realities of Theo's life.

Fuck, *Galen* and Theo weren't forever.

When Theo won back his throne—and Galen would make damn sure he did—he'd have to marry and have a small herd of children, and women willing to share their husband's bed with his best friend were few and far in between. Especially noble women. Even if they somehow won the lottery there, it wouldn't be an equal triad. Theo and his wife would always be married, and Galen would always be the third. They'd have to take precautions to ensure that when she got knocked up, the bloodline remained uncontested.

It was fucking exhausting to even contemplate, and the probability of it happening at all was so slim, it might as well be impossible.

All they had was right now.

Theo smoothed Meg's hair back and then ran his hand over Galen's jaw. "You two are beautiful."

"We're not always going to be the three of us together," Galen murmured in her ear. "Does it bother you that Theo and I will fuck without you sometimes?"

She shivered. "No, of course not. I might be bummed out I didn't get to watch, but I don't expect to be in the middle of it every time."

"That's how we feel about you, princess." Theo smiled. "Never apologize for one-on-one with either of us. We might give you shit for it, but it's in good fun."

She finally relaxed against them. "I don't know the rules of this sort of thing. It's entirely new territory for me."

Galen stroked his hand over her hip, liking the way she fit between them. "Only one rule—open communication. You want something, you tell us. You don't want something, you tell us. And we'll do the same for you."

Meg let out a slow breath. "I'll try."

It was better than he hoped to get.

Theo reached over them both and snagged the book Meg had dropped. He examined the cover—a shirtless man in a kilt wielding a sword and looking particularly intense. "Interesting." He turned to the back and raised his eyebrows. "How filthy is this book, princess?"

"Very." She said it so primly, Galen chuckled.

He kissed the back of her neck. "Are you harboring fantasies about Fabio in a kilt? Should we buy Theo a wig so we can play out this particular scenario?"

She elbowed him. "One—Fabio might have been cool back in the day, but he's a crazy right-wing asshole now so we'll never speak his name again. Two—if anyone is going to play Viking, it should be *you* in the kilt."

"She's right." Theo opened the book and flipped a few pages. "I'll be the doting husband and you'll be the pillaging Viking she wants but can't admit it aloud."

The scenario skittered too closely to where Galen's thoughts had gone just a few moments before. He wasn't the third in this scenario. If anyone could claim the position, it would be Meg, but the lines had blurred until they ceased to exist, and he preferred it that way. The thought of Meg with Theo's wedding band around her finger left him with a tangled mess of emotions in his chest that he didn't know how to deal with. "That's not what she wants, Theo."

Meg snorted. "Please, do tell me what I want instead of asking me."

"I don't need to ask you, baby." He kissed her neck again, just because she was close and he liked the taste of her on his tongue. "I know what you want. You want both Theo and I to play Viking to your village girl. You'll run. We'll chase you. How long do you think you can evade us before we catch you and take our reward out on your pretty pussy... and your mouth... and your tight little ass?"

She shivered and pressed her ass more firmly against

him. "Okay, fine. That sounds like a lot of fun and I would one hundred percent be down for it."

"Thought so." Galen reached around her and ran his hand down Theo's chest. "Now, baby, you've been selfish. Theo is hard and ready to fuck. Should we let him choose who he gets to take his frustration out on? Or should we choose for him?"

"You." Meg didn't hesitate. "I want to watch him take it out on you."

That's my girl.

Chapter 11

Despite the early start to the day, they left the house a full hour later than Theo had planned. Fucking Galen had led all three of them to the shower and it was hardly anyone's fault that they'd gotten distracted all over again. And then they had to hold off until Meg could file the paperwork for her deferment, which had taken yet more time.

Meg seemed to have shelved her fury at them both for the moment, but Theo had no illusions—it would arrive again. She clung too tightly to her plan for her *not* to resent them if they held her back for too long.

The sooner they got this fucked up situation resolved, the better for all involved.

As soon as you are reinstated, the whole thing ends.

He pushed the thought away. He spent enough time borrowing trouble without adding more to the balance. They had right now, and right now would have to be enough. Once things untangled, he and Galen would go back to Thalania and Meg would resume her life in New York with the major difference of financial status. He hadn't told her that he'd made a deposit to her personal account, because she'd just yell at him all over again. Money wouldn't give her back the time she'd lost or eliminate the memory of the fear she'd experienced because of Dorian's men, but it would give her a freedom he suspected she'd never had before. She could hate him for that gift if she wanted, but she'd damn well keep it.

Theo glanced at Galen as the climbed into the car. "You found the backup files?"

"I found a place that *might* have the backup files." Galen held the door open for Meg and then took the driver's seat. "My German is rusty and we had to go around a few times, but the secretary claims that the fire didn't destroy all the records, just their copies of them."

Thank fuck.

Meg leaned forward. "If this is out of line, let me know, but… what records are we trying to track down?"

Theo and Galen exchanged a look. They hadn't exactly decided whether or not to loop Meg in on all the details. Galen shrugged, leaving it up to him. He sat back. If she was involved enough to be in danger, she was involved enough to know the plan. "I was stripped of my rank because my uncle claims that my mother was still married to her ex when she and my father got married and got pregnant with me. While there's no doubt in anyone's mind that I'm Teddy's son, rather than her ex's, the marriage wasn't legal and so I'm not legitimate. With those considerations in play, I cannot be King of Thalania."

Fuck if it didn't still hurt to say it aloud. There were times during his teenage years where Theo wanted nothing more than to run away and leave the country to sink or swim without him. To hand off the responsibility that weighted his every step. To just be a normal civilian who worried about normal civilian things.

He'd made his peace with being the next King of

Thalania in his early twenties, and he'd spent the next ten years learning everything he could from his father to be the best king possible. The one his people deserved. The weight never decreased, but he learned to bear it without complaint.

And Phillip had taken it all away.

Meg reached out and touched his bicep. "He waited until after your father passed, right? So there was no way for him to formally adopt you and make the whole thing legal."

Smart girl. He nodded. "It was a brilliant play."

"Not brilliant enough," Galen muttered. "He faked it. There's no way he didn't fake it."

"The marriage certificate dates hold up." His mother had married an American, and he and Galen had tracked down the records and had them verified. There was no record of a divorce, and there should have been within the same state where they were married. For there to be no record meant it had never happened.

Which meant Phillip was right.

Meg gave his arm a squeeze. "So that's why you're in Germany—the birth certificate."

"Yes. It was the one item missing from Phillip's presentation that dethroned me before I had a chance to actually be on the throne. He's not the kind of man to leave a loophole for someone to walk through, so there had to be a reason he chose not to include it." A long shot for the record books, but at this point long shots was the only thing they had left.

"Hard to get a birth certificate from a burned-down clinic."

"And yet that's exactly what we're going to do." No guarantee that the backup records would hold the information he sought, but Theo wouldn't leave Germany without at least trying. He stared out the windshield as Galen guided them down the winding road. Trees practically blocked out the gloomy skies that promised rain later in the day. Despite that, it was a beautiful area and he relaxed back into his seat. "If this doesn't work, we'll just have to set out to seduce Meg into marrying us."

She let loose a satisfying squeak. "That's not funny."

"Who's joking?"

"You are, you asshole," Meg hissed. She smacked him, hard enough to sting. "You can't say stuff like that, Theo. I know what this is. We all know what this is. Don't pretend like it's something else. It's too cruel."

He opened his mouth to contradict her, but Galen gave a slight shake of his head. *Fine, then.* Theo ran his hand through his hair. "I'm hurt you don't want to keep us, princess."

"Wanting something has nothing to do with the reality."

He knew what she'd say next—a long list of their theoretical differences, starting with the number in his bank account. To Meg, his finances mattered more than anything she might share between them. It was interesting that she'd looked to Galen to help during that first argument. Theo could have been petty as fuck and told her that Galen's holdings were double his own. He'd lost a lot when Phillip stripped him of his titles, all the money and properties, except what he'd had in his personal accounts. It was only because he'd enjoyed playing the stock market and was more than passably good at it that he had anything to his name at all.

Galen was still titled. He had two residences in Thalania—one in the capital Ranei, and one in the middle of his holdings, which included three towns and a small city, all of which he collected an income from in the percentage of a small tax. All of it could be stripped from him, but they'd already made arrangements to combat that eventuality.

Not to mention Galen had trusted Theo to invest his money for over a decade. He was wealthy even without any of his connections to Thalania.

Theo couldn't tell Meg any of that. She saw a kindred spirit in Galen, someone who stood in Theo's shadow or some shit. And they saw *him* as the heir apparent, the one who would reclaim his throne and leave them both behind in different ways.

He didn't have an answer for that.

He didn't have an answer for a lot of things right now.

So Theo let the conversation fade into silence, rather than spark into an argument that would ruin the flickering happiness they'd claimed for their own. It wasn't forever, but it didn't have to be. He had to be content with that.

When have I ever been content leaving something I wanted behind?

Galen took a turn onto a wider road. They still had a good thirty minutes of driving ahead of them, so Theo leaned forward and clicked the radio on, picking up on one of the local channels. His German was just as rusty as Galen's, but the station played Top 40 hits, and that was good enough for now.

To one side, the road fell away into a ravine, dark and twisted with old growth. It made the hair stand up on the back of his neck. Theo straightened. "Galen—" He never got the rest out.

One second they were cruising along, and the next they were airborne. Up was down. Down was up. Theo hung suspended in his seatbelt as the world rushed by for one breathless second.

Then they hit and everything went dark.

—

MEG MUST HAVE LOST CONSCIOUSNESS. The last thing she remembered was looking out the window and now she was upside down and blinking blood from her eyes. She touched the bright spot of pain on her arm and cried out at the feeling of something big and sharp protruding from her skin. *Glass*, her mind so helpfully supplied. She knew better than to yank it out, so she swiped the blood from her face and tried to figure out what happened.

Theo hung from his seatbelt, his body limp. Unconscious. That was all. He'd passed out. He wasn't dead. He couldn't possibly be dead. Theo's life shone too brightly to be doused like this. It had to.

You're going into shock, Meg.

Galen's seat sat empty, door closed. The windshield was gone, but she couldn't tell if it had happened during the crash or afterward. It didn't matter. The only thing that mattered was getting out of this car and then getting Theo out as well. Cars didn't really explode as easily as the movies made it look, right?

Oh god, what if they did?

She fumbled for her belt clasp, her movements slow and uncoordinated. *Must have gotten knocked on the head...or it's blood loss.* The roof of the car over her head was stained a wet red that made her stomach lurch. How long had she been unconscious?

Too long.

She pushed on the latch, but it resisted. Jammed. "Oh, fuck."

Footsteps outside her door. Meg blinked, but she didn't get a chance to react before someone wrenched her door open and then Galen was there. He looked just as shitty as she felt, small cuts peppering his face. It didn't seem to bother him, though. He touched her head and then cursed as the sight of the glass shard in her arm. "Hang in there, baby."

"Theo."

"He's breathing. He just knocked his head really good. *He's* not bleeding out." He pulled a knife from somewhere, a viciously long serrated blade that had her heart leaping into her throat. Galen guided her uninjured hand over her head to brace on the ceiling. "I'm going to cut you out of your seatbelt."

"Okay," she whispered.

"Try not to crack your head."

This was right about the time she should fire off a snappy reply, but Meg didn't have anything. She just nodded and locked her elbow as best she could. Galen sliced through her seatbelt and her arm went out. He must have expected it, though, because he caught her around the chest and helped ease her down. "Almost there, baby. You're doing great. We need to get out of the car and then I can get a better look at your arm."

"*Theo*," she insisted.

"I know." Galen dragged her out of the car and propped her against a nearby tree. He paused, staring up the embankment where they'd been driving not too long ago. She couldn't see the road from her position, couldn't hear anything that might be a car driving past. Galen turned back to her. "Are you going to pass out again?"

She shook her head slowly, not liking the way the world swam around her at the movement. "I don't think so."

"Good. Don't." He pointed at the embankment. "If something moves up there, you say my name."

Meg nodded carefully. "Okay." She watched Galen fight open Theo's door and give him the same treatment he'd given her. Theo murmured something, the sound of his voice washing over her. Theo was okay. Galen was okay. Things would be okay.

She shivered, cold despite the relative warmth of the day. *Definitely shock.* Nothing moved except Galen and Theo, and her thoughts drifted in lazy swirls as she contemplated that. *Galen thinks someone did this to us and might finish the job.* Meg blinked and blinked again, the scene in front of her moving in stop-motion snapshots.

Galen checking Theo for injuries.

Blink.

Theo and Galen going still, their gaze trained on something she couldn't see.

Blink.

Theo crouching in front of her, his blue eyes worried. Galen nowhere in sight.

Blink.

"Meg. Meg, stay with me." He said it with the quiet patience of someone who'd been talking to her for some time with no response.

Her body flashed hot and cold and she looked down in time to see him extract a six-inch shard of glass from her arm with a pair of tweezer looking things. *Where did he get those?* Theo held her arm braced between his big hands and she belatedly realized she was struggling to get away from him. "I know, I know, I'm sorry," he murmured. "It's going to get worse before it gets better." He prodded the wound, sending agony searing through her. "I have to make sure there's no more glass in here or we run the risk of shredding something important when the bandage puts pressure on it.

"Theo." She gasped, a buzzing in her ears nearly drowning out his steady voice. "Theo, it hurts."

"I know, princess. I've got you. Trust me." He cursed

softly and pulled another shard from her arm. "That's the worst of it. We'll clean it when we get somewhere safe." He used one hand to dig through a white box with a distinctive red cross on the front and then set to work bandaging her up. "It didn't nick an artery, which is a fucking miracle. You would have bled out before Galen had a chance to get you out of the car."

Meg gave into the dizziness and closed her eyes. It was easier to breathe without seeing his ministrations. "Your bedside manner leaves something to be desired."

"There she is." Pressure on her arm as he wound some kind of flexible tape stuff around it. "You scared the shit out of me."

"That makes two of us."

He stroked a hand over her cheek. "You can open your eyes now. I'm done."

The light had changed overhead, but she couldn't tell if it was because she'd lost time or because there was a storm coming. "How long have we been out here?"

"Too long."

She looked around, cautious of too-quick movements. "Galen?"

"He's doing what he does best."

That wasn't any kind of answer at all. She shuddered. "Shouldn't we call for help?"

"Doing that just ensures that we're bringing civilians into this, and paves the way for them to separate us into ambulances and finish the work they started."

She tried and failed to make sense of that. Galen had seemed to think this wasn't an accident, but how could someone possibly attack them and then pose as a paramedic? Things like that only happened in fiction, didn't they? "Theo, what's going on?"

"We'll talk about it when we get out of here. I've got your wound stabilized. It's time to move."

She started to climb to her feet, but he didn't give her a chance to fail. He scooped her into his arms and started through the trees in the opposite direction of the road. Meg bit her lip to avoid asking him more questions. He was right. Answers could wait. She tucked her face against his neck and tried to keep her shivers contained. There was no telling how much blood she'd lost. What if she needed a transfusion? How would they know or even accomplish it if they were too paranoid to go to a hospital?

I thought I knew the stakes. I had no idea.

"I've got you, princess. You'll be safe." He murmured against her head as he picked his way through the thick trees.

Germany seemed like such a small country on a map—smaller than many US states—but it might as well have stretched for hundreds of miles in all directions. The forest felt vast and ancient, even though part of Meg's brain pointed out that the trees couldn't possibly be as old as her imagination wanted to believe. The danger, she couldn't write off as easily. "Are there wolves in Germany?"

"I won't let you turn into a real life Little Red Riding Hood."

"Oh god. There are totally wolves in Germany," she whispered. "You know, when I put a pin in this country, I thought for sure that it would be a trip filled with schnitzel and amazing beer and cruising the Rhine and dancing all night with some blond guy named Hans."

"Hans isn't a German name, and he sounds like an asshole."

She smiled against his skin, letting their low conversation distract her from the steady pulse of pain in her arm and the danger all around them. "He was nice in my dream."

Theo walked for several minutes without saying anything. Just holding her close and watching everything around them. "Why a pin?"

Maybe it was blood loss or maybe it was the terror bleating in the back of her mind, but Meg didn't even think of lying. "I grew up poor and miserable—things that don't have to go hand in hand, but they did in my family. It was... ugly. Really ugly. I spent a lot of time fantasizing about running away, but even when I was young and stupid, I knew better. Nothing good happens to runaways. I stayed. I kept my head down as much as I could. And the only thing that got me through it was my map filled with places that I'd someday go. My escape."

Theo hugged her closer. "When we're through this, Galen and I will take you on a Rhine river cruise. Fuck, we'll take you anywhere you want to go."

"When we're through this, you'll be King of Thalania again." Her eyes were getting heavy, the weights of them pulling her toward the darkness. "I'm really tired, Theo."

"I know, princess. We're almost there."

Almost where?

Light played across the backs of her eyelids and Meg opened them to find them on the edge of a hill. The forest lay behind them and fields upon fields rolled out at their feet over the gentle hills. Theo hitched her higher and readjusted his grip. "See that village?"

She squinted against the weak sunlight, barely making out a little cluster of buildings camped out three hills over. They were some kind of brick or mortar or whatever buildings had been made out of back in the day, and they looked almost as if she and Theo had stepped into a time warp into the past. The steep roofs were a charming red and even at this distance, she could see flower boxes blooming in many of the windows. "I see it."

"Galen is going to meet us there. And then we're out of here."

Out of here. She clutched his shoulder. "What? No. You need that birth certificate."

"Phillip's not going to stop coming or sending Dorian and his men after us. If he's taking these measures before the coronation, then he's desperate. The whole reason I brought you with us was that I thought our presence would protect you." Theo gave a sharp laugh. "I should have known better."

She'd never seen him like this before. Laughing Theo. Sexy Theo. Infuriating Theo.

Never Bitter and Despairing Theo.

"Theo, you're doing the best you can."

"My best isn't fucking good enough." He started down the hill, and despite the anger in his voice, he held her gently and moved in a way that didn't jar her. "I should have stayed and fought when Phillip first pulled this bull-shit. I had leverage and power as the Crown Prince. If I'd stayed—"

"What would have happened to Thalania? Answer me." She fought against the fatigue seducing her eyes closed and grabbed the front of his shirt. "You know what would have happened. What always happens when two factions fight for power."

"I wouldn't have let it come to a civil war."

"It wouldn't have been your choice to make once you decided to fight. Phillip has a lot of support among the first circle of families. He wouldn't have gone down easily, if it at all. You made the only choice you could have given the circumstances."

He looked down at her, blue eyes filled with things she

wasn't willing to put a name to. "When did you become an expert on Thalanian politics?"

In for a penny, in for a pound. "After that night with you two, I was curious. I didn't think you would call, but I wanted to know more about the place you two came from." She forced herself to release her grip on his shirt. "You can't leave Germany without what you came for, Theo. I won't let you."

"In that case, we'd better get a move on. Galen will kill us both if we're late."

Chapter 12

Galen didn't breathe until he saw Theo and Meg walk into town. Leaving them had been the hardest fucking thing he'd had to do, but with someone hunting them in the trees, Galen was the best equipped to handle the problem. He started the car he'd stolen from the guy and drove to them. Theo carefully set Meg in the backseat and followed her in. Good. She looked three seconds from passing out, though the patch job on her arm was well done.

Theo scrubbed a hand over his face. "Let's go."

"No." Meg shifted on her seat like the car might explode around them. "Theo needs to get the birth certificate."

Theo spun on her with a curse. "We talked about this. You need a fucking doctor and probably a blood transfusion."

"Probably." She sank back into the seat and closed her eyes. "But I'm just going to keep fighting with you until you do what you need to do, getting weaker all the while."

It was a brilliant play.

Theo glared at Galen, but he just shrugged. The truth

was they needed that damn birth certificate and as much as he wanted to gather up them both and get the fuck out of this country, they'd come here for a reason. The cause was greater than all of them as individuals. But he knew his friend and he knew that Theo wouldn't agree to shit without some kind of compromise. "We know a doctor."

Theo's jaw went tight, his thoughts obviously following the path Galen's had taken. "Not her."

"She's all we have."

"Fuck. Fine. Call her." He turned back to Meg, pressing a hand to her forehead. "Hurry."

Galen made the call, got the address. It was two villages over, which was the only silver lining in what had become a shitshow of a day.

"She's asleep," Theo murmured. "Tell me."

"One man. He was trained too well to give up who sent him, and I didn't have time to convince him to see things my way. He went for his knife. I got to mine faster." He kept his voice monotone. Theo didn't like the lengths Galen was willing to go for him—for them—but Galen had made his peace with his role a long time ago. No monarch made it through their reign without getting their hands bloody. He spared Theo as many of those hard decisions as he possibly could.

It was the least he could do after what Theo had done for him.

"It's not safe to go back to the house."

Galen checked the rearview and kept driving. "I'll take care of it." He didn't trust this doctor, but he could bank on her hating Phillip enough that she wouldn't turn over information about them. That was *all* he could bank on. After they dealt with the marriage certificate, Galen could stash them somewhere to rest and circle back to the house to get the things they needed.

They weren't going to get far without their shit.

"No. No more risks. You've done more than enough. I'll do it."

He tightened his grip on the wheel. Theo wasn't normally squeamish about letting him handle shit, but this morning had shaken all of them. When he'd wrestled himself out of the seatbelt and turned around to find Theo unconscious and Meg bleeding out from a huge gash in her arm... Galen hadn't known fear like that in years. Not since they were nineteen and Theo's horse had thrown him.

He shuddered at both memories. "We can't risk you, and you damn well know it. Learn to delegate."

"Don't you dare talk to me about delegating. You would carry the whole fucking world if I let you, and it's not right. If something happened to you—"

"You would keep going." Galen took a turn and entered the village. It was larger than the last one, more of a town really, sprawling at twice the size of the place where he'd picked them up. "You are more important than any one part, Theo. If you fall, then Phillip wins. Edward becomes puppet king to your uncle, and Phillip twists him into a man of his own making. He'll marry Camilla off to some douchebag who will break her spirit, because he can't afford for anyone to rise up against him." Not that Galen could see sweet Cami leading a rebellion, but stranger things had happened.

Theo was silent for several breaths. "Stop throwing my role in my face like it makes me special. I have a job to do, same as anyone. Just because you're not a Fitzcharles doesn't mean you're expendable. You are *not* fucking expendable, Galen. If something happens to you..."

"It won't." He had no business making promises, and he knew better than to try. "And even if it did, you'd finish this. You'd connect with the other people loyal to you and you'd see this plan through." He parked and turned to meet Theo's gaze. His blue eyes were filled with anger and something like despair. Galen leaned forward and lowered his voice. "You are going to be the motherfucking King of Thalania, Theo. Every single person can be sacrificed except you. Every. Single. One."

For a long moment, he thought Theo would argue with him. But he finally gave a short nod and sat back. "Let's get this over with."

It wasn't a win, not by a long shot. In fact, this whole day was a mark in the loss column. They were down and hurt and Phillip had obviously decided to stop pussyfooting around and take out Theo directly. All of that translated to one undeniable fact.

Things were about to get a whole lot worse.

━━

MEG WOKE up as Theo tried to carry her out of the car. She shook her head. "I can walk. Just hold me up." A girl could only handle being carted around so much, and his arms had to be exhausted after their earlier trek. She caught sight of Galen and went still, running a critical eye over his body. No outward signs of injury and he was moving okay as he rounded the front of the car. "You made it."

"*You* made it." He neatly stepped between her and Theo and scooped her into his arms.

"Hey! I can walk."

"You're about to fall over, and Theo is weaving on his feet. Don't make my job harder than it has to be." He slowed and lowered his voice. "I'm glad you're okay, baby. We're going to make sure you stay okay."

A wave of dizziness left her lightheaded as he picked up his pace. "Galen—"

"Hush." He stalked to the building they'd parked in front of, a cheery little house with white walls, flowers growing from every available surface, and a charming brick walkway leading up to the bright red front door. Galen shifted her closer and spoke in her ear. "Keep your mouth shut in here, no matter what she says. She's the best doctor around, but her help comes with thorns. Got it?"

She started to tell him exactly where he could stick his advice, but Meg forced herself to stop and think instead of jumping straight into conclusions. Galen could be a dick, but he wouldn't give her instructions like that unless they were walking into a dangerous situation. They'd just been run off the road—or whatever happened that resulted in their car in that ravine. She wasn't playing in the shallow end anymore. She wasn't even in the deep end. She was in the fucking ocean.

Meg finally nodded. "Okay."

"We'll get you through this. Trust me." He half turned to look at Theo. "Ready?"

"Not in the least. Let's go." Theo took the lead, shouldering open the door and holding it so Galen could walk through with her after him.

Meg wasn't sure what she expected, but the adorable factor from the outside spilled over into the interior. They stood in a small living room with cozily worn furniture that spoke of a lot of time spent there. On the other side of the room, a tiny kitchen with perfect white cabinets and not a dish out of place overlooked an equally small backyard that appeared to have some sort of garden. It was perfect, the kind of house Meg would have built for herself if she was interested in living in a small town again, but she wasn't.

Theo crossed his arms over his chest, every breath conveying barely concealed aggression. "We're here, Alexis. Let's get this over with."

Footsteps above them and then the narrow stairs to their right creaked. Galen tensed as if expecting an attack. None of this made any sense. If this person was so dangerous, why had they brought her here? They were acting like they'd stepped into hostile territory, instead of somewhere they were safe enough to recover from the crash.

What's going on?

The woman who walked down the stairs a few seconds later was as out of place in the cute little house as a shark in a kiddie pool. Meg automatically sized her up. Understated designer clothes—jeans and a blouse. Blond hair that likely cost several hundred dollars an appointment to maintain, if not more. Bright red lipstick and low-key day makeup. This woman had money up to her ears, and she'd probably been born into it because she didn't feel the need to show it off. She moved with a confidence that blatantly ignored how both Galen and Theo tensed at the sight of her. Meg placed her age somewhere around forty-five, though she could very well be over fifty with the kind of money she sank into her appearance.

None of that explained the men's reactions.

The woman, Alexis, walked up to Theo and pressed an air kiss against each of his cheeks, once again ignoring the fact that he didn't return the gesture. "It's been too long, Theodore." She had a faint German accent that gave her words a pretty lilt.

"With respect, we're not here to catch up. You said you'd help."

"Of course." She turned bright blue eyes on Meg and smiled, though there were glaciers warmer than her expression. "Darling girl you've got here."

Galen tightened his grip on Meg as if he wanted to yank her away, but he held still as Alexis prodded the bandage on Meg's arm. She frowned. "This isn't a half bad patch job. I'd say I was proud if the sentiment wouldn't curdle your stomach."

"Alexis," Theo warned.

"This way." She headed through the living room and down a short hallway to what was probably a spare bedroom or office at one point. It contained a bed, but that's where the familiarity ended. The bed was more hospital cot than a place for sleeping, and there was what appeared to be a full medical set up. Meg avoided hospitals like the plague unless she *had* the plague. Doctors were expensive and being a bartender didn't come with benefits. She used the clinic at NYU if pressed, but she had to be knocking on death's door to even consider it.

Galen set her down on the bed and gave her hand a squeeze. Then he moved to stand just inside the door. Theo took the chair on the other side of the cot, apparently so he could glare daggers at the woman helping them. There was a history there, but hell if Meg could make sense of it.

Alexis took her blood pressure, pulse, and temperature, and then checked her eyes. "She shouldn't need a transfusion." She put on gloves and unwound the bandage, her touch cold and careful despite the light mocking in her eyes. "Theo is something of a drama queen, but I'm sure you know that." She tossed the bandages into a nearby trash can and probed the wound. "I'm going to wash this out to make sure we're not closing it up with glass still in there. It'll be a bitch, but you'll thank me for it later."

Meg nodded and braced herself. A large hand closed around her uninjured one and she glanced over to see Theo holding her. He gave a half smile. "It'll be okay."

"Of course it'll be okay. I'm the best doctor in the southern half of this country." She snapped her fingers at Galen without looking over. "I need saline. Top drawer."

He looked like he wanted to snarl some choice words, but he retrieved the bottle of saline and handed it to her. Alexis pulled out a pair of large tweezers and raised a dark eyebrow. "Will you hold still or do you need assistance?"

Do I need someone to hold me down?

Meg cleared her throat. "I'm fine."

"Have it your way." She doused Meg's arm with saline, clearing away the dried blood, and then did it again. "Try not to scream in my ear." And then she probed deeper into the wound.

Meg had to look away. Pain made the room around her hazy and too bright, and her stomach tried to rebel. She clamped her teeth together to contain the wounded animal sounds her tongue wanted to make. Instead, she held tightly to Theo's hand, as if gripping him until his bones ground together would actually lessen *her* pain.

On and on it went as Alexis pulled three separate slivers of glass from the wound. Several more minutes and she pronounced herself satisfied. "It's not wide enough to require stitches if you aren't an idiot." She dumped the bloody gloves into the trash, grabbed a new pair, and clean bandages. Through the whole process, her expression hadn't changed. She could have been sitting down to tea or a book club or a conversation she was only mildly interested in.

She stared hard at Meg. "Though you're obviously dating these two fools, so that makes you an idiot if I've ever seen one. Maybe stitches would be a better choice. ."

The pieces clicked into place. She looked at Alexis's blue eyes and then over to Theo's. "She's your aunt."

Theo's expression went dark. "She's a fucking traitor."

"If I was a traitor, boy, I would have called that uncle of yours instead of playing doctor with your girlfriend." She put a trio of butterfly bandages over the cut and then a pad of gauze over that. "How is Phillip these days?"

"As treacherous as always."

"I assumed as much." A roll of bright pink bandages went over the gauze, row after row of it until it was completely covered. Alexis sat back. "This needs to stay on at least a week. The bandage is waterproof, so you can shower as soon as you can stand without toppling over. No baths for a week or so. If the pain gets worse instead of better or you start showing signs of infection, either come back or get to a hospital. After a week, change the bandages but don't mess with the butterfly bandages until it's healed shut."

"Okay."

She looked over Meg at Theo. "He's not going to stop."

"I'm aware."

"I told my sister not to run off with that dickhead from America, and look where that ended up. Then she pairs up with another dickhead from Thalania." Alexis laughed bitterly and pointed at Meg. "Be smarter than Mary was, girl. Nothing good comes from the Thalanian royal line. It's all heartbreak and backstabbing and bullshit. Get out while you still can."

Meg swallowed hard. "I'll take it under consideration."

"You won't, just like she didn't." Alexis pushed to her feet. "You two might as well get cleaned up and go take care of whatever you need to before you leave the country."

Theo didn't move. "What makes you think we have things to take care of before we leave the country?"

Alexis gave a mirthless smile. "Because my dear son

told me what you've had him looking into." She shook her head. "You should have just asked me. I have copies of all the family records."

"If I'd asked, you would have said no."

She shrugged a single shoulder. "Perhaps. I suppose we'll never know." Alexis turned and walked out of the room.

Galen pushed away from his spot on the wall. "I'll be back in an hour. If you can convince her to give you a copy, great. If not, you will damn well wait for me to get back before you go after those records. They know what you want. They'll be waiting for you."

A muscle in Theo's jaw jumped, but he nodded. "Be safe."

"I'll do my best." And then he was gone, leaving them alone.

Theo leaned forward and studied her face. "You need rest."

The only thing Meg wanted in that moment was to curl up and sleep, but it wasn't a luxury they had. She started to rub her eyes and realized she was covered in blood. "We both need a shower. We look like victims in—"

"An attack designed to look like a car accident?"

She sighed. "I was going to say that we look like victims in a teen slasher movie, but thank you for taking the wind out of my sails."

"I'm sorry, princess." His serious tone said he was apologizing for a whole lot more than cutting her off.

"You couldn't have known." She should be pissed. She might be later on, when she wasn't so bone-crushingly exhausted. Maybe. Meg didn't know anymore. She really had stepped through a mirror into another world and while the rules and players didn't make sense, there was one thing she knew beyond a shadow of a doubt.

Theo and Galen would never intentionally put her in harm's way.

A week ago, their unintentionally doing exactly that would have had her screaming the roof down. But that was before seeing Theo's despair and his body hanging limp and unconscious in his seatbelt. Before Galen stepped between them and danger again and again without thought to his own safety. Both men carried their own demons.

She wouldn't add to them. Not when the circumstances were beyond their control.

She squeezed Theo's hand. "Why don't you get one of those showers and then you can help me with mine?"

He gave another of those tired half smiles that still managed to warm his eyes a little. "I think my aunt might kill us if I take you in the shower in her house."

"Get your mind out of the gutter." She said it with a smile of her own, though. "Go, Theo. We should be ready for Galen when he gets back."

That got him moving. He nodded and disappeared through the doorway. A couple minutes later, the sound of water running upstairs reached her. Meg tried to relax and counted slowly in her head. Before she made it to sixty, Alexis walked into the room.

Now that she knew the woman was Theo's aunt, she could see the resemblance. It was there in the proud line of her nose, the way she carried herself, and of course her blue eyes. She sat in the chair he'd vacated and folded her hands in her lap. "What my nephew is doing is foolhardy at best, and suicidal at worst."

So we're going to play it like that.

Meg made a noncommittal noise. As suspected, that didn't slow Alexis down any. "My sister was the same way —impulsive and too inclined to see the glamorous big picture instead of the nitty-gritty details required to create her vision. She died because of that."

"I was under the impression that the late Queen of Thalania died because of an illness."

Alexis shook her head slowly, her eyes hard. "Oh, honey, you're playing in the big leagues now and you have no idea what's at stake. She died because someone took exception that their queen was a foreign commoner, rich or no, and poisoned her. Just like someone very likely poisoned Teddy last year." She leaned forward and lowered her voice, every line of her barely concealed fury. "That place might look like a paradise, but it's a viper's nest. No sex is good enough to put yourself at those people's mercy."

Meg searched her face. She'd known Alexis would come back to make her pitch, but for the life of her she couldn't figure out if the older woman was sincere or if she was playing at a deeper game. "I appreciate the help you gave me today."

Alexis sighed and sat back. "But you're going to make your own way regardless of the advice of people who know better. I see."

"Do you really blame an entire country for your sister's death?"

"I place blame where blame is deserved. My sister was a good girl with terrible taste in men. Her first husband nearly beat her to death, and she ran straight into the arms of Theodore Fitzcharles II. For all that she thought he was a literal prince charming, *he* was the one who ended up killing her. It doesn't matter whether his hand wielded the poison, because he was responsible." Alexis rose. "Some things are unforgivable. Theo should have taken his exile as the gift it was and started over. He'll regret his choice before the end of this. You all will." She walked out of the room.

It was only then that Meg realized the shower overhead had turned off. She tried to situate herself more firmly against the headboard, thinking hard. She didn't have siblings, and though part of her had always wanted them, her rational brain was all too happy to provide a bullet list of reasons why she was lucky her mother had chosen not to have more children.

But if she did…

Meg shook her head. Her family wasn't like Theo's or like his mother's. They weren't close. There was no magical bond holding them all together no matter what life threw their way. Her aunt and uncle and their respective children lived the next town over, and she'd only seen them roughly once a year at a very uncomfortable Christmas dinner. They were simply people who happened to share blood by virtue of birth.

That said, she knew all about carrying around a chip in her shoulder a mile wide. Hers was a different flavor than Alexis's, but ultimately that made no difference. She understood the other woman, at least in part.

Theo strode back into the room. He wore a pair of sweatpants and a white T-shirt and his hair was wet and slicked back. The man always looked good enough to eat. It was downright criminal. "My aunt was dripping her poison in your ear, I see."

"I get why she is the way she is." She obviously cared very deeply about her sister and grief and guilt had turned into hate. In her position, Meg couldn't say that she'd have reacted any differently. "What I don't get is the relationship or lack thereof." She motioned between Theo and the rest of the house.

"Come on." He helped her stand and kept his arm around her as he guided her up to the bathroom upstairs. Only once he'd closed the door behind them and flipped on the water did he speak. "Let me help you." He touched her dress and grimaced. The blood had long since plastered it to her skin and dried. "I'll buy you a new one." He ripped it down the center and helped her slide the sticky fabric off her body.

Meg very pointedly didn't look in the oval mirror over the sink. She stepped into the glass shower and bit back a cry as the hot water hit her skin. *Safe. We're temporarily safe… Probably.* She wrapped her arms around herself and ducked under the spray, letting it work the blood from her hair and body. It swirled around the drain in red and then pink, and finally clear. Only then did Meg shampoo her hair and wash her body as best she could with one arm.

Through it all, Theo stood just outside the door, ready to jump in if she needed him.

"If you don't want to tell me, it's okay," she said softly.

He sighed. "As much as my aunt blames my father for my mother's death, she blames me, too."

"Why?" Mary Fitzcharles had died something like twenty years ago. Theo couldn't have been more than ten when it happened—far too young to be held responsible.

"Alexis holds to the belief that my mother used my father to get out of her abusive relationship, but she never had any intention of staying, until they realized she was pregnant with me. Which is when my father married her, apparently despite the fact she was still married to her first husband."

To blame an innocent kid for something like that… "That's bullshit."

"Maybe." His phone beeped and he paused. "Galen's got our stuff and is on the way back. It's time to go."

Chapter 13

Pressure built in Theo, a great crushing monster he couldn't deny. Seeing Galen walk through the door, whole and hale, helped. A lot. But every time he looked at Meg, too pale and determined to power through the weakness caused by her injury, he wanted to break something.

This was his fault.

Galen hustled Meg out to the car—a different one than what he'd left with—and Theo went to find Alexis. His aunt stood in the backyard, smoking a cigarette, her eyes on the clouds overhead. "You're determined to see this through."

"I don't have another option. I never did, despite what you want to believe." Once Phillip got a taste of power, he'd never stop. He might be content to play the puppeteer behind the throne now, but eventually that wouldn't be enough. Theo's brother and sister were vulnerable now that their father was gone. He was raised as the heir, with no veil over his eyes when it came to how things worked. They were sheltered and kept coddled. When Edward hit eighteen, that would have changed, but their father died before he could ease them into the realities of being part of Thalania's ruling family.

Theo couldn't abandon them any more than he could abandon his country.

"I have to do this," he said.

Alexis exhaled a long stream of smoke and looked at him. "You might get both of them killed."

He tensed at the very idea of it. Galen could take care of himself, but he thought of Theo first, rather than his own safety. Meg was smart and savvy, but she was out of her depth in this situation. A world without either of them would be unthinkable. "I won't let that happen."

"You're so much like your father, it makes me sick." She shook her head and took another drag from the cigarette. "You're not a god, Theodore. You can't save everyone."

He could stand here and argue with her until he was blue in the face, but she would never forgive him for being the reason her sister stayed in Thalania, or for having that country's stamp all over him. Theo was who he was. And Alexis might not believe it, but Mary had been happy until she died. However his parents' relationship started, it ended in mutual affection and love. He couldn't say as much to his aunt, though, without being accused of lying.

Instead, he went with the reason they were in Germany to begin with. "Will you give me a copy of her birth certificate?"

"You should let this go. Settle down with your cute little polyamorous life. Have babies or don't. Grow old at a normal pace instead of accelerated through the stress of holding an entire country together."

Theo held onto his patience by his fingertips. "Phillip is actively trying to remove me from the equation now, Alexis. He won't stop, because as long as I'm alive, I'm a threat—even if I'm living what passes as a normal life. This is as much about survival as it is about reclaiming my birthright." He paused. "And my mother deserves to have her reputation cleared."

Alexis gave a bitter little laugh. Her blue eyes, so like his mother's, held no warmth or sympathy. "Mary's dead. Who gives a fuck about her reputation?"

"I do. And I think you do, too." He glanced over his shoulder. Galen would have Meg in the car by now. They were waiting. "Alexis, please."

She sighed and walked to a small table situated between two wicker chairs to snuff out her cigarette. Alexis bent and pulled a faded blue folder from beneath one of the chair cushions. She handed it to him. "Next time you're going to bring violence down on us, don't involve my son."

"I won't." It was the least he could agree to. "The renovation is complete, as agreed. Thank you for the use of the house."

Alexis shook another cigarette out of her pack and lit it. "I'm still contemplating burning it to the ground."

He bit back a protest. The house belonged to her, and as such, it was her choice. No matter how little he liked it. There was no guarantee Theo would make it back through Germany again any time soon, but hell if he wouldn't have bought that house from her outright if he thought for a second she'd sell. They'd only been there for roughly twenty-four hours, but the memories he and Meg and Galen had created within those four walls would stay with Theo for the rest of his life.

He flipped open the folder and read the equally faded birth certificate for one Mary Mortimore. "Thank you."

"Don't thank me. I'm assisting in your determination to get yourself killed." She turned away.

There was nothing else to say. He'd got what he came for, and there was no mending bridges when it came to Alexis. There hadn't even been a bridge to begin with. "Stay safe, Alexis."

"Go."

He went.

Theo made sure the door was locked behind him and then walked to where Galen had a beige Audi station wagon running and slipped into the back seat next to Meg. Galen barely waited for the door to shut before he took off. "You got it."

He looked at the birth certificate again. *Mary Louise Mortimore.* His mother. "I got it." It didn't seem like anything special, though. He had no idea why Phillip had specifically not included it in the evidence he'd compiled, but Theo had every intention of finding out.

After they got to safety.

He leaned forward. "Greece."

"Figured."

Meg had found a blanket somewhere—Galen, no doubt—and had it wrapped around her so that only her face was visible. "What's in Greece?"

"A property Galen owns that no one in my family or his knows about. He purchased it through a shell corporation within another shell."

She gave a wan smile. "I'm sure the fact that Greece borders your country has nothing to do with that decision."

"Well, there is an infinity pool."

She laughed softly. "Of course there is."

"Next he'll try to convince you that naked sunbathing is the thing to do." Though there was a thread of amusement in Galen's voice, the tense line of his shoulders gave lie to it. He glanced at Theo in the rearview. "Why don't you both rest for a bit? It's a long drive, and we're going to have to make it longer to muddy the trail."

"I'll take over in a few hours." He should have said he'd drive now, but the truth was that his head pounded hard enough that it was a wonder it didn't fly right off his shoulders. Theo needed a handful of meds and a couple hours sleep and he'd be as good as new.

Mostly.

"Works for me."

Theo touched Meg's knee. "How are you holding up?"

"Oh, you know, I'm peachy."

Right. Ask a stupid question, get a stupid answer. He motioned. "Come here, princess. We both need some rest while we can get it."

She unbuckled her seatbelt and moved to the center seat. Once she had buckled herself back in, he arranged the blanket around them and tucked her against his side. The tension bled out of her as the space between them warmed. She shivered. "God, this is the most insane experience of my life, and that's saying something. What the hell did they do—shoot us?"

"Not us. One of the tires." Galen didn't look back. "It's not an impossible shot, but it took a lot of skill to set it up so that the tire would go out right as we hit a curve and send us into the ravine."

"They really want you dead, don't they? I thought you had until your brother's coronation."

He should shield her from this, but even lies of omission tended to blow up in his face when it came to Meg. Better to put all their cards on the table and let her decide for herself. "They think you might get pregnant."

She shot up fast enough that she almost clipped him in the jaw. "*What?*"

Galen took the entrance ramp onto the Autobahn and

picked up speed. "If you get knocked up with Theo's kid, then it bring other factors into play."

"Why? If Theo isn't in line for the throne right now, then why would his kid be a factor?"

Theo sighed. "Because my uncle knows he's spun a web of lies and my brother is barely more than a child. He's not going to be married and settling down anytime in the next few years, even if he wasn't taking the throne. That leaves our sister as his only heir, followed by Phillip. And Phillip has no kids of his own. You mentioned a civil war, but having our line die out *would* cause a civil war. There are two lines who could argue that they hold enough royal blood to be next in line after Phillip, and neither of them are going to compromise. It would be England's War of the Roses all over again. While there are members of both families that would be happy to see that happen, the majority of them prize Thalania and their business interests over their ambitions. If they know that I have an heir, they might be willing to support me despite the evidence Phillip provided. I'm a known quantity, and even though you're not one of the marriage candidates they'd been pushing on me since I hit twenty-one, it wouldn't matter. Stability is everything."

"So many strings." She gave a sigh of her own and resumed her position tucked against his side. "I think I'm going to try to sleep now."

He'd said something wrong again. Theo held Meg close and let the hum of the car's engine sooth his eyelids shut. He never usually had a problem talking to people, especially women, but from the start Meg had cut through the bullshit. She didn't like words twisted into games, didn't get off on the push and pull of power plays the way some women did.

She didn't want his money, but she wanted him.

She didn't seem too keen on the fact he was a prince, but she didn't blink at his unconventional relationship with Galen—or that they wanted her to be part of it.

She'd agreed that this should be temporary, but every time he said something that supported that agreement, something shut down in her hazel eyes.

The truth washed over him in a slow surge. *She doesn't like the thought of this ending.* She might not want to keep them in any real way, but it would hurt her to walk away.

He stroked a hand over her temple without opening his eyes. It would be so easy to get her to stay. No games. All he'd have to do is tell her the truth. *I've gone and fallen for you, princess. I think we both have.* It would be a long road, but at the end of it, it would be the three of them together.

Theo couldn't do it.

His wants didn't matter in the grand scheme of things. He wasn't his own person. He wasn't free to choose.

That truth had never mattered all that much to him. It was just the way things were. He always knew things with Galen would get complicated, but they'd always been complicated in their own way. That was just another truth he worked around as necessary.

If he wanted to have his cake and eat it, too, he'd convince Galen to marry Meg. Galen was titled, but he had a shit ton more freedom than Theo did. It would tie her to them, would allow them to stay together…

Until Theo married.

He was a lot of things. A cheater wasn't one of them. Any woman he married would expect him to be faithful, and rightfully so. A theoretical wife who didn't mind that her husband snuck away to fuck his best friend and *his* wife… No, it was an impossible dream. One that would turn to ashes if he tried to force it. That way lay resentment and the fracturing of his and Galen's relationship, to say nothing of bending Meg until she broke.

Theo could be selfish. Fuck, he was born that way. But this thing between the three of them was too precious to poison with his plans. It would hurt to let Meg go. It might even break something in him.

But he'd do it.

There was no other option.

THE NEXT TWO weeks passed in a blur that consisted of the hum of the car's engine and the scenery sliding by too fast to really enjoy. They drove through countries that peppered Meg's pin board, but the most she got to enjoy them was hitting gas stations and drive-thrus to keep them going. Galen was too paranoid to let them stay overnight in a hotel, so the only bed she got was an hour here and there when they'd make pitstops to shower. During those stops, he disappeared to do whatever it was Galen did to keep them safe. A direct route only should have taken them about twenty hours to make, but something happened between her falling asleep that first time and when she woke up. The plan changed. The easy camaraderie between them dissolved into tense silence and tenser conversations.

It wasn't quite hell, but it was definitely hell-adjacent.

She woke to the realization that the car had stopped. When had she fallen asleep? Sometime after they crossed the border into Greece, the lull of Galen's big body wrapped around her too comfortable to deny. He was gone now.

Meg opened her eyes. She lay across the backseat, her

head pillowed on Galen's jacket. She started to sit up, but stopped when the men's voices reached her.

Theo cursed. "It doesn't make any sense. The birth certificate is just a birth certificate. It's not anything special. There's no secret clue that's revealing why Phillip didn't include it. Maybe it really was that the clinic burned down and he couldn't be bothered to search a copy out."

"You're wrong. It means something. We'll figure it out."

"We keep saying that, and we keep fucking up. Phillip is acting erratic and paranoid enough that he might just send someone with a rocket launcher after us if we don't do him the favor of dying in a so-called accident."

"I won't let that happen."

"You aren't a god, Galen. You can't control everything, and if you throw yourself in front of a bullet for me, I swear to all that's holy, I will bring you back to life so I can kill you myself."

Galen was quiet for a beat. Two. "My life is yours, Theo. It has been since I was sixteen."

She shouldn't be listening to this. Eavesdropping when they were withholding information was one thing, but listening in on what was obviously a private conversation was something else altogether. The raw truth in Galen's voice tolled through her. He wouldn't want that vulnerability witnessed, and he wouldn't thank her for having done it. *Fuck.* She couldn't sit up now. It would ruin everything.

Theo's voice moved closer, lower. "Knock that shit off. You don't owe me shit."

"Your father was going to send me into exile with them, and you stepped in. Fuck, Theo, that's a debt I can never repay."

Theo cursed. "And look where it took you—right into exile with *me*. Being mine hasn't done you any favors, so you can climb right off that self-sacrificing cross of yours. My life isn't worth more than yours. It never was."

Galen's parents had been exiled?

Meg obviously needed to up her research game. She knew about the fallout surrounding Theo's parents' marriage, but apparently the political upheaval went back further. She hadn't been aware that exile was so commonly used in today's world. She sighed. Damn it, what she needed was a week and a computer with good Wi-Fi just to catch up.

Above her head, the car door opened. She rolled carefully onto her back and stared up into Theo and Galen's faces. "Oh. Hey."

Galen shook his head. "What did we tell you about eavesdropping?"

She had no self-righteous anger to hold her steady this time. "I woke up and you were talking, and there didn't seem to be a good time to interrupt."

"Mmmm."

"What? You were having a moment. I wasn't going to be the asshole who ruined the moment."

"And yet here we are."

Theo surveyed her. "How are you feeling?"

Surely, he couldn't mean to have this conversation with her flat on her back and them standing over her? She struggled into a sitting position. "I'm fine." Meg caught sight of impossible bright blue behind them. She nudged Galen out of the way and her breath caught in her throat. "That's... That's the Aegean Sea."

"Yeah."

Her eyes burned and she rushed to climb out of the car. Theo was there with strong hands to help her to her feet, and he held on a few extra moments as if she might topple over. Maybe she would. Meg couldn't bring herself to care, not with the sight before her. She took a cautious step forward, half sure it was a pain-induced mirage that would dissipate if she got too closer.

But no. It was real.

Once upon a time, she'd been infatuated with the idea of living in Greece. It was before the political upheaval and shit in the last ten years, which had dampened her desire to visit but hadn't managed to remove it from her pin board.

They had parked the car next to a house that looked about as one would expect—very square and very, very white—but never in Meg's dreams did said house include an infinity pool. And it certainly didn't include what appeared to be a private dock into the Aegean itself. It was all stark low cliffs that the house was built into and the almost painful blue of the water and...

Meg pressed a hand to her mouth. "It's the most beautiful thing I've ever seen."

Arms wrapped around her as Galen came to stand behind her. A few seconds later, one of Theo's hands settled on her hip, and she knew without looking that he'd taken up position pressed against Galen's back the same way Galen was pressed against hers.

In that moment they just...were.

There was no future lined with pitfalls and danger. There was no past littered with pain and betrayal and bullshit. It was just the three of them watching the sun creep toward the horizon.

She moved first, turning in Galen's arms to look up at both of them. "This is your house."

"This is Galen's house."

Galen shrugged. "It used to have something else on this land, but I wanted somewhere private so I had the house built."

Not just a house he'd purchased, but one he'd picked

for himself from the ground up. Meg's curiosity perked up. She turned to look at it with new eyes. "Show me?"

"Sure." He led the way around the side of the house and up to the front door. It was bigger than she'd expected, and it looked sturdy enough to repel a small invasion. He keyed in a number into a security pad next to it and pushed it open so she could walk through.

She gave him a look. "Are you sure you don't want me to hide behind you so you can clear this house?"

"I have cameras set up inside that are linked to my phone. No one's been here but the maid, and nothing has been messed with."

"Security systems can be hacked."

He paused, closed the door, and turned to face her. "You don't trust me to keep you safe."

It wasn't that at all. She didn't think *anyone* could have kept her perfectly safe from the odds they faced, not that Galen would ever admit that. Every time he looked at her, his gaze touched on her arm as if reminding himself how he'd failed her. He did the same thing to the impressive bruise that had bloomed and faded on Theo's face. She glanced at Theo, but he had taken up a perch on the staggered stone wall that seemed designed to keep the steep hill behind the house from toppling the whole building into the sea. There would be no help from there.

Fine.

She lifted her chin. "It was a joke, Galen. People make them sometimes. *You* make them sometimes."

"Not about this." He crossed his arms over his chest. "And to answer your question, no one can fuck with my security system because I have someone who handles it, and they're one of the best there is. You won't be hurt again."

Now they got to the crux of the issue. "My being hurt wasn't your fault."

"Wrong, Meg. It is my fault. It's my job, and I'm trained for it. I should have seen the attack coming and maneuvered to avoid it."

God, she wanted to shake him until he realized he wasn't infallible. "Hmm. In that case, maybe you should just stage a coup of your own. Take over Thalania for Theo since you're a one-man army who has thought of everything, and who is responsible for everyone." She motioned to the rock wall. "Should Theo sit there? Because what if that rock scratches him and you have to go to battle against it, brooding all the while?"

"I protect, baby. It's what I do."

"Sounds like you need a hobby."

He moved toward her, backing her against the door and bracketing her in with his hands on either side of her head. "Sounds like you didn't learn your lesson before."

"My lesson was not to eavesdrop. No one ever said anything about having a, *gasp*, opinion." She flattened a hand against her chest and gave him her best damsel in distress look. "Should I go sit over there next to Theo so you can babysit us properly? Maybe you can get us an adult-sized playpen to keep us from getting into trouble since apparently you're the only one here who is responsible for the lot of us."

He cursed long and hard, the gruff tone doing delicious things to her body. "You're impossible."

"Only because you know I have a point." She leaned forward and planted her hands on his chest. Meg couldn't change Galen, no matter how much she wished she could relieve him of the burden he carried—one just as heavy as Theo's. She couldn't take it from him, but maybe she could convince him to lay it down for a few hours.

She gave him a soft smile. "You won't believe me that you're not super human, and I guess that's something we have to live with. But this is your place and your territory and we're safe here. Put down the burden for a little while."

"Don't coddle me, Meg. I don't like it."

She rolled her eyes. "God forbid you actually be human." She reached up and cupped his jaw. "Show me your house, Galen. Please?" She wanted to get another look at the man beneath the harsh exterior, the one he kept offering tantalizing glimpses of.

And once he relaxed, she'd work on a *really* effective way of distracting him.

Chapter 14

Galen followed Theo and Meg into the house. It had been years since he was here last. Before Theo's father got sick. Before the world came crashing down around them. They used to make an effort to visit once a quarter, to unplug and spend some time recharging where their every move wasn't scrutinized.

He stood in the entranceway and let the memories wash over him. Eating with Theo around the small kitchen island. Scrolling through the endless selection of movies on the massive television in the living room before they decided they were their own best entertainment. Spending days wrapped up in each other on the bed situated in the other half of the loft. Fucking in the shower, the pool, against the windows that stretched the entire length of the back of the house.

Theo moved unerringly to the liquor cabinet tucked in the corner of the kitchen and pulled out a bottle of bourbon. As he began setting out three glasses, Galen turned to watch Meg.

The open floor plan was really more suited for a loft

than a house, but he'd always liked the smallness of it. Everything in Thalania had been opulent and over-sized, a race to the most ridiculous display of wealth. Theo participated by virtue of his birth, though his heart wasn't in it. Galen just flat out didn't play. But being surrounded by people with those kind of priorities wore a person down. This was more home than his various houses in Thalania because it was *his* in a way that was independent of his role for his country and his future king.

Meg moved around the house as if in a daze, her eyes growing bigger by the second. He tried to see things from her perspective, but there was nothing particularly special about this place, aside from the location. Maybe the pool. It was just a house, albeit one that mattered to him.

"Oh, Galen." Her soft words washed over him like the morning mist. "This is wonderful."

"I designed it." He didn't mean to say the words. He just opened his mouth and they emerged fully formed. "For me and Theo. It's our place." He hesitated, and then cursed himself for hesitating. Galen walked up to stand next to her where she stood looking out over the pool and the Aegean Sea. From certain angles, the infinity pool looked like it actually merged with the sea itself. He watched her face in the reflection in the glass. "It could be your place, too."

A true sanctuary for the three of them.

She gave him a smile weighed down by sadness. "I think we both know that I'll never make it back again, but I appreciate the thought. It feels like magic here." She wrapped her arms around herself, the movement mostly unhindered despite the bandage still wrapping her arm. The physical reminder of how badly he'd fucked up. "This whole experience has been like magic. I keep thinking I've stepped through a mirror or climbed into a wardrobe. I don't know how I'm supposed to go back to reality after this." The last was said so low, he had no doubt she hadn't meant to voice it.

Stay.

He clenched his jaw to keep the word inside. It wasn't his place to offer that. Things between them worked now because they were perfectly equal. Going back to Thalania —taking *Meg* back to Thalania—would skew that. It had to. Even if he somehow convinced Meg to stay, to be with him publicly and with Theo privately… Theo would still marry someone else. They'd only be borrowing time against a future heartbreak.

It might be worth it.

"I was serious before, Galen." She kept her voice pitched low. "You didn't fail. You were working with the parameters of what you knew. Theo lived. I lived. We got out of there because of you."

"It's my job to keep him safe—to keep both of you safe." A job he'd spent his life doing. Theo might think it was a debt long since paid, but even after all this time he didn't understand how thoroughly he'd changed Galen's life. Theo was loved by his parents, and when his mother died and his father remarried, he was loved by his step-mother as well. He never wanted for anything, emotional or otherwise.

Galen's path to his teenage years differed greatly. His family had the money and power, but his home life was… less than ideal. He shook his head. "You've done enough. Though I suppose you could offer that sweet pussy up in the way of comfort."

"Don't do that." She turned to face him, her hazel eyes large in her face. "I love the dirty talk and you know it, but don't throw it between us like some kind of weapon because you're done with the conversation."

He sighed. "Look, I don't do this shit."

"This shit." Meg gave a half smile. "Have conversations?"

"Relationship shit." He ignored her surprise and kept going, well aware that Theo had drifted closer again. Things were easier between Theo and Meg. Their personalities complimented each other. Theo might drive her up the wall, but he'd pull her out of her shell the same way he coaxed Galen out of his. There was no resisting Theo when he set his mind to something. And Meg gave Theo a piece of something he'd never had access to before—normalcy. A woman who cared about *him* first, and his power and rank and country second.

For Galen and Meg, it was different. Fucking her was as easy as breathing. They fit. They fit even better with Theo in the mix. Conversations? Emotions? The rest of that shit? Not so easy.

But he hated the wounded look in her eyes when he shut her down, and he couldn't seem to stop himself from trying to fix it, even knowing he'd likely make it worse. "Theo and I have been friends for so long, sometimes it feels like we're two halves to a whole. We don't have misunderstandings. We know each other as well as we know ourselves. Fuck yeah, we fight. We're both stubborn bastards and that throws wrenches into the gears sometimes. It's not effortless, but I know what Theo needs from me and vice-versa. This is different."

"This is temporary."

"Yeah, you keep saying that. Are you trying to convince me or yourself?"

She didn't seem to have an answer for that, so he kept going. "I won't use sex as a weapon again." He allowed himself a slow smile. "Though I meant what I said. I *am* going to take my frustrations out on your sweet pussy."

She blushed a cute pink. "Yeah, I got the memo." Meg turned to face Theo. "Are those shots?"

"Indeed." He passed out one to each of them and raised his own. "We're alive. A celebration is in order. Bourbon, good food, and fucking until dawn."

Meg laughed. "That's a toast I can support."

They took their shots as one. Theo met Galen's gaze and raised his eyebrows, and then turned to Meg. "Why don't you grab that shower while I get food started?"

She looked between them and sighed. "If you needed time to talk, you could just say so."

"We could," Galen agreed. "But you have a nasty tendency to eavesdrop. It's a terrible habit."

This time, her smile was bright enough to light up the room. "You love it. What's the point in devising all those ways to punish me if I never do anything to deserve said punishment?"

Theo chuckled. "She's got you there."

"Shower. Now."

"Yeah, yeah, I'm going." She blew them both a kiss and strode to the only door in the interior. There was a spare bedroom and second bathroom downstairs, but no one had ever used them. They were an eventuality that Galen had planned for without ever following through on. He'd had Theo here. Why would he want to bring someone else?

Meg sure as fuck wouldn't be using the spare bed.

They waited for the shower to start going before moving to the kitchen. Theo poured another set of shots and slid on toward him. "What if this wasn't temporary?"

"Don't."

"I'm just saying—"

Galen downed his shot. "This *has* to be temporary, Theo. You have to marry one of the nobles to keep everyone in line. Your mother was a foreigner, and if your father had married another outsider for his second wife, the Families would have revolted."

"Fuck the Families."

"You can say that and get away with it. No one else can." He couldn't let Theo do this, couldn't let him offer hope where there was none. "With most things in life, you can power through them and bulldoze people into doing what you want. This isn't one of those things. We're taking back our country, Theo. That comes with responsibilities for you. A marriage. Being king. You don't have the luxury of choosing."

Theo looked at him a moment too long. "This isn't only about Meg, is it? You're already working on the wall you're going to build between us. How does that look in your head, Galen? This future you're planning without talking to anyone."

Of all the variations of Theo, Galen hated the reasonable one the most. His friend was so much easier to deal with when he was being sardonic or driven or fanciful. He clenched his jaw. "Like I said—you marry one of those noble girls. She has your babies. Your children inherit. There is no place for me in that picture, not outside of being your head of security."

When they were young and dumb, they'd gotten blindingly drunk one night and talked about what it would be like if they got married. It was a pretty thought, but it couldn't happen. The succession had to be cemented, and it had to be cemented without anything too complicated fucking it up. Theo and Galen getting married had complicated written all over it. An impossible dream, just like a future with them and Meg together. Emphasis on *impossible*.

"What if we just walked?"

"That's not funny."

"Who's laughing?" Theo took his shot and set the glass down on the counter with a clink. "Phillip might be fucking evil, and Edward might be a child, but I have no doubt they want what they think is best for Thalania. They aren't going to drive it into the ground and scatter its people to the wind. Maybe it was narcissistic to think that I should be king. I have you. We have Meg. We have more money than we could spend in a lifetime. Why the fuck do I need a country, too?"

Galen snagged the bottle and put it away before either of them could give into the temptation to get shit-faced. "No, Theo. You're not going down the road. Your father wanted you to be king. He trained you to be king. You have visions for Thalania that are a damn sight better than not driving it into the ground and scattering its people to the wind. That *matters*."

"Why?"

He turned to look at his friend. Theo seemed to have aged years in the last few weeks. It should have made him look strung out and exhausted, but the stress had only sharpened his good looks. He really was a pretty fucker. Galen shook his head. "You know why."

Theo was meant to be king by more than birth. He genuinely loved his people, and he'd been in the process of putting policies into place that would bring their country to the world stage in a big way. That was important. More than that, Theo knew Phillip wouldn't be satisfied until he sat on the throne, instead of behind it. Right now, he stood as third in line. The only way he could achieve his ambition was if both Cami and Edward were removed from the equation. He couldn't pull the same trick of picking the legalities of *their* parents' marriage apart. Their mother hailed from one of the oldest Families in Thalania. Her relatives would never stand for it.

Phillip would kill them.

It might take years. He was never one to do something to cast suspicion on himself, but he would do it.

Galen didn't say any of that. He didn't have to. Theo knew the truth, just like Galen knew why he was letting despair creep in. He walked around the corner of the island and pulled Theo into a hug. "We had a setback. It's not the end. Don't let this fuck up your head."

"I know. Fuck, I know." Theo's lips moved against his temple as he spoke. "It's hard to see the positives in this. I'm fighting and fighting and if we succeed, the prize is that I have to sacrifice two people that are most important to me."

"Heavy is the head that wears the crown."

Theo huffed out a laugh. "Now I know you're worried —you're misquoting Shakespeare at me."

Galen clasped the back of his neck and rested his forehead against Theo's. "You were born for greatness. You were born to keep your people—*all* your people—safe. That matters more than anything as mundane as happiness."

"Fuck, Galen, you're terrible at pep talks."

"It's not one of my skills." He couldn't let Theo diverge from his path, no matter how attractive Galen found the idea of walking away and never looking back. It wouldn't work. Theo was too ambitious to sit back and meander through life without some great cause to fight for. He might think he could leave Thalania behind, but the truth was he'd change his mind.

Or he'd spend the rest of his life resenting Galen and that resentment would poison everything.

No, there was no other way.

Theo had to be king.

Galen would do whatever it took to make it happen.

———

SOMETHING HAD CHANGED while Meg was in the shower. After pulling on one of Galen's T-shirts, she'd walked out to find Theo brooding, his normally expressive face closed down and discouraging questions. Galen's mood hadn't lightened, either. Meg picked at her pasta and promised herself that next time she would most definitely eavesdrop. It was the only way to get reliable information with these two, for all that they claimed they wanted open communication.

Apparently, that only applied to sex.

It shouldn't sting. They hadn't promised her forever, despite Galen's comment earlier, and she'd be a fool to want it.

She *was* a fool to want it.

Sometime in the last few weeks, Meg had slipped. Her anger and desire had morphed into a deeper emotion that she wasn't quite ready to put a name to. It didn't matter. It *couldn't* matter. When this was over, she'd go back to her life in New York and she'd only have her memories with these two men and the magic the three of them created together.

It wasn't perfection. They were too human for something so flawless. What they had was messy and complicated and filled with an intimacy she hadn't expected. Meg wasn't sure of much in this world, but she was sure that Galen and Theo cared about her.

It wouldn't stop them from leaving, but it still warmed her.

"Why an accountant?"

She jumped at Theo's voice filling the silence at the table. Meg looked up to find both of them watching her. Had he asked the question more than once? She took a quick sip of water. "What?"

"Of all the things you could pursue a degree in, why did you choose something as boring as accounting?"

He would see it that way, wouldn't he? She fought down her instinctive urge to bristle and tried to sort out an honest answer. "My home life wasn't a dream when I was growing up. I worked my ass off to get enough scholarships to get the hell out of the town I grew up in, but I knew the only way to stay gone was to go into a stable career. You know that old saying about death and taxes? There is never a lack of demand for accountants."

"Stability."

She glanced at Galen. "Yes. There's the added bonus that numbers make sense to me. There's no gray area or emotional bullshit. It's just cold, hard facts. Black and white and red."

Theo considered the bourbon in his tumbler. "What would you do if you weren't so concerned with stability?"

"I don't understand the question." He shot her a look and she sighed. The joke *had* been flat. "I don't know, Theo. I never put much thought into it. Pipe dreams don't pay the bills. They don't put food in the fridge. They sure as hell don't keep a roof over your head. That's what matters to me—not following some half-baked dream."

He took a long drink. "Indulge me, princess. If money wasn't an issue and you had no ties, where would you go? What would feed your soul?"

He didn't understand how much that question hurt. He couldn't. "Theo, I grew up in a double-wide that was one inspection away from being condemned. My mother drank herself stupid most days of the week, and when she didn't have the cash to pay for that alcohol, she used other methods. My childhood was *hell*. And when she went on a particularly brutal bender, she'd rant about how things were supposed to be different for her. About all the dreams her pregnancy with me had dashed to pieces. Dreams won't get me anywhere but following in her footsteps." She set her fork aside. "I'm sorry. I'm not trying to be an asshole, I swear. But what is an entertaining theoretical question for you is one that brings up a whole lot of emotional bullshit for me."

"It seems we're all destined for futures that are practical and stripped of dreams." He downed the entirety of his drink and gave himself a shake. "I'm the one who should apologize. I'm feeling particularly morose today. It's not a good look for me."

Galen pushed to his feet and gathered their plates. "Thanks for telling us, Meg." Here, in this place, he was softer than she'd ever seen him. Not *soft*. She didn't think there was a scenario where Galen could be soft. But it was as if the sea and the house had dulled some of his sharper edges. The anger that had rode him so hard for the last two weeks was nowhere in evidence.

She stood and walked around the table to press a kiss to Theo's lips. "You don't have to apologize for having a full spectrum of emotions, Theo."

"Don't I?" He shook his head. "I need some air." He held up a hand before Galen could speak. "I'm not leaving the property. I'm going to take this bottle and go sit on the chair by the pool for a little bit." He walked away before either of them could say anything.

Meg joined Galen at the sink. She grabbed a hand towel. "You wash. I'll dry." Through the window, she watched Theo stalk to one of the chairs and drop into it with a grace that he possessed even when angry. "Is he upset about the birth certificate or something else?"

"He's pissed because I reminded him that we can't have it all, no matter how much we want it." He scrubbed a plate, rinsed, and handed it to her. "In a perfect world,

Theo's uncle wouldn't be trying to kill us. He wouldn't have a country he needs to serve more than he needs to pursue his own happiness." He shot her a look. "You wouldn't be going back to New York without us."

"Galen…" She dried the plate. Meg didn't usually make a habit of asking questions unless she knew she was willing to hear the truthful answer. But she couldn't seem to help it with these two. "What would a perfect world look like for him?"

"For us," he corrected. Galen kept washing, as if mulling it over. The tightness in his shoulders gave lie to that assumption, though. He knew what he wanted. He was just working around to voicing it. Finally he handed over the last pot and turned to face her. "You'd go back to New York, and we would, too. Theo would keep playing the stock market because it entertains him, though eventually we'd have to find some kind of business to buy to focus his ambition." He leaned against the counter. "You'd go back to school, and we'd spend the next year or two going round and round while you yelled at us that you had your own life and yet somehow you'd end up in our bed again and again until we convinced you to stay. Eventually, you'd get over the fact we have money, and when you got bored with the accounting shit, you'd figure out that dream of yours and we'd go chase it down together."

For a moment, she let herself picture it. Being with them. Creating a life together. It wouldn't be easy. They were all strong personalities and there would be countless clashing in the future as they found a way to piece themselves together into a whole. But It was a lovely dream. "I'd make you work for it."

"I know." His lips twitched. "And without a doubt, you'd find ways to break the rules just so we'd punish you."

She finished drying the last pan and set it aside. "It's too bad it's only a dream."

"Yeah. Too bad." He pulled her to him and wrapped his arms around her, both of them facing the window. Galen rested his chin on her head. "That man right there is destined for great things. He's not ours, no matter what any of us want. He's Thalania's. If Theo had his way, he'd find a path forward where he gets us and he gets the throne. It doesn't exist. And it's breaking his fucking heart."

THEODORE HAD THE BIRTH CERTIFICATE.

Phillip cursed. Read the report. Cursed again. He should have known better than to let Dorian handle this mess. The man was both inventive and cruel, but he had a soft spot for his son that prevented him from taking the necessary measures. He still thought the boy would fall into line, and so he hesitated.

Phillip couldn't afford to hesitate.

Theodore might not know what that birth certificate signified yet, but he was too smart for anyone's good. He'd figure it out.

It was time to escalate matters.

He reached for the phone and paused. Doing this through unofficial methods hadn't worked. Calling for an official assassination of a former Crown Prince... It would get out. He didn't have full control of the various departments yet. Theodore's influence went too deep and though no one had stepped in when he was exiled, there was still a simmering resentment aimed directly at Phillip. They blamed him for making the choice he did, and there were key administrators who actively worked to make his life more difficult than it needed to be.

If it got out that he had ordered Theodore killed...

No, that wasn't an option.

There had to be another way.

Ah. Yes. That will work nicely.

He dialed his head of security—well, technically, Isaac Kozlov was Edward's head of security—and waited. A few seconds later, a gruff voice came on the line. "What can I do for you, my lord?"

"I need to see you immediately."

"I'm on my way."

Exactly two minutes later, Kozlov walked into his office and shut the door. He was a giant of a man, well over six feet tall and looked like he could lift the solid mahogany desk over his head without effort. A particularly brutal scar wrapped around his neck, and in the years that Phillip had known him, Kozlov had never once even attempted to hide it. It was distasteful.

Kozlov sat across from him. "What can I do for you, my lord?"

"I have just received information that Theodore is in danger. I need him extracted and brought back to Thalania."

Kozlov didn't blink his eerie gray eyes. "I haven't seen this information. What is your source?"

Damn it, why couldn't the man just obey instead of asking questions? Phillip fought down his ire. "My source is none of your concern. Someone targeted Theodore two weeks ago, and I have every reason to think the attacks will only escalate. We can protect him better than he can protect himself at this point. He doesn't have the resources."

Still no expression on Kozlov's face. "Theo has Galen.

That's resource enough." He straightened in his seat. "It's against the law for an exile to return. If he sets food on Thalanian land, he would be incarcerated. That doesn't sound particularly safe, my lord."

"I know the law," Phillip gritted out. "I'm prepared to temporarily lift the exile ruling, at least until we can get to the source of these attacks." When Kozlov didn't blink, he forced a worried expression onto his face. "For god's sake, Kozlov, he's my nephew. I can't let him die."

"Huh." Kozlov finally nodded. "I'll get a team on it." He pushed slowly to his feet. "And forgive me, my lord, but I'm not ordering him brought across the border until that exile is rescinded."

"Don't forget who you answer to."

"I'm well aware of who's in charge, my lord." Kozlov shook his head. "But I can't guarantee my men would follow my orders if I gave that one. They were Galen Mikos's men before they were mine, and on top of that, they like Theo. There's only so much I can ask of them where those two men are concerned."

Phillip glared. "I'll take care of it. Go."

"My lord. I'll see to this personally." Kozlov dipped his head in a move that was barely a bow and walked out of the room.

His head of security couldn't be trusted. Oh, Kozlov never quite stepped out of line, but Phillip couldn't guarantee his loyalty, and that made him a potential problem down the line. Goddamn Theodore and Galen. Between the two of them, they inspired love and loyalty in a way Phillip couldn't compete with. People who didn't like Theodore's posh manners adored Galen's grittier attitude, and vice-versa.

If he removed Theodore, he'd have to remove Galen as well. The man wouldn't stop until he found and punished the responsible parties, which would lead him right to Phillip's door. While he was at it, they might as well take care of the girl in the process. Have the whole thing tied up in a neat little bow.

First, Phillip had to get them all back on Thalanian soil.

The sooner, the better.

Chapter 15

Meg convinced Galen to watch a movie to kill some time, but it ended and Theo still hadn't come back inside. She twisted on the couch and watched him through the glass. "Does he do this often?"

"No." Galen cursed. "He just needs time."

It was such a man thing to say. Not that there weren't instances when distance was exactly what a person needed. But Theo wasn't nursing some restless irritation or letting anger cool or recharging. He was hurting and frustrated and letting him stew would only make it worse. "I think you're wrong."

"That so?"

"That's exactly so. He doesn't need time to get even more wrapped up in his head. He needs a distraction."

Galen snorted. "I bet you have a specific kind of distraction in mind, don't you?"

"In fact, I do." She started to stand, but stopped when he caught her wrist. Meg looked down at Galen, read the pain in his dark eyes—pain she had no doubt he intentionally revealed to her. "You have something to say."

"It's not going to fix anything. Your distraction. It's going to put a Band-Aid on a gushing wound. Our time is winding down."

Strange how what originally felt like a gift of limitations had begun to strangle all three of them. Meg had no answers. They weren't normal people, and they just happened to be sharing the road for the time being. Their destinations stood on opposite ends of the world.

Knowing all that didn't mean she'd leave Theo to stew in his misery any longer than strictly necessary.

She forced herself to smile, forced herself to let go of the future that was never meant to be hers. "Come on, baby. Let's go make Theo feel better."

"I still think it's a mistake."

She huffed out a breath. "Your complaint has been heard and registered. Trust me when I say he needs this." Maybe they all did. The magical night two weeks ago seemed a small lifetime away, and she wanted to reclaim it for herself and Galen as much as she wanted to for Theo. "Come on, Galen. What's going to happen is going to happen, and sitting here in misery in anticipation for it isn't doing us any favors."

He finally allowed her to pull him to his feet. "Did you read that in a book? Because if ever there was someone who obsesses about all the things they can't control, I'm looking at her."

"Ha ha. You're hilarious." She rolled her eyes. "Yes, I had my life planned down to the barest detail. Didn't make a damn bit of difference, did it? I still ended up along for one hell of a ride." Life was messy. She knew it better than most.

But then, so did both of these men.

Meg released his hand and walked to the sliding glass door that opened to the back patio. The sun had lost its battle with the moon, though it took its time sinking low in the sky, begrudging missing out on even a second of its evening. It painted the sky in pinks and oranges and indigo, transforming a beautiful view into something otherworldly.

The man sitting on the patio, glaring at the sea, only made the sensation all that more acute. Theo was pretty enough to be a fallen angel, but being in his presence was like bargaining with a crossroads demon. It felt good—so good that it made her ache sweetly—but in the end, it would take something vital when he walked away.

Her breath. Her heart.

Her very soul.

Stop it. You told Galen that brooding didn't help, so take your own advice. You have this moment.

It has to be enough.

Meg didn't look back to see if Galen was following. He was. He might not know what to do to help Theo out of this moment, and he might give her shit about her methods, but in his heart of hearts, he trusted her to see them through. This time *she* held the reins.

Theo didn't appear to notice that he was no longer alone. Just as well. He was just as stubborn as they were—more so in his own way—and if she came at him head on, he might snap. Whatever that looked like for a man like Theo. She was usually pretty good at reading people, but Theo flipped through masks the way women flipped through lipstick shades. He was so good at offering the safe, careful version of himself. The jokes. The ambition. The politically savvy future king.

But she'd been around him enough to see the flickers beneath. The man who'd lost his mother, lost his father, lost his purpose when he'd lost his kingdom. Galen might be the warrior, but Theo was a wolf cut off from his pack. Had he even had a chance to mourn his father's death?

She didn't think so.

She also doubted that he'd thought too hard about what came after he succeeded. Oh, he'd trained for this his entire life. It wasn't the running the country that she worried about—it was the fear that he'd become brittle when everything crashed down on him at once. A marathoner who made it through excruciating obstacles, only to have their body fail them two feet past the finish line.

Galen will take care of him. The fallout isn't for you to worry about.

Too bad she couldn't control her feelings any more than she could control everything else going on in her life at that moment.

Meg pulled off her shirt, leaving her naked. She dropped it onto the chair on the opposite end of the pool from where Theo sat. He didn't look over. *Broody McBrooderson.* She stretched her arms over her head and turned to face the sunset. This place was a perfect flavor of paradise, and she let herself soak it up for a few seconds.

She turned to find Galen standing next to the stairs into the pool. He still wore his jeans and customary white T-shirt, but there was nothing relaxed about the way he watched her. *Mmmm, yeah. Not quite as good as sex, but it's up there.* She gave him a saucy grin and walked toward him, putting a little swing with each step. "How deep is this pool?"

"Five feet." His gaze flicked to her bandaged arm. "Do you think that's wise?"

"I'm healing up fine." And if she could soak in a tub, she could soak in a pool. She stopped in front of him and ran her hands up his chest. "Galen?"

He let her inch closer, his eyes going so dark they seemed to swallow up the light of the sunset. "Yeah?"

"Mmmm. God, I love your body. Though I can't pick my favorite part. Ass. Shoulders. Chest. Thighs. You're a fucking masterpiece."

"Not me." He started to glance over his shoulder, but she caught the band of his jeans, drawing his attention back to her.

"Yes, you." She pressed the heel of her free hand against his cock. "I would commit unforgivable acts just so you'd let us tie you to a bed and have our filthy way with you." Meg gave a happy sigh. "It makes me wet and tingly just thinking about you like that, all flat on your back and helpless to do anything but use those filthy words to convince Theo to give you what you want."

"And what do I want?"

She released his pants and stroked her hands back up his chest. Meg went up onto her tiptoes, the merest breath separating their lips. "Him in your ass. Me on your cock."

"If you're offering—"

She pushed him into the pool. It shouldn't have worked—Galen was every inch an immovable object—but he was too close to the edge and hadn't expected it, so he went down like a felled tree. He burst through the surface with all kinds of retribution written across his face, and Meg laughed. "Catch me." She jumped, hitting him in the chest and wrapping her legs around his waist. He wasn't ready for that, either, and they both went under.

Galen finally got his feet under him and stood, her still wrapped around his waist. "I'm going to paddle your ass for that."

"Promises, promises." She laughed again. She couldn't help it. Galen looked as disgruntled as a cat in a bathtub and twice as murderous. Tightening her legs around him, she worked his shirt off and lobbed it onto the patio, where it landed with a wet splat. "Not quite there yet, but we're getting warmer."

He disentangled her from him with ease and tossed her farther into the pool. Meg yelped as she hit the surface, and by the time she surfaced and wrestled her hair away from her face, Galen had managed to lose his jeans. He stalked toward her, the water creating tantalizing glimpses of his hips and cock before it climbed his chest. Damn it, she should have taken up her position in the shallow end.

Galen snagged her around the waist and pulled her to him. "I ought to drown you for that."

"Ooooh, big scary man." She wiggled against him. "I'll make it up to you later."

"Damn straight you will." He launched her into the water again, a cat with his toy. This time, Meg didn't get a chance to yelp before he was on her again. He caught her hips and twisted to pin her against the side of the infinity pool, his chest to her back.

She looked down, down, down to the sea below. "Did you have to build your damn pool on a cliff?"

"The whole house is on a cliff." He lowered his head until his lips brushed her ear. "He's watching."

"Of course he is." She pressed back against him, shivering at the feeling of his hard cock against her ass. "Are you ready for me to make it up to you?"

He nipped her ear. "I'm listening."

"The pool steps."

Galen didn't need more urging than that. He tossed her over his shoulder, dunking her in the process, and carted her across the pool to the steps. Where he dropped her into the water again. Meg came up sputtering. "You're such a dick."

"Guilty."

She pushed on his shoulders, guiding him back to sit on

the top step. They sat at an angle, so Galen faced Theo. His gaze flicked over her head before settling on her face, all the confirmation she needed. Theo was watching them instead of lost in his own thoughts.

Now they just needed to tempt him into the water.

Kind of like how Theo and I had to tempt Galen into playing with us that first night.

She smiled at the memory and licked her lips. Galen looked like some sea god who'd wandered into the wrong body of water. His dark hair was slicked back, and droplets of water clung lovingly to his chest, descending in tantalizing drips to his stomach. Lower.

She ran her hands up his thighs as she stepped between them. The water didn't quite hit her waist. This whole thing would work better if it was shallower, but she liked the picture Galen presented too much to tell him to move out of the pool. His cock jutted thick and heavy against his stomach. *Oh yeah. This is going to be good.* Meg shifted her hair over one shoulder, took a second to adjust her angle, and then dipped down and took Galen's cock into her mouth. It would have been more comfortable to go to her knees on the bottom step, but they were giving Theo a show.

Galen, of course, figured it out immediately. "He's starting right at your ass, baby. Water's low enough, I bet if you lift your hips, he can see your sweet pussy. That's where you want him, isn't it? Driving into you while you suck me off." He wrapped her hair around his fist and leaned back. "Fuck, if you could see yourself right now." He went still. "Spread your legs a little more. Yeah, like that. Arch that spine, baby. He's getting up."

Meg obeyed. The water lapped at her pussy, its touch nowhere near strong enough to get her where she needed to be, and all the more erotic for the teasing. With Galen's words wrapping around her, she could feel Theo's gaze on that most private part of her, just like he described. *Come play with us, Theo. Touch us. Suck us. Fuck us.*

Us.

Was there ever a more erotic word in the English language?

Galen gave her hair a tug. "Don't let his eye-fucking your pussy distract you from how you're going to make up that little stunt to me. Suck me like you mean it."

She shivered and ran one hand up to brace herself on his thigh and hip. With her free one, she cupped his balls, letting the water and her fingers play with him as she sucked him harder. Her jaw already ached from his size, but it was more than worth it to hear his quiet curse when his cock bumped the back of her throat. Meg withdrew completely and flicked her tongue around his crown and then down to his base. She belatedly realized that she'd closed her eyes somewhere along the way and opened them.

The way Galen watched her stole her breath from her lungs. He wasn't just a man getting the blow job of a life-time from a naked chick in a pool while his best friend looked on. His dark eyes held something beyond lust, beyond desire, beyond even possession.

"Brace yourself, baby."

Her mouth was full of his cock, so she didn't get a chance to ask him what he meant before hands closed around her hips and a cock was shoved deep inside. Theo withdrew and shoved into her again, hard enough that she lost control on Galen's cock and took him deep enough to make her eyes water. Galen moved before she had a chance to. He yanked her off his cock—off both their cocks—and spun her around to land in his lap, with her legs on either side of his thighs. "You want to pound her pussy, Theo? To take your frustration out on her?" He dragged her finger through her wetness on display. "Here she is."

She'd never seen Theo out of control before. His blue eyes held a legion of storms. He closed the new distance between them and shoved into her again, filling her completely. Galen braced her hips, holding her in place to take Theo's thrusts, goading him on with his words. "That's right, Theo. She's wet and tight and ready for whatever you give her. Let go. She can take it."

There it was again—that delicious feeling of being their plaything.

Theo caught her hip with one hand and Galen's shoulder with the other, driving into her again and again, both of them holding her in pinned and open for him. It was…

There were no words.

Theo gave one particularly savage thrust and bent down to set his teeth against her neck. "This is what you wanted."

"Yes." She couldn't wrap her legs around him so she ran her hands up his back, holding him as close as she could. "Give it to me, baby. Give it all to me." All his anger and frustration and desire. Galen was right. She could take it.

She *wanted* to take it.

Galen hooked the back of Theo's neck, towing him up for a kiss. "Let go. We've got you."

Theo's started moving again, fucking her against Galen's chest as if he could merge the two of them—the three of them—if he just applied enough force. Meg relaxed into it, letting herself be buoyed between these two men. As if sensing her surrender, Galen shifted one hand down to stroke her clit, tightening the spiral of pleasure already coursing through her. With Theo's face against one side of her neck and Galen's breath ghosting across the other side... Perfection didn't begin to cover it. They encompassed her. Overwhelmed her.

They made her feel safe.

Galen kept his stroking her clit to the tight little circles she loved even as Theo drove into her. He growled against her skin. "When he's done with you, it's my turn, baby. That blowjob just got me going, and I'm going to take it out on your pussy the same way Theo is right now." He laughed, low and mean. "He's riled up. A couple minutes to recover and he's going to be ready for you again. How long can you hold up before you cry for mercy?"

"I can take it," she gasped.

"Good. Because you damn well will." He pressed down hard on her clit.

It was too much, just like he must have known it would be. Meg came with a cry, and Galen kept up that gloriously delicious touch as Theo went wild inside her, his strokes losing their rhythm as he cursed and came. He didn't immediately pull out, though. He kept them sealed together as he ran a hand up the center of her body to bracket her throat. "Meg."

He said her name like he owned her.

Like maybe she owned him, too.

He lifted her off Galen and nodded at his friend. "Chairs."

"Yeah."

Theo tossed her over his shoulder and walked up the stairs out of the pool. Meg slapped his ass. "I'm getting tired of being hauled around like some kind of war prize."

"No, you're not."

No, she really wasn't.

By the time they made it to the chair set Theo had

been on earlier, Galen was already there with three towels. He draped one around her as soon as Theo set her on her feet and passed one to Theo. They dried with quick, efficient movements, but Meg couldn't help glancing at Galen's hard cock. He had made her a promise, after all.

"See something you like?"

"You know I do."

He shook his head. "Shameless."

"You like it."

"Children," Theo warned. He dropped into the same chair he'd occupied earlier. "Bend over the table, princess. Legs wide."

The table was some kind of faintly rough rock—granite, maybe—and she shivered as she obeyed. It was cold against her damp skin, rough against her sensitive nipples. She braced her hands flat on the table on either side of her head, giving herself over to whatever Galen would do. Doing something she spent so much of her life fighting tooth and nail against.

Surrendering.

Galen stepped between her spread legs, the hair on his thighs coarse against her skin. He speared a single finger into her. "You've filled her up, haven't you, Theo? Left her all wet and ready for me."

"You can thank me by sucking my cock later."

Galen's laugh rolled down her spine. "Believe me, I will." He guided his broad cock into her in a single, steady thrust. She expected him to lose control the same way Theo had, but Meg should have known better. They were too well balanced to lose it at the same time, though she couldn't help wondering what it would be like if they did.

If she'd survive it.

It would be a glorious way to go.

He leaned down, pressing himself against her back,

pinning her between the cool rock and his warm body. "How you holding up, baby?"

Checking in.

Her chest felt too full, and it took her several breaths to formulate a response. "I'm good."

"Mmmm." He pumped slowly, letting her feel every inch of him. He touched her bandage, as if reassuring himself that it was intact. "I changed my mind. We're going to do this a different way." Galen pulled out of her and jerked his thumb at Theo. "Bed. Now."

She half expected him to haul her in there, but he just took her wrist and towed her after him into the house. Galen sank onto the bed, seemed to consider and positioned himself with his head near the foot of the mattress. He pulled her on top of him and angled his cock into her. "Better."

He was letting her control the pace. Letting her decide what was too much for her. The feeling in her chest got worse. Or maybe it was better. She couldn't be sure. Meg bit her bottom lip. "Yeah. It's good."

Theo stood over them and gave his cock a rough stroke. Just like Galen had predicted, he was already growing hard again. God, what did they *feed* these Thalanian men? Theo glanced at her bandage, a flicker of guilt in his blue eyes. He met her gaze and some of wildness retreated. "Did I hurt you?"

"No."

His mouth twisted. "Would you tell me if I had?"

"*I* would tell you if you had." Galen reached up and grabbed Theo's hands, pulling him to the edge of the bed. "Focus, asshole. You want that blowjob or not?"

Theo traced them with his gaze, starting at the top of Meg's head, caressing her face, lingering over her breasts and where she was joined with Galen's cock, and then up Galen's chest to this face. "Yeah, Galen, I want you to suck my cock. I'm just as irritated at you for that little show as I am at her."

"I know." He didn't sound the least bit sorry.

As Theo braced himself on the mattress and guided his cock into Galen's mouth. Meg started moving as she watched him disappear through Galen's lips. "Oh god." It had been good watching them fuck. Better than good, though there was a healthy dose of longing and spurned lust in there. Riding Galen's cock while he sucked off Theo? She braced her hands on Galen's chest and moved faster, chasing her pleasure even as Theo's danced across his expression.

"You two are nothing but trouble," Theo muttered, thrusting deep, his blue eyes gone dark. "How am I supposed to figure out a way through this with you playing in the pool, sucking his cock and flashing that pussy at me as if I'm going to ignore such a blatant invitation." He rode Galen's mouth even as she rode his cock. "That's right, Galen. You know how I like it."

It was too good. Too good and too perfect and she just wanted to make it even more so. Meg leaned back and reached down to cup Galen's balls. "Think I can make him come before you blow?"

Theo gave her a wicked smile. "We'll find out."

Galen shifted, grasping her hip with one hand and Theo's thigh with the other. He urged on her strokes and as she played with his balls. It wasn't enough. His control was too good. Already, pleasure danced along her nerve endings, teasing her with another orgasm to match the first. She fought it, trying to prolong the perfection of the moment. Meg pressed two fingers to his ass as she thrust down, grinding over him. Galen's hand spasmed on her hip and then he was coming, filling her up. *Oh god, oh god, oh god, that feels so good.*

Theo withdrew from Galen's mouth. "On your stomach." He glanced at Meg. "She looks like she needs another orgasm, don't you think?"

Galen hauled himself up, toppling her onto her back. He kissed Meg like he needed her more than he needed air, and then shifted to the side and stroked a hand down to cup her pussy. "Next time, you ride my mouth, while he rides my ass."

She shivered and opened her legs wider. "Yes." Meg watched Theo grab the lube and position himself behind Galen. *Yesyesyesyesyes.*

Galen laughed against her neck. "You love watching us, don't you?"

No point in lying. "It gets me halfway there just by being in the room."

Galen pushed two fingers into her as Theo guided his cock into his ass. His hand mimicking Theo's hips, fucking her even as he was fucked. Meg twisted and kissed him, riding his hand as she came. She melted back to the mattress, watching them through her haze of pleasure. "You're the most beautiful men I've ever seen. Especially like this." The way Theo watched Galen… There was no doubt in her mind that they loved each other. She'd never doubted it.

For the first time since this all started, Meg allowed herself to dream that they might look at her the way they looked at each other.

That they might love her, too.

Chapter 16

Meg woke up wrapped around Theo. On his other side, Galen spooned him as if trying to protect Theo with his own body, even in sleep. Both their expressions were relaxed. It didn't exactly make them look innocent—nothing short of a miracle could do that—but it was as if they'd put down their respective burdens for a little while. They were lighter.

She wanted to bundle them up and keep them here forever. To say to hell with their respective obligations and responsibilities and to throw out her life plan and just be together and pursue their happiness.

I love them.

Meg's breath caught in her chest, fluttering on panicked wings. No, she couldn't possibly love them. They hadn't even been together three weeks. People did not fall in love in three weeks. Not even with funny, calculating, ambitious exiled princes. Or with their grumpy, driven, protective bodyguards.

She could tell herself it was the sex clouding her judgment, but it would just waste precious time to circle back to the same conclusion. Somewhere along the way, she'd gone and fallen for them both. Maybe it was when Theo had carried her across an entire fucking field to get them to safety. Or when he'd spoken about his parents, his country. The exact moment didn't matter, because he'd slipped beneath her defenses and compromised her heart.

With Galen, she could pinpoint the exact moment.

Yesterday. In the kitchen. With his concern for Theo palpable in the room. The softness beneath his spiky exterior.

God, she was so screwed.

She slipped out of bed and made a quick trip to the bathroom. After doing her business, she splashed water onto her face and stared at her reflection in the mirror. She didn't look *that* different than she had three weeks ago. A little more tanned, maybe. Her body all sorts of marked up with the evidence of amazing sex with two men. She'd put on a little weight and had lost a little of the gaunt look she'd fallen into over the summer.

But she just looked like herself.

Like Meg.

She shook her head and slipped out of the bathroom. Both men were still asleep, but even after the time away from New York, she wasn't used to resting so much. The last two weeks were different, because she'd been healing, but now that she felt better all around, restlessness stole through her. *Maybe hiding out here for the rest of our lives isn't such a foolproof plan.*

The house was set up in an upside-down U, with the kitchen and living area on one side and the bedroom on the other. There were no doors between them, but it gave the illusion of privacy without sacrificing an inch of the view from the windows that stretched along the entire wall facing the Aegean Sea.

She padded into the kitchen and rustled around until she found the coffee. It took another few minutes to decipher the coffeemaker, but eventually Meg had it going. She stretched as the tantalizing scent drifted through the kitchen and smiled. *Coffee makes everything better.*

Meg turned to the windows and froze.

A man stood on the other side. He was tall—taller than both Galen and Theo—and dressed entirely in black from his shirt to his jeans to his boots. Brown hair with the kind of bronzed skin that spoke of either hours spent in the sun or really excellent genetics. A gnarled scar around his throat where it looked like someone tried to garrote him.

And he had a gun pointed directly at her chest.

She lifted her hands, but considering she was standing there naked as the day she was born, the gesture didn't make sense. He pointed at the sliding glass door, and she hesitated. Was the glass bulletproof? It seemed like something Galen would have installed in a house he owned. He was paranoid like that.

But she couldn't guarantee it.

If she let him in, he could kill them all.

If she didn't let him in, he could shoot his way through the window and kill them all.

Her options sucked.

"Open the door, baby."

She jumped. She couldn't see Galen around the section of the wall separating the bedroom from the rest of the house, but apparently his spidey senses had tingled and he was awake. *Thank god.* She inched to the door, painfully aware of the gun trained at her chest. She flipped the lock and scrambled back.

The gunman wasted no time. He stepped into the house and shut the door behind him, never once breaking eye contact with her. To his credit, he didn't ogle her nakedness, but considering he'd just forced his way into the house at gunpoint, she wasn't inclined to grant him any brownie points.

"That's far enough, Kozlov." Galen's voice came from her right. He stepped out from behind the wall, his own gun trained on the stranger. *He* had found time to throw on a pair of pants. He passed her a robe he held in his free hand. "You good?"

She hurried to wrap it around her and tie the belt. "I'm fine."

Kozlov gave them both a long look and held his hands up, making a show of putting the safety on his gun. "I'm just here to talk."

"Then talk." Without looking over, Galen snagged her arm and pulled her over to stand behind him, putting his body between her and this Kozlov.

Hands closed on her shoulders and then Theo was there, moving to stand next to Galen. "Isaac. Been a long time."

Kozlov—Isaac—started to bow and seemed to realize Theo was no longer Crown Prince. "Your Highness."

"Not anymore."

Isaac eyed Galen's gun. "Phillip sent me to bring you in. He claims there are attempts on your life and he's worried about you." He slowly holstered his gun. "Struck me as funny. If he cared so much, why the fuck did he exile you in the first place. So that got me to thinking."

"You should never think, Kozlov. It's bad for your health." Galen showed no signs of putting his gun down. His big back blocked most of her view of Isaac, but she wasn't willing to peek around him for a better look. Obviously, they had history.

"Now, Mikos, don't be like that. You know damn well that I could have walked in here and taken all three of you out while you slept. I'm the one who set up the fucking security in the first place. You think I can't get past it?"

Meg blinked. *Huh. Well that's a twist.*

Galen cursed and let his gun fall to his side. "What are you doing here?"

"Like I said, Phillip gave me an order. I'm obeying."

Theo snorted. "Maybe the letter, if not the spirit. Did he want me trussed up like a turkey or just the traditional black bag over my head?"

Meg slid between them just enough so that she could actually see what was going on. Theo had his easy smile in place, but she knew him well enough to recognize it for the mask it was. Galen just looked like he was ready to shoot Isaac in the head and toss him into the sea. "I could really use some coffee." She didn't realize she'd spoken aloud until all three men looked at her. She swallowed hard and refused to wilt. "This sounds like it's going to be a conversation they need to pay attention to, and coffee helps."

Galen's eyes flashed, but Theo nodded. "Coffee." He motioned Isaac toward the table situated by the kitchen island. "You'll forgive me if I ask you to put your weapons on the coffee table."

"Of course." Isaac strode to the coffee table and set his gun carefully onto it. Followed by another gun that had been tucked into his boot. And three knives he pulled from…somewhere. Finally, he walked to the dining room table and took up a position with his back to the solid wall perpendicular to the glass one.

Meg hesitated, but Theo pressed his hand to the small of her back. "Show no fear, princess," he murmured. "Chin up."

She could do this. She could drink coffee while a man who'd pointed a gun at her told her two lovers… whatever he'd come there to tell them. It wasn't any stranger than being shot at or getting patched up in a cute little cottage in Germany or any of the other things that had happened to her since meeting Theo and Galen.

While she got mugs down from the cabinet, Theo sat in the seat directly across from Isaac. Galen took up a position against the kitchen island, just far enough back that he was almost in Isaac's blind spot. *Pinning him between them. He couldn't possibly avoid attacks if they both came at him from that position.*

Or maybe she'd seen too many action movies.

She brought coffee to the men and then retreated back into the kitchen. If shit hit the fan, she could duck behind the heavy cabinets or bolt out the front door. Though she doubted Isaac showed up here alone. That would have been stupid, and he didn't strike her a stupid man. One in an impossible situation, most definitely, caught between his current monarch and the one he obviously had supported pre-exile. There was history with Galen to consider, too.

Better to be quiet and still and let the men take point on this. It had the bonus of decreasing the chances of one of them ordering her away and then her having to eavesdrop yet again to keep up on the current situation. Meg leaned against the counter and sipped her coffee.

Theo leaned back, as regal as the king he almost was despite his surroundings. "You have my full attention."

THEO STUDIED Isaac as he drank his coffee. "Let me see if I have this straight. My uncle wants you to retrieve all three of us and return us to Thalania… for our supposed safety."

Isaac flicked a glance to Galen. "That about sums it up." He leaned forward with a suddenness that had Galen reaching for his gun, but Isaac's eyes were only for Theo. "He's not my king. Edward could be if given a chance, but he won't have that chance with Phillip playing puppet master."

"What you're saying is dangerously close to treason." It was also exactly what Theo had feared. Edward was a good kid but his mother had pampered and sheltered both her children as much as she could. A gift, but one that had long since grown teeth. His skin was too thin, his control was too incomplete, he craved other people's approval. None of those things were terrible in a normal person. He was seventeen. He'd outgrow a good portion of them when he figured out who he was.

But in a king?

Phillip would have no difficulty manipulating Edward into doing whatever he wanted, whenever he wanted it.

Not that Theo would say as much to Isaac. He might have served as Galen's second in command for the last ten years, but he was still sworn to serve Thalania, and at the moment, Theo and Galen stood in opposition to what the regent of Thalania wanted.

Isaac didn't move. He barely seemed to breathe. "You're trying to take the throne back. That's why he's determined to bring you back under his thumb." The slightest pause. "He's going to kill you."

"To be fair, he's already tried." Theo leaned back, affecting a relaxed pose as he contemplated his coffee. "How long do we have before he gets suspicious?"

"Twenty-four hours. I'm the best, and he knows it." He shot another look at Galen. "Well, second best. But I have an edge because I know Galen better than almost anyone. Phillip's aware of that history. He'll expect me to be able to dig you out of any hidey-hole you've crawled into." He motioned at the house around them. "Case in point."

Twenty-four hours wasn't enough. They still didn't know what the damn birth certificate signified, how it was the key to unlock the entire puzzle. *If* it was even the key. At this point, Phillip could very well have left it out because of some perverse desire to offer hope, only to snatch it away after Theo had gone through so much trouble to obtain it. "And after that you'll follow orders."

Isaac had the grace to look uncomfortable. "I might not agree with Phillip's way of doing things, but your brother and sister are the royal family and the next in line for the throne." Another of those micro hesitations. "If there's a way for you to retake the throne…"

Theo held up a hand. "If there was a way, I wouldn't tell you what it was because it'd put you in a shitty position. I respect you too much to do that." He let his hand drop. "Just like you'll respect our privacy for the next twenty-four hours before you do what you came here for."

"I'll respect your privacy." He jerked a thumb over his shoulder. "From a distance where I can see everything to ensure you don't bolt again."

He expected as much. Theo set his mug down. "One last thing."

"Yeah?"

"Meg stays out of it." He wasn't ready to end things with her, but if the alternative was to haul her back to Thalania and into more danger than they'd been in up to this point combined… No. Theo was selfish—he was the first to admit that—but he wasn't *that* selfish. "We're putting her on a flight back to New York. As far as you're concerned, she was never here."

Isaac's eerie blue eyes flicked from him to Galen to Meg. "I have my orders."

Galen shifted, breaking his line of sight with her.

"Phillip's more concerned with us than with her. He'll be satisfied."

"I have my orders," Isaac repeated. He turned back to Theo. "You know he'll just send someone to collect her if you try to dodge this."

Yeah, he would. Theo made a show of looking at the clock over Isaac's head. "Twenty-four hours. Isaac. I expect you to honor it."

"Yes, Your Highness." He stood, gave a half bow, and walked out the way he'd come, scooping up his weapons in the process.

Galen moved to the door and locked it behind him, for all the good it would do. It hadn't kept him out the first time, and it wouldn't do it a second time if he changed his mind or Phillip altered his orders. Theo sighed. "Our time-line just got a whole hell of a lot more complicated."

Meg moved around the kitchen island to frown down at him. She was a vision in her short, white robe, her dark hair tangled around her face, her mouth looking distinctly just-fucked. The robe parted as she moved, revealing a slice of skin down to her stomach that drew his gaze. She snapped her fingers near her eyes. "Up here, Theo." She frowned harder. "You're seriously going to toss me onto a plane and ride off to meet your uncle, knowing that he's planned something nasty for you?"

"I'm going to put you on a plane *precisely* because my uncle has something nasty planned." Phillip would use the three of them against each other to obtain what he wanted, and then he'd make them all disappear.

Meg stared for several long moments. "I don't like this."

"No one does." Theo pushed to his feet and took her hands. He glanced at Galen. "We promised not to let anything happen to you, princess. We've already fucked that up, but that doesn't mean I'm going to stop trying—that either of us is going to stop trying."

"What about you? If something happens to you…"

"Nature of the beast."

Meg reached up and touched his face. "Don't do that. Don't act like it doesn't matter what happens to you. It matters."

Galen walked over and set his gun on the kitchen counter. "He's right. There's a decent chance Phillip will let you go if he's got us both in his control. We're Thalanian, exiled or not, which puts us under his jurisdiction. You're American. If word gets out that Phillip Fitzcharles is ordering American girls snatched off the street, it will be a diplomatic nightmare. He's too smart to risk that."

Theo permitted himself a small smile. "I see you've been talking to Alaric." If there was one thing his cousin was good for, it was running his mouth. Theo still hadn't confirmed one way or another if Alaric was reporting directly to Phillip, but he had quite the internet following by virtue of being related to the late Queen of Thalania and being too handsome for his own good.

Theo just insured that, should Phillip make the wrong move where Meg was concerned, Alaric going public with it would benefit him greatly. He'd go publicly speculating on how *very strange* it was that Thalania had taken a particularly nasty interest in some poor American girl who just happened to date the wrong guy.

It wasn't foolproof, or Theo would have put it into play earlier, but if Phillip already had what he wanted, he might hold off going after Meg to avoid bringing more trouble down on his head.

Galen shook his head. "You should have told me that you looped in that idiot. There's got to be a less round-about way to protect her."

"*Her* is standing right here." Meg stepped back enough that she could look at both of them. "This isn't a decision you get to make without me."

"This is what you wanted, princess. To go home, back to your life. To follow your plan." She'd already sacrificed enough just by being with them. He still hadn't gotten around to telling her about the money, but to be fair, he hadn't told Galen, either.

Meg sighed. "This is so screwed up. I had a plan. It was a very good plan, and now…"

"It can't matter." Galen's dark eyes held the same emotion squeezing Theo's chest until he felt like he'd never draw a full breath again. *Love. He loves her, too.* Galen couldn't tell her any more than Theo could. It would be unspeakably cruel to say those three little words before they launched her back into the life she'd claimed for her own. She'd grown up at the mercy of others' whims, and she'd fought tooth and nail to free herself.

He wouldn't be the one to wrap her in chains again.

Neither of them would.

Galen stroked her hair back from her face. "There's not a way through this where our shit stays intact. No matter which way it plays out, compromises will be made that will break us. Better for you to go back now and resume your life. Get your degree. Be the best fucking accountant out there until you figure out what you really want to do with your life."

He knew what came next. *Find a man who worships the ground you walk on. Let him love you. Marry him. Make a family with him.*

Fuck. He swallowed, his insides turning to shattered glass at the thought of Meg settling down with some asshole. Except he wouldn't be an asshole. She was too smart for that. She'd find a nice guy with a little edge, one who wouldn't bore her to death. It would take him a while to get past the many walls around her heart, but if he was worthy, he'd manage.

She'd be happy.

Happier than she could be in some compromised semi-secret bullshit of a relationship with him and Galen.

Meg stepped away from Galen's touch. "Rationally, I know you're right. This just sucks."

"Yeah," Theo ground out.

She pressed her lips together and squared her shoulders. "No use in arguing about it. Let's just…" She gave herself a shake. "Let's get another look at that birth certificate. You need a plan for when you go back there or you really will be walking into a trap."

God, he loved her so much, it made his heart feel like it could beat itself right out of his chest. Theo cleared his throat. "Yeah. Sure. Let's do that." He walked to where they'd stashed their stuff and pulled out the folder where he'd kept the various documents they'd painstakingly collected over the last few months.

They laid them out on the kitchen island. Theo read over them for the millionth time, but nothing had changed. No secrets jumped out and smacked him in the face. No path forward revealed itself.

Useless.

"Hold on a minute," Meg murmured. She picked up the birth certificate and held it next to the first marriage certificate. "These are both correct?"

"The marriage certificate is a copy we got from the courthouse in Las Vegas, so it's official. Safe enough to assume the one Alexis gave us is, too." It had the right marks, at least.

Meg pointed at the birthdate listed on the marriage certificate. "This is wrong, then."

Theo frowned and moved closer. The marriage certificate listed Mary's birth year as 1969. He lifted the birth certificate. It was so old and faded in places, he hadn't even noticed that the last digit was different. It had just looked like a faded out nine. It wasn't.

It was a seven.

He did some quick math in his head. "But that would mean she was—"

"Sixteen when she married her first husband. Which is technically legal if she had at least one parent's written consent."

"She didn't." That much, he knew. Mary had run away from home. Her parents didn't even know she was in the States until she was already married.

Galen leaned forever to look. "Not to mention they would have the right birth year if she had parental permission. They didn't. She lied." He held Theo's gaze. "She *lied*. It didn't matter that she never got divorced because the first marriage wasn't legal in the first place."

Meg gave him a smile that barely wavered at the edges. "Congratulations, Theo. Or should I say, Your Highness? You were right. You're the rightful King of Thalania."

Chapter 17

They drove Meg to the airport.

Galen stood next to Theo as they watched her work her way through the line to the ticket counter. In a few short hours, she'd be safe on a plan headed back to New York. On a plane out of their lives for good. "You sure about this?"

"Do you love her?"

Galen jerked around, surprise rocking him back on his heels. "What the fuck kind of question is that?"

"One you might as well have shouted your answer to." Theo gave a small smile. "Have you thought about leaving it all behind? I know you liked New York."

What was he on about?

Theo answered the question he hadn't voiced. He held up his phone, the screen displaying an airline ticket with Galen's name on it. "You should go with her."

"*What?*"

"I took you for granted." Theo slipped his phone into his pocket. "You've always been there, and I never put much thought into a day when you might not. It's not fucking right, Galen. The only reason you don't leave my side is because you feel like you owe me. You don't. There was never a debt, and if there had been, you would have repaid it a thousand times over. *I* owe *you*." His blue eyes held something akin to grief. "You've given half your life to me, sacrificed every chance at happiness you had along the way."

He was going to fucking kill Theo. Galen closed the distance between them. "I love you, you idiot. You make me happy."

"I made you happy. Made—past tense. It's not going to work. Fuck, you know that better than I do." Theo gave him a sad smile. "You deserve more than to be someone's dirty little secret."

"Who's going to watch your back if I'm not there to cover your ass?" The thought of Theo moving through the tangled politics of Thalania without Galen at his six left him sick to his stomach. Who could he trust with Theo, besides himself?

He stopped short.

What the fuck kind of question was that? He had no business even considering how Theo would function without him, because he had no intention of going anywhere.

"I see that look in your eyes." If anything, Theo's smile turned even more bittersweet. "You're just like our Meg, so focused on the path in front of your feet that you've never stopped to wonder if it's the right one."

"I'm not leaving you." It was unthinkable. His life and Theo's were inextricably linked. They had been for nearly two decades.

Theo cupped his jaw and stroked his thumb across Galen's bottom lip. "Yes, you are. Go with our girl. I can't have her—I can't have either of you—but I think you two could be happy if you both retract your spikes a little." He dropped his hand. "Besides, she's going to need someone to stop her from hopping the next flight back to kick my ass the second she checks her bank account."

For fuck's sake. "What did you do?"

"Go to New York with her and find out." He half turned away. "Ah, here he is."

Kozlov walked up with a bag in hand and passed it to Theo. "Packed to your specifications."

"Thank you." Theo turned back to Galen and shoved the suitcase into his hands. "You're checked in. Here are enough clothes to keep you for a couple days while you get your feet under you. The apartment's already been switched over to your name only." He chuckled, the sound dry and unconvincing. "I considered putting Meg's name on it as well, but then she really would fly back to Europe to kick my ass."

"Why are you doing this?" It was already decided. One look at Theo's face told him that. If Galen tried to follow him, Kozlov no doubt had orders to knock him out and toss him into the cargo hold or something equally underhanded. No matter what he said, Theo would make sure he got on that plane.

Theo's smile dropped as if it'd never existed and he let Galen see through all the bullshit to the staggering loss beneath. It was like an abyss opened right in front of him, and one wrong move would send him tumbling in. Just like that, Theo's grin was back and his mask firmly replaced. "Two out of three isn't bad odds. Marry her. Have a small horde of Mikos babies. Figure out what you both want without all the bullshit of responsibility and plans involved. Be happy together." *Someone has to make it out of this happy.*

The words he didn't speak lay between them like a live thing.

Galen took a step back, the chasm in his chest growing deeper, more jagged. "You're not giving me a goddamn choice."

"Wrong. I'm giving you every choice." Theo nodded at Kozlov and headed for the doors. "Be happy, Galen. Do it for me."

You son of a bitch.

Galen spun on his heel and stalked to where Meg had just emerged from the ticket counter, her bag tucked under one arm. Her eyebrows shot up at the sight of his suitcase. "What's going on?"

"Theo decided to play matchmaker."

"Wait." She caught his arm, and he dragged her a few steps before he finally slowed and turned to face her. Meg looked over her shoulder to where Theo had stood a few moments ago. "I'm going to need you to explain what the hell you're talking about."

"Our favorite almost-king has upgraded to playing god. He's decided that since he can't have you, I should. I guess I'm the fucking consolation prize."

"Not a consolation prize." She bristled. "He's being a noble selfless idiot, isn't he? Just like he was when he decided that I'm getting carted off home. I didn't hear *you* complaining about that decision."

"Because it's the right fucking decision. You don't have a stake in this game. You're just a walking liability, and you deserve better than to play second fiddle to whatever noble Theo marries."

Meg looked up at him with hazel eyes that saw too much. "It sucks when someone else makes the call for you, doesn't it?"

Fuck, he hated having his choices thrown back in his face, but hell if she wasn't right. Galen clenched his jaw.

"Fine. I'll play. What would you do if we didn't decide to cart you back to New York?"

"I love you." She reached out, almost tentatively, and pressed her hand over his heart. "It seems stupid to say it like it means nothing, but it does to me. I love both of you." Meg hesitated. "This was never in my plan, and I don't have some neat little answer for you. I would have gone with you to Thalania. I would have done whatever Theo needed from me to help him take back the crown. And after... I don't know what would have happened after. But I would have made my own decision about where I ended up."

They turned almost as one to look at the airport security line. Galen had been following orders his whole fucking life. First with his father, and then to Theo's father, and then to Theo. Granted, it was different with Theo. He loved that idiot, and Theo usually knew when to back down and let Galen's expertise take over.

Not this time.

"If something happens to him, I'll never forgive myself."

She poked his chest. "That's cute. Try again."

Damn it, what did she want from him? But he knew, didn't he? "We keep saying there isn't a way for the three of us to be together, but we haven't even fucking tried. Maybe it'll blow up in our faces. Fuck, it probably will." He caught the edge of her smile and it made something in his chest twist. "I love you too, Meg. Both of you."

Theo did, too. He wouldn't be this determined to see them happy if love wasn't involved. The emotion made people do stupid, noble shit like sending them off to be together while he resigned himself to a life apart.

No. Fuck that. Galen wasn't leaving.

Neither, it seemed, was Meg.

He did some quick calculations. "They'll have driven. Kozlov hates flying and avoids it whenever possible. If we leave now, we'll barely be an hour behind them." He knew Kozlov well enough to know which route he'd take back. The man was cautious and he'd be overly careful with Theo as a passenger.

They might even be able to make it across the border before Theo did.

Meg's eyes lit up and she gave him a grin that was downright wicked. "What do you say we go get our man?"

He hooked the back of Meg's neck and pulled her to him. Galen kissed her hard, loving the way she melted against him. When he finally lifted his head, they were both breathing hard. "I love you, Meg. I said it before, but I fucking mean it."

"I know." She nipped his bottom lip. "If you didn't, you would have let me get on that plane and gone after Theo yourself."

It would be complicated. He didn't see a way forward for them that didn't involve a shit ton of compromise and a healthy dose of pain.

Galen didn't give a fuck.

For so long, his life had boiled down to one hard task: keep Theo safe. That wouldn't change, but now there was somehow room for more. He'd *make* room for more.

He took Meg's hand and tugged her toward the doors. "Let's go get our man."

━━

WHEN THEY DROVE across the border between Greece and Thalania, Theo expected to feel relief. Like he was finally coming home. Unfortunately, relief was in short supply.

Peace had left the building, too.

He had one chance to get this right or Phillip would no doubt build a dungeon just to throw him into it for the rest of his life. But all Theo could think about was Galen and Meg. They'd be close to landing in New York by now. Meg would want to go back to that threadbare little apartment, but Galen would growl at her until she snapped and agreed to go to theirs.

No, not theirs anymore. Galen's.

Damn it, he made the right call. The *only* call. If Theo couldn't have what he wanted, then he'd make damn sure the people he loved could. They were both too stubborn by half, but they'd figure it out. Galen just needed to learn to give a little instead of stepping onto the battlefield, and Meg needed to be coerced into believing that bending was better than throwing herself against every problem she came across until she broke.

They'd figure it out.

They had to.

Isaac cleared his throat. "You're sure about this, Your Highness?"

"Yes." He checked his phone again. The heads of the seven noble Families in Thalania formed a Parliament that worked in conjunction with the King or Queen. They didn't have the power of the sitting monarch, but that wouldn't matter in this scenario. There *was* no sitting monarch, and there wouldn't be for months yet. All he needed was for the majority of them to publicly confirm that the marriage between Theodore Fitzcharles II and Mary Mortimore was legal based on the documents they'd seen with their own eyes. Phillip couldn't fight both the public and the Families, and Theo had already taken steps to get the public on his side.

One thing at a time.

"I'm not talking about taking the throne back—it was always yours. I'm talking about Galen."

He didn't look up from his phone, couldn't risk Isaac seeing the way his whole body clenched in agony at Galen's name. "There's nothing to say about Galen."

"He's one of your greatest assets and you put him on a plane heading in the wrong direction."

"Galen is much more than an asset and he deserves to be treated as such."

Isaac exited the highway and stopped at a light at the bottom of the ramp. He turned to face Theo. "Forgive me for being blunt—"

"If you're not blunt, there's nothing to forgive."

Isaac ignored that and kept talking, each word a hammer chiseling away at the wall Theo fought so hard to build around himself when he walked out of the airport and left behind what had become two of the most important people in his life. Isaac cleared his throat. "Forgive me for being blunt, but you made a dumb ass move leaving him behind. Probably the girl, too, based on how you looked at them. A king needs allies, people he trusts beyond all political machinations, people who are there for *him* and him alone. Do you really think you're going to find it in Thalania when you just sent the only two people that applies to away?"

"I don't remember asking your opinion."

Isaac snorted. "Galen's not here to offer his, so I figured I'd step in. You already know what he'd say."

Yeah, Theo knew what he'd say. The same thing Isaac had. The same thing Meg had. That they wanted to come with him to face this together. He couldn't allow it. If he let himself, he'd find a way to convince them to stay. To try to find a way forward.

He'd destroy them all in the process.

They would be happy together, damn it.

"What if there *was* a way?" Isaac kept going, kept outline possibilities that were beyond impossible.

Now more than ever.

Ten minutes after they hit the capital city, Ranei's, limits, Isaac checked his phone and cleared his throat. "I need to make a stop."

"What?" Theo twisted to look at him as he turned and then turned again, guiding the car into a little alley between two tall buildings. They weren't far from the palace—another thirty minutes or so—but there was nothing in this area of Ranei that should have required Isaac to stop. Theo took a slow breath, centering himself like Galen taught him. "My uncle's orders."

His door was yanked open and strong hands gripped his shoulders and pulled him out into the alley. Theo swung. He wasn't going down without a fight. If he had any say in it, he wasn't going down at all. His fist connected at the exact moment he registered Galen's angry dark eyes.

Galen's head snapped back and a feminine voice cursed. "What the fuck is wrong with you, Theo?"

He turned, nightmare slow. Meg. "You're supposed to be on a plane."

"Yeah, well, plans changed." She smacked his arm and slid between him and Galen to check his friend's jaw. "Any loose teeth?"

"I'm fine." Galen picked her up and set her aside so he could turn to face Theo fully. "Stupid move, letting Kozlov take you somewhere you didn't want to go."

Yeah, it had been. He glared. "You aren't supposed to be here."

"You're not king yet, and I stopped being your head of security when we went into exile together. I don't take orders from you." He opened the back door and waited for Meg to climb in, and then he followed her and shut it with a snap.

Theo stared. "What are you doing?" When Galen ignored him, he jerked open the back door and leaned down, getting in his friend's face. "What the fuck do you think you're doing?"

"You need witnesses. I'm titled. Meg's a civilian, but she works as a second witness."

"Gee, thanks," she murmured.

"Hush." Galen turned back to him. "Phillip doesn't care about the truth. He cares about being the puppet master behind the next king. He'll kill you if he thinks he can get away with it."

Theo clenched his hands to keep from reaching into the backseat and strangling the man he loved. "That's wonderful, Galen, I most certainly hadn't thought of that. Just like I hadn't thought to arrange to have the entirety of the sitting Parliament at the palace waiting to witness the evidence I'm presenting."

Galen gave him a long stare. "Be a shame to make them wait."

He wasn't going to get them out of this car without an all-out brawl. Theo looked at Isaac, but the other man seemed to find the steering wheel intensely fascinating. "You're going to be punished for this."

"Can't wait." Galen crossed his arms over his chest and nodded at the front seat. "Shall we?"

"I'm going to throw you in the fucking dungeon."

Meg leaned over to peer out the side windows, taking in the city. "Kinky."

Galen snorted. "That threat would be a lot more effective if the dungeon hadn't caved in and been walled over about fifty years ago."

"Don't you dare say another word—either of you." Theo turned around to face the windshield and pressed his fingers to his temples. Walking into this confrontation with them was out of the question. How the fuck was he supposed to keep them safe when neither Galen nor Meg seemed that concerned with following his expertly-reasoned orders?

The drive to the palace felt like it took ten times as long as it should have. Isaac parked in one of the lots several blocks away and led them into the apartment building that was manned entirely by security staff. No one looked directly at their little group, which told Theo all he needed to know—everyone was waiting to see how things fell out before they declared their allegiance one way or another.

He didn't hold that against them.

This wasn't their fight.

Isaac used his fingerprints to open a padlocked door that led down a narrow set of stairs. Theo had frequented this path more times than he could count as a teenager, usually with Galen by his side. Whenever palace life got to be too constricting, the large rooms filled with too little air and too many needs, they'd sneak out and spend a few hours walking the streets of Ranei. Theo's father always sent someone to shadow them, but he'd given them the freedom they needed.

Fuck, he missed his father.

Ghosting their way through the tunnels that ran beneath the palace grounds felt like walking back in time. He half expected to come out the door at the end and find his father in his study, glasses perched on the edge of his nose, embroiled in some ancient history book. Theo rubbed a hand against his chest, as if he could physically draw away the pain blossoming there.

After his father died, everything happened so quickly.

Phillip's coup. The exile. The plan to reverse the exile and retake his birthright.

This chapter would be over soon.

For better or worse, he'd have to deal with the consequences.

A hand on his arm drew him back to the present. Meg looked up at him with those pretty hazel eyes, her smile warm. "You aren't alone, Theo. I get why you sent us away, but that's not what this is. We've got your back."

"What is this, then?" A question he should know better than to voice *now*.

Her smile went soft. "It's love. And love doesn't stop when it's no longer convenient. This isn't a battle we can fight for you, but we can stand at your back and support you while you fight it for yourself."

The aching in his chest increased tenfold. In all his scenarios, he'd never once stopped to think that love might actually be the result. He'd loved Galen since they were kids. That relationship was as known to him as his own heartbeat, steady and sure and always present. Even when he sent Galen away, he never doubted their feelings for each other.

Meg was different.

She had a life that didn't include him. She had goals and a plan that he didn't factor into—goals and a plan that she'd staked her entire future happiness on.

When this started, he never planned on derailing her. He'd just wanted her and a window of time where they could all enjoy each other. Crossroads were supposed to be temporary, after all.

"You love me."

"Yes." So simple, that answer. No dicking around, no playing hard to get. She just met his gaze and gave him the one thing he never dared hope for. "And you love me, too."

It was not a question, and why should it be? Of course he loved Meg. How could he not? "You know I do."

"Yeah. I do." She gave him another of those achingly sweet smiles and squeezed his hand. "You've got this, Theo. And we've got you."

In front of them, Isaac slowed. They had reached the door to the palace.

It was time.

Chapter 18

Meg fell into step next to Galen as Theo started up the stairs. Galen leaned down and took her hand, steadying her despite the fact her steps were sure. "Stay by me. Don't say anything. Theo's got this dog and pony show planned down to the last second, no doubt, but Phillip will lose his cool at some point and I may have to step in."

He said it so casually, as if his protecting Theo was as second nature as breathing. *That's because it is.*

She nodded and squeezed his hand, and then they were through the door at the top of the stairs and into another world.

Meg hadn't had nearly as much time to examine Thalania when she and Galen were rushing to beat Theo there, and the tunnels were just tunnels. Impressive for their scope, but not particularly jaw-dropping.

The palace changed that.

She stopped short and took in the great domed ceiling, the tile beneath her feet that looked positively ancient despite being shined within an inch of its life, and the framed paintings lining the wall that had to be priceless.

She recognized a few of the styles, though Meg had never been particularly into art. The fact she recognized them at all spoke to their value. *This is where Theo grew up. This is where Galen's spent the last decade and a half.*

"This room used to have double the amount of art, but Theo's mother thought it should be enjoyed, so she spread it out through the rest of the palace. After Mary died and Teddy remarried, Katherine kept things the way they were." Galen gave her hand one last squeeze. "Stay close."

Theo smoothed a hand down his shirt. He'd changed since they'd seen him last and now he wore slacks and a button-up. He glanced at her. "After this, we'll talk. All three of us."

Talk about the future.

She nodded, her heart a caged beast in her chest. Meg had meant every word she'd said to Galen, and every word she'd said to Theo. She loved them. She wanted to figure it out. Find some sort of compromise that wouldn't drive them all insane.

It had to be possible.

She really, really hoped it was possible.

"Let's go." Theo led their strange little procession out of the room and down an equally impressive hall, its thick white walls making her think of the home in Greece they'd left not too long ago. But where Galen's place was sparse and strangely comfy, this one radiated cold power. It was a reminder of how different the worlds they came from were.

And, for the first time, Meg just didn't give a fuck.

Theo and Galen might have been raised completely different than her, but if she was going to fight so hard to scrub off her history, she would allow them to do the same. The only thing that mattered was the future. It had enough hurdles without her throwing a few more up because of her issues. She would likely never be comfortable with their wealth, but she was willing to try to get over the money stuff if it meant having these two men in her life.

She half expected him to lead her to an honest-to-god throne room, but the door Theo walked through ended in a glorified sitting room. The room held an array of chairs and couches that were all artfully arranged to create an intimate setting where deals were obviously made. Seven people filled them, four men and three women.

Meg automatically categorized them as she took up a position next to Galen, three steps behind Theo. The older man with the distinguished mustache was a good tipper, and he had kind eyes that didn't quite mask the intelligence and ambition there. She would have pegged him as a CEO or someone high up in a corporate office based on that combined with his expensive suit. The two women under fifty looked at Theo as if he was a piece of prime rib that had been delivered specifically for them. The older woman had to be approaching ninety, but from the other six's body language, she was the one to watch. The final three men were cast from the same mold—rich and ambitious— though they couldn't look more different in their coloring, ranging from pale and blond to dark brown skin and black hair.

She couldn't see Theo's face from her position, but the line of his shoulders told her everything she needed to know. He moved like a solider stepping onto a battlefield he wasn't sure he'd survive. "Thank you for coming."

"Curiosity, my dear Theo," the mustached man said with a smile. "It's not every day that a prince returns from exile."

"Former prince." This from the young-ish blond woman. She wore a designer dress in a tasteful baby blue that showed off her lean legs.

Meg glanced at Galen, but he was too busy watching

the seven to notice her. It reinforced her feeling of being embattled, though no one had said anything particularly vicious yet. She pressed her lips together to stifle her questions. If they made it out of this the way Theo obviously had planned, then she'd have time for her questions later.

The door swung open and a man walked into the room. He was like a smaller, diminished version of Theo. Narrower in both shoulders and face, his hair thinning on top, his eyes so cold Meg doubted they ever warmed. His step hitched when he realized who occupied the room, but the surprise didn't show in his expression. "Interesting gathering, Theodore."

This had to be Phillip, Theo's uncle. There was no one else it could be.

Theo pivoted easily to meet Phillip without ever actually offering the rest of the people his back. "Uncle. I bring glad tidings." His smile lit up the room, and she would never know by looking at him that he loathed his uncle, or that the man had attempted to have him murdered.

A born politician.

But then, you knew that. It's just another facet of Theo.

He turned back to the gathered people. "You see, there's been a mistake. Let me explain."

———

THEO DIDN'T GIVE Phillip a chance to take control of the conversation, and he didn't give *himself* a chance to react to seeing his uncle after all these months. They had never been close, not when Phillip always had his eye on the throne, but family should have meant something. He knew better. Of course he knew better.

The bastard didn't even wait a week after his brother—

Theo's father—died to make his move. *That* was what Theo couldn't, wouldn't, forgive.

Then there's the rumors of poisoning…

He turned with a practiced smile to the nobles gathered. "It seems my uncle was a little too trigger happy about declaring my parents' marriage a fraud."

Pierce Huxley pulled at the edge of his mustache and raised his eyebrows. "We examined the evidence provided, and I don't see how that's possible. The dates speak for themselves."

"That would be true if my mother's first marriage was legal."

Phillip finally recovered and moved forward, attempting to inject himself between Theo and the nobles. "It seems my nephew has taken the loss of this throne a little too hard and has brought you here to spin his conspiracy theories. I apologize for the inconvenience of you making a trip for nothing, but I will see him suitably dealt with." He flashed a look at Theo over his shoulder that promised the kind of pain that could break a man.

If he didn't win this, Theo wouldn't be walking out of this palace alive.

Neither would Galen or Meg.

"Let the boy speak." Yael Nibley, rose. At five foot-nothing with a cloud of white curls around her head and a jeweled cane she used to get around, she was still an imposing presence that silenced everyone in the room. Likely because she had been head of the Nibley Family longer than any of them had been alive. She turned dark brown eyes on Phillip, the force of her personality snapping at him. "I, for one, would like to know what new evidence he's brought."

Theo didn't hesitate. "Of course, Lady Nibley." He pulled out the documents he'd kept on his person since

Meg discovered the truth. "If you'll allow me." Theo moved to lay them on the table in front of her. He went through what Meg had found, and the legalities behind it.

Pierce frowned. "You're sure the birth certificate is legitimate? I was under the impression that something had happened to make it irretrievable."

"A fire," Phillip cut in smoothly, all honeyed words and false sympathy. "The clinic where Mary Mortimore was born was a small one in Germany and hadn't had a chance to move their full backlist of paper documents to a digital format. The records were lost."

Oh, no you don't. Theo kept his smile firmly in place. "That's true. This didn't come from the clinic. This was a family-owned copy that I retrieved from my aunt, Alexis Mortimore."

Phillip blanched. "I was informed that no such copy existed."

"I'm afraid my aunt doesn't hold much love for Thalania or the Fitzcharles family name. She wasn't inclined to do you any favors." If she had, Theo held no doubt that the birth certificate would have conveniently disappeared somewhere on the trip back to Thalania. He turned back to the gathered lords and ladies. "As you can see, because my mother was underage when the marriage certificate to her first husband was issued, that marriage wasn't legal and is null and void. As such, her marriage to my father stands as her one and only marriage."

"On the contrary—"

Theo spun on his uncle, his control slipping. "I realize this is not a convenient realization for you, uncle, and I'm dreadfully sorry for that, but the fact remains you declared me illegitimate in error." He should have left it there, but long-banked fury got the best of him. "You should have hired more efficient assassins if you wanted to remain the right hand of the future king."

"I don't know what you're implying, but I resent it."

"I'm implying nothing. I'm flat out telling you that I have a firsthand account that you hired someone to attempt to kill me and make it look like an accident."

Phillip's face went a dangerous shade of purple. "You're out of line."

Lady Nibley adjusted her spectacles and set the birth certificate back onto the table. "The boy's right, Phillip. You made a mistake." She folded her hands in her lap, as regal as any queen who'd ever sat on the Thalanian throne. "Seeing as it required a vote to strip Theodore Fitzcharles III of his rank, based on the evidence provided by Phillip Fitzcharles, there's no reason we can't take a vote to reverse the order and reinstate him."

"You can't do that," Phillip snarled. His composure cracked and fell away like a badly fitted mask. "He's a bastard and some bullshit paper isn't enough to prove that he isn't."

Lady Nibley ignored him the way she would ignore a toddler throwing a tantrum. "All in favor of reinstating Theodore Fitzcharles III as rightful King of Thalania?"

Slowly, hands went up around the room. Theo noted that three—Hollis Vann, Doyle Bakaj, and Yancy Popov— hesitated before raising their hands. They didn't want him back, but with four already voting to put the motion into effect, they didn't want to bring attention to themselves.

I'll deal with you three later.

Lady Nibley nodded. "Welcome back, Your Highness."

"Thank you, Lady Nibley." It was done.

He'd won.

Theo turned to look at Galen and Meg, but stopped at

the sight of Phillip backing toward the door. "Going some-where, Uncle?"

"You son of a bitch." He *moved*, yanking the gun from Isaac's holster and pointing it at Theo. "You can't inherit if you're dead."

Phillip never saw Galen coming.

He grabbed the hand holding the gun and forced it to the ground as Phillip squeezed off two shots, and then Galen delivered a devastating punch to the older man's jaw, sending him to the floor in a heap.

It was over in seconds.

He handed the gun back to Isaac. "Next time someone gets the drop on you like that, I'm going to kick your ass myself."

Isaac went pale. "Noted."

Theo took a careful breath and turned back to the nobles, all watching with varying degrees of surprise and alarm. "If you wouldn't mind staying in the palace for a little while longer before going about your day, I have an announcement to make once I've taken care of this issue."

Once again, Lady Nibley spoke for all of them. She walked over and patted his cheek. "You're a good boy, Theodore." She stepped over Phillip's prone body without missing a beat and walked out of the room.

The others followed more slowly. Lord Huxley clasped Theo on the shoulder. "I'm genuinely happy to have you back, Your Highness."

"Thank you."

And then the room was empty except for the three of them and Isaac and Phillip. Theo stared down at his uncle. He'd like nothing more than to remove the man perma-nently, but doing so would alienate people he couldn't afford to anger. "Isaac, arrest my uncle. He'll be held on charges of treason while we conduct an official investigation into the events surrounding my father's death and everything that's happened since." It was possible that Phillip had covered his tracks too well, but they would find out one way or another through the investigation. If his uncle was found guilty of treason through an official investigation, not a single one of his allies would stand with him. It was the only way to ensure Phillip didn't become a martyr.

He waited for Isaac to pull Phillip to his feet. "Once you have him secured, send a team to collect Dorian Mikos." Galen's father would receive the same treatment as Phillip—an official investigation followed by a trial. It would effectively take their fates out of Theo's hands, and more importantly, out of Galen's hands.

Isaac nodded. "Yes, Your Highness. I'll see it done immediately." He hauled Phillip out of the room and shut the door softly behind him.

Theo walked to the door, locked it, and finally gave Galen and Meg his full attention. Galen had an inscrutable look on his face, but there was relief in his dark eyes. Meg grinned bright enough to blind him. She threw herself into his arms. "You did it."

"*We* did it."

"You were amazing." She kissed his jaw, his chin, his mouth. She wiggled out of his arms before he could fully enjoy the feel of her. Meg tucked a strand of hair behind her ear. "Congratulations, Theo. I mean it."

But she thought he'd turn her away now, send her back to New York. Reinforce the barriers he'd tried to put into place between them.

Fuck. That.

Theo walked to Galen and snagged his neck, pulling him in for a kiss. He told his best friend with teeth and tongue what he'd already said with words. *I love you. I'm sorry*. The last needed to be voiced, though. Theo broke away. "I shouldn't have sent you away."

"No, really?" Galen gave him a tight smile. "Congratulations, Your Highness."

"Don't pull that bullshit." He walked to the nearest chair and dropped into it. They drifted to stand next to each other, though he doubted they meant to. It was just sheer magnetism, drawing them together with both proximity and chemistry. He felt the pull, too, a hook in his gut that demanded he go to them, touch them, hold them close and celebrate this win.

Not yet.

Theo considered how to broach the subject, but in the end, he wanted nothing between them but perfect honesty. No good intentions. No self-righteous bullshit. Just the truth. "I want you to stay. Both of you."

Galen crossed his arms over his chest. "We've talked about this. Several times."

"Yeah, we have. Things change." He leaned forward. "Princess, you have another year of school and I'd never ask you to sacrifice that, but you don't start back up again for another eleven months. Stay with us. Figure out if we can make this work. I know we can, but it will take time to work out the kinks."

She looked torn between hope and fear, her hazel eyes too large in her face. "What happens when eleven months is up?"

"That's for you to decide. Go back to NYC and finish out the degree. Visit us on your breaks, and we'll visit you in between breaks. Or do your year remotely. It's your choice."

Galen shifted. "You have to marry, Theo. It's part of the gig."

252

This, at least, he had an answer for. "If you agree to stay, to be with me, I'll name you Consort. Both of you."

Meg blinked. "What?"

Theo couldn't help a grin at their confusion. "There's an old clause in our laws—so old, I'd completely forgotten about it until Isaac brought it up. Thalania's always been a small country, and as power rose and fell around us, one of my many times removed great grandfathers decided that if he had to marry a foreign princess to save the country, he would, but he wouldn't share full power with her. So he named her Consort to his King. It put her above the noble families, but below his position. Their children were legitimate, of course."

"Charming."

"It was a different age." He shrugged. "Only two of the monarchs in the entire Thalanian history utilized that clause, so it's not well known. The reason I bring it up now is because there's no limit on the number of Consorts a monarch can have."

Galen looked away, and back. "It will cause problems. Triads aren't exactly an accepted thing, here or on the world stage."

"It won't cause any issues that we can't deal with together." Theo pushed to his feet and crossed to them. He took their hands, and hesitated. This had to be their choice, damn it, but fuck. He wanted them to make the one that would bring them all the most happiness.

He flat out wanted *them*. "It won't be easy. There will be unique challenges, and things will be messy while people get used to the idea that their king is in love with two people. It's worth it to me. More than worth it. I love you. Both of you." He hesitated, trying to control his racing heart. He might as well have tried to control a stampede. "But if you don't want all the strings that come attached to loving a king, I can't blame you for that. Or if you want to take the eleven months and figure it out at the end of it, we can make it work."

"That means keeping things secret," Galen said.

"Yes."

"No," Meg said. "No secrets. If we do this…" She gave herself a shake and lifted her chin. "I want you, Theo. And I want you, Galen. I can't pretend that I'll be graceful and easy about every challenge that shows up, but I'm willing to fight for you—for us." She gave him a tentative smile, and then turned it on Galen. "What do you think?"

"It might be a mistake."

Meg rolled her eyes. "No shit it might be a mistake. It could blow up in our faces—literally, apparently. The question isn't what could go wrong. It's whether you are willing to fight for what you want—what you love."

Fight for us, Galen.

Galen looked them both. "This is what you want—what you really want?"

"Yes," Theo said.

Meg took longer. "I never expected any of this, but… I'm not willing to walk away just because it wasn't part of my plan. We can make it work. I know we can."

Finally Galen nodded. "Then I'm in."

Theo pulled Galen in for another kiss, and then Meg. "We need to change and address the media." He kept a hold of Meg's hand and tugged her behind him to the door and down the hall toward the private living quarters.

They'd agreed.

He'd barely dared hope that they would, and now he wasn't about to pussyfoot around on following through on his end of things.

It took an hour to get them changed and find clothes for Meg that were appropriate for a press conference. After spending so much time being a civilian, it felt strange to be back in this place. He looked around, seeing evidence of his father everywhere. His mother's influence was smaller, more diminished with time, but still there nonetheless.

And then there was no more waiting.

Theo led the way to the press room. He stopped just outside the door and turned to look at Meg and Galen. Galen was as handsome as ever in one of his many black suits, though he'd left off a tie like normal. Meg looked resplendent in a gunmetal gray dress that managed to be demure and make him want to rip it off with his teeth at the same time. "You look beautiful. Both of you."

"Thank you." Color dusted Meg's cheeks, though she looked a little ill as she took in the door they were about to go through. A low murmur on the other side was the only indication of the rat race they were about to set off.

"Second thoughts?"

"No. Nothing like that. This is just… new."

"We've got you, princess." He pressed a careful kiss to her lips, mindful of her lipstick. "Let's go."

Camera flashes blinded him as he stepped through the door and walked to the small podium set up at the front of the room. Even after all the time away, Theo fell into autopilot, smiling though spots still danced across his vision. He leaned down and spoke into the mic. "I've missed you."

Questions were fired from every single person packed into the room. He let them yell it out for a few moments, and then held up his hand. "There will be time for questions later this week. This press conference is purely to inform you of the new development." *Should have found Edward and Camilla and told them before I did this. Fuck, I didn't even think of it.* Too late to go back now. He kept his smile firmly in place. "New evidence has come forward to correct the mistake made several months ago. My parents' marriage was, in fact, legal, and Parliament has already voted to reinstate me as Crown Prince of Thalania." Another uproar at that. He let them have longer this time before he called for quiet again. "My coronation will be scheduled shortly, and you'll be the first to know once the details are finalized. In the meantime, there's one more matter of business to attend to—or matter of the heart, as it may be."

That got their attention.

Perfect silence fell, filling with the kind of anticipation that only a reporter on the verge of a particularly juicy story could manifest.

He glanced over to where Meg and Galen stood just inside the door, both of them watching him closely. As he met their gazes, they each nodded. No change of heart there. *Thank fuck.* He turned back to the mic. "Once I am King, I'll be naming my Consort. Meg Sanders... and Galen Mikos."

No going back after this.

Good.

He wouldn't have it any other way.

Theirs for the Night

A Thalanian Dyanasty Novella

Chapter 1

"Don't give me that look—you're coming out tonight. It's your birthday, Meg, and there's only one proper way to turn twenty-three. It's not home alone, stressing about things you can't control."

Meg Sanders finished restocking the beer fridge and pushed to her feet. After a twelve-hour shift of bartending, everything hurt from her worn-out tennis shoes to her shoulders. Even if she wasn't exhausted, she'd still be looking for an excuse to say no. Just like she always did when Cara tried to convince her to go out after their shift.

She loved her friend, but Cara couldn't seem to get it through her big, beautiful brain that Meg was *broke*. The combination of no money and aching feet wasn't one that motivated her to go dancing. When she'd first landed in New York, she'd racked up more than her fair share of credit card bills living beyond her means, the freedom of answering to no one going straight to her head. She couldn't afford to make those same mistakes again—even for a night. "I have to work tomorrow."

Cara mimicked a buzzer noise. "You don't work until three tomorrow. Try again."

Meg leaned against the bar and cast a look over the room. Despite being a Saturday night, they were in the magic hour between rushes. Too late for those pre-gaming it before hitting the clubs. Too early for those same people stumbling in for the Satellite's fabled breakfast and Bloody Mary's to get their hangover started right. "We're in a bar. I spend all my time dolling out alcohol to drunk people. The last thing I want to do right now is go out and be around *more* drunk people."

"Honey." Cara grabbed her arm and towed her through the doorway and into the short hallway that led back to the kitchen. She frowned, her big brown eyes serious for once. "I know you're broke and stressed and worried about fall tuition, but if you don't take some time to cut loose, you're going to explode into a Meg-shaped puddle of anxiety and brains."

Meg made a face. "You say the nicest things."

"I say the truest things." Cara yanked her mass of blond hair out of her ponytail and ran her fingers through it. "Come out with me tonight and we'll celebrate your birthday right—just for a little bit. The bouncer at Bliss owes me a favor, so you don't have to worry about cover and if you let me pick your outfit, you won't buy a drink all night." She held up a hand, forestalling Meg's refusal. "Even if that drink is ginger ale. I'm not saying you need to get shit-housed. I'm saying you need to put the stress on the backburner for a few hours. All your problems will still be there in the morning."

The only thing I want is to go to bed and sleep for twelve hours. She opened her mouth to say exactly that…but it was a lie. If left to her own devices, Meg would go home, reread the letter for the thousandth time. It would say the exact same thing it had from the moment she opened that red-stamped letter—her financial aid had run dry. Spending hours trying to make the math work in a way that didn't spell the end of her dreams, just like she had every night this week, wouldn't make a damn bit of difference.

Spoiler alert—the math didn't work.

Maybe Cara was right. Maybe she just needed some time away from reality. Meg knew from years of experience that if she couldn't find a way around a problem, sometimes the best thing to do was to check out completely and let her brain work on the solution in the background. A night of dancing might be just the thing to shock the solution loose.

Hopefully.

If it wasn't, she didn't know what she was going to do. Every plan Meg had for her future hinged on her ability to get this degree and leverage it into her dream job—a dream job that paid the bills. Being an accountant wasn't glamorous and likely wouldn't make her rich, but it was steady work that would never go away. Taxes and death were the only certainties in life, just like old Ben Franklin had said.

She would have happily broken dozens of laws as a child to have a reliable income that paid the bills. Nothing —*nothing*—would stop her from carving out the kind of safe space that financial security created.

But not tonight.

Nothing would happen tonight but more stress and worry and plotting half a dozen contingency plans that made her sick to her stomach to even think about.

Meg sighed. "Two hours—tops."

Cara let loose a squeal to shake the windows and pulled Meg in for a tight hug. "You won't regret it, I promise. It will be fun." She bounced back. "Let's get the hell out of here, run by my place to change, and go dance our asses off."

Her friend's enthusiasm spread through her until she managed a smile of her own. "Sounds like a plan."

An hour later, wearing the smallest dress known to mankind, Meg wondered what the hell she'd been thinking. She tugged at the hem again. "You sure you didn't have something with more yardage?"

"Oh, hush, you look amazing and you know it." Cara nudged her toward the front of the line of people that snaked down the block. "Besides, you used to own a dozen just like it."

Yeah, she had. Before she'd gotten in over her head with credit card debt and sold every piece of clothing that wasn't vital—and clubwear didn't make the list.

"It's been a while." It took four years to undo six months' worth of damage, and she was never, ever going down that road again. Meg smoothed down her dress again and pushed the old thoughts from her mind. Tonight was about letting go. She could let go. She used to be able to compartmentalize with the best of them.

She was just out of practice.

Though she'd pushed a magnificent red dress on Meg, Cara had picked something similar in black that showcased her mile-long legs and pressed her boobs to gravity-defying heights. She grinned. "You look amazing. Own that shit."

Meg forced herself to straighten her shoulders as they approached the bouncers. She might be an inch away from indecent exposure on both her chest and ass, but she'd be damned before she let anyone know exactly how uncomfortable she was. There had been a time in her life when dresses like these were the rule instead of the exception, but that was a small lifetime ago. She was out of practice with that, too.

Cara sidled up to the giant of a bouncer and went onto her tiptoes in her sky-high heels. Whatever she said worked, because he nodded, gave her ass a playful smack, and unclipped the velvet rope to let them in. He winked at Meg as she passed, but thankfully kept his hands to himself.

Inside, it was just another flavor of every other club in NYC. A bass she could feel in her bones, low lights, and a packed dance floor. Meg stepped to the side as she walked through the door, trying to get her bearings. The DJ booth overlooked the dance floor that took up most of the main floor, and the bar stretched across the wall opposite in front of a truly impressive display of bottles. Stairs curved up to a second floor with what looked like booths and plenty of spaces to watch the dancers—the VIP lounge.

She checked out the people near the railing out of sheer habit—when one was a bartender, it paid to know one's patrons. The woman in the tiny jumper with the cut-outs likely hadn't paid for a drink all night and, even if she had, she wouldn't tip. Two other women seemed more focused on each other than they were on their view. They didn't touch, despite standing close enough to mingle their exhales—they were on their first date, maybe second, and it would get hot and heavy after they left the club. A few feet from them, two men leaned against the railing. One had his back to the dance floor, his attention focused on his friend. The other...

The other was staring straight at *her*.

Meg froze, her breath a trapped thing in her throat. Even across the distance, those blue eyes pinned her in place and stoked a heat inside her that had no business existing. His face was all angles that should have been too sharp for beauty, but was painfully attractive all the same. Dark hair cut tight against the side of his head and left slightly longer on top, begging for someone's fingers to sift through it. He wore jeans and a T-shirt that should have downplayed his presence, but she couldn't shake the feeling that this was a man who was at home in expensive suits as he was in the clothing he currently wore.

Trouble.

He said something to his friend, and the man turned to face her. Where the first guy was almost pretty—if a woman was willing to cut herself to pieces on his beauty—this one was rough and unfinished and screamed danger in a way that made her nipples go tight.

Holy shit, what is wrong with me?

She tore her gaze from them and searched the crowd for Cara. *I should have known the red dress was too loud. Black would have been better.* There were bartenders who were loud and put themselves out there, drawing people in and making bank off the tips that invariably followed. Meg didn't number among them. She blended. She was damn good at it, too.

It was so much easier to move through a crowd when no one was paying attention to her, and there wasn't a more attention-grabbing color than fire engine red.

Since Cara didn't materialize in front of her, Meg headed for the bar. She'd bet her next paycheck Cara had already charmed a drink out of some guy. She drew in men the way honey drew bees, though she never seemed to go home with any of them. Meg had her own theories about that, but Cara was her friend so she tried not to psychoanalyze her.

Speak of the devil.

Cara peered out from behind a guy in a cheap suit and waved at Meg. She grinned at Meg's raised eyebrows and gave an unrepentant shrug, a drink in each hand. A few seconds later, Cara was at her side, having brushed off the guy. "What?"

"One of these days that is going to backfire."

"Without a doubt." She held up the drinks. "Cranberry-vodka or Crown and Coke?"

Meg rolled her eyes and motioned to the darker drink. "You already know the answer to that." They had to lean close and yell to be heard, which didn't make for ideal conversation, but it was just as well.

Meg sipped the drink and took her first full breath in what felt like weeks. Her shoulders relaxed a little and she took another sip, letting the music drive the tension from her body. Cara was right—it would still be there tomorrow. She could take tonight and enjoy herself.

Against her better judgment, she glanced up to the two men she'd seen at the bar.

The spot where they'd stood was empty.

Irrational disappointment surged her. She tried to shake it off, the same way she'd shaken off her day. They were strangers who probably had half a dozen women ready to jump them at the slightest crook of a finger. Or they were gay. Given how her luck had been going lately, it was probably the later. Either way, neither one of them were the least bit interested in *her*.

Determined to put it out of her mind, she downed her drink and set it on a nearby table. "Let's dance!" She waited for Cara to finish her drink and then towed her friend into the crowd. They carved out a neat little spot for themselves and started moving with the beat. Before long, a guy had grabbed Cara's attention and she was happily grinding on him, stroking his biceps as she spoke in his ear. Meg's laugh was eaten by the music. On her own again, she lifted her arms over her head, tilted her face back and let the strobing lights wash over her.

It was going great until a rough hand closed around her hip and jerked her back into a hard body.

She barely had a chance to register that someone had grabbed her when both hand and body were gone. The absence left her unbalanced and her ankle turned, sending her tipping to the side—right into a large male chest. The stranger caught her easily, his hands cupping her elbows as she found her balance again. Meg looked up...and kept looking up until a pair of devastating blue eyes stole her breath much the same way they had earlier.

The pretty guy from the VIP lounge.

She looked over her shoulder in time to see the other half of the pair dragging a drunk dude through the crowd and toward the exit. *Oh.* One hand released her elbow and gentle fingers clasped her chin, drawing her attention back to her apparent savior.

Not that I needed saving...

He gave a tight smile and mouthed. *You okay?*

How was that even a question? Women got grabbed in clubs all the time. It wasn't okay, but it was hardly worth this level of reaction. Still, it was kind of nice and he was seriously attractive and she found herself nodding slowly.

The second guy returned a few moments later, and Blue Eyes grinned. The expression lit up his face, giving him a playful edge that had her rocking back in her high heels. He leaned down, giving her plenty of time to react, and spoke in her ear. "Dance with us?"

Wait a minute—us?

She angled back enough to look at both of them, at this smiling stranger and his much more serious partner. The vibes coming off the two were so damn strange, Meg didn't know what to do with them, but she found herself nodding as if it was every day that two gorgeous dudes wanted to dance with her at the same time. As if they were a pair and she was…

She didn't know what she was if they were a pair.

They're probably gay, right? This doesn't make sense otherwise.

Straight guys did not share a dance partner the way these two did. They moved seamlessly, transitioning her between them as if they done this a thousand times before. They always seemed to know where the other was, and both kept a careful distance between them and her, touching her only on her hips and nowhere else.

It was so freaking sexy, she could barely stand it.

By the second song, she already had good idea of their personalities. Blue Eyes seemed to be enjoying himself immensely, always ready with a grin that lit up his expression even as the heat in his gaze damn near melted her panties right off. This one was the kind of guy who threw himself full-tilt into life and to hell with the consequences. His sinful lips promised one hell of a good time and the way he stared at her mouth had her fighting not to lick *her* lips in response.

Dark and Broody was his perfect counterpart. He was bigger than Blue Eyes, his broad shoulders practically blocking out her view of the club. His short black hair was cut serviceably in a way that was just shy of military, and his short beard gave the impression of forgetfulness, rather than following any hipster trend. He wore a plain black T-shirt and jeans, and she would have thought he was just going through the motions except for the fact that he matched his hips to hers with an effortlessness that left her whole body tight. She had no business imaging how he'd use that particular skill in bed and yet…

And yet there was the way he watched her, as if he already knew what she'd taste like and savored the flavor on his tongue like his favorite kind of candy.

The song changed, shifting to one that was on every radio that month and the dance floor surged as people abandoned their drinks and crowded in. The space between Meg and her partners disappeared and she found herself sandwiched between the men. Dark and Broody had his hands on her hips, and she was braced on Blue Eyes's chest. Dark and Broody acted as a wall at her back, keeping the worst of the crowd off them. Blue eyes lifted her hair away from her neck and his lips brushed her ear. "Have a drink with us."

There it was again. That word, ripe with meaning. *Us.*

As if they were a unit and she could take them as one or reject them as one.

Getting ahead of yourself, aren't you? He asked you to have a drink, not to…

The crowd surged again, pressing them ever more tightly together and she froze. There was no mistaking the fact that they wanted her—that they *both* wanted her. Her fingers flexed on Blue Eyes's chest, kneading his pecs, and his hands dropped to her hips, just above where Dark and Broody held her lightly. *His* hands shifted the slightest bit, his pinkies drawing across the bare skin of her thigh just below the hem of her dress. Just that. Nothing more.

But she felt branded right down to her soul.

"Meg!"

Cara appeared at her side, her dark eyes saucer-wide. She gave what barely passed as a polite smile to the men and then grabbed Meg's wrist and towed her into the crowd and away from them. She didn't stop or slow down until they burst through the door of the ladies' room.

In there, the music was slightly less deafening, so Cara didn't have to yell when she said, "Holy crap, are you okay? I'm sorry. I didn't mean to abandon you. I thought you were dancing alone and then I turned around and they had their dirty paws all over you and—"

"Cara." Meg grabbed her hands and gave them a squeeze. "Cara, I'm good. They asked to dance. I said yes. It's good."

"They…" If anything, Cara's eyes went wider. "Oh *shit*, I am the worst wingwoman in the history of wing-women. You were getting busy, weren't you? Look at you, you're all flushed." She laughed and leaned against the counter. "God, I thought you were freaked out and couldn't escape and that's why you looked like that. But it was *lust*." She gave Meg a playful smack. "Get it, girl!"

Meg glanced at herself in the mirror and, sure enough, a flush of pink stained her chest and cheeks. Even more telling, her nipples pressed against the thin fabric of her low-cut dress. She cleared her throat and tucked her dark hair behind her ears. "It's fine. I'm sure they'll get another partner."

"*They?*" Cara waggled her brows. "I know you don't really hookup, but this might be the time to make an exception. If I had one guy—let alone *two*—looking at me the way they were looking at you, I'd consider breaking my rule about going home with strangers."

Meg adjusted her dress, half sure she could still feel the imprint of their hands on her hips, could feel Blue Eyes's chest under her hands, could *definitely* feel Dark and Broody's fingers dragging over her skin. She cleared her throat. "How were they looking at me?"

"As if you don't know. Come on, honey. I know you're out of practice, but you're not *that* rusty." Cara laughed. "They were looking at you like they wanted to take turns eating you up." She sobered a little. "But, for real, you should go for it. You're only twenty-three once. And it's your *birthday*. I couldn't have come up with a better present for you if I'd tried." She drew her short frame up and took Meg's shoulders. "I give you permission to go home with them and do the kind of filthy things you'll embarrass your grandchildren with stories about when you're old and senile and drunk on red wine."

Meg gave a nervous laugh even as her gaze skated to the bathroom door. "It's okay, Cara. Like I said, I'm sure they found someone else to dance with. And dancing is *not* the same thing as them taking me home. If there's even a *them*. They're probably not into women. It's probably some game they play before they go home with each other and…" She opened the door and stopped short, causing Cara to bump into her.

Blue Eyes and Dark and Broody leaned against the wall opposite, twin expressions of heat in their eyes. Meg swallowed hard. "Oh."

"You were saying?" Cara laughed in her ear. The music should have covered up their words, but Meg couldn't shake the feeling that both men knew every word of the conversation they'd just had. Cara squeezed Meg's shoulder. "You sure you're good with this? I fully support it if you are, but if you need a save, I will hustle you out of here like you're the nuclear football and I'm the head of the Secret Service."

Meg licked her lips, and two pairs of eyes followed the movement. "It's just a drink."

"Sure, honey, whatever you have to tell yourself." Cara didn't release her. "If you change your mind, text me. Just don't leave the club until you're sure."

"Yeah, okay." That was smart. She took one step forward, and then another. Blue Eyes held out a hand, every move as imperial as a king. As if he already knew how this played out and every move she'd do before *she* knew.

It irritated her despite the lust beating a drum through her veins. She might want him—want both of them—but she wasn't a goddamn sure thing.

Meg cocked her eyebrow and met first Blue Eyes's gaze and then Dark and Broody's. And then she took off into the crowd.

Chapter 2

The woman was a challenge if Theo had ever seen one. She cast a look over her shoulder, as if he hadn't managed to get the hint the first time. Her look might as well have hollered, *Come and get me.*

He took a single step toward the dance floor, but Galen stopped him with a hand on his chest. He leaned in and spoke directly in Theo's ear. "This is a mistake."

"You want her, too."

"Fuck yes, I do." He leaned harder into Theo's chest. "But I know you, and I know that look. This is just for tonight, Theo. You can't afford anything more—and *she* doesn't know enough to sign on for more."

His mouth twisted at the ever-present reminder that his life wasn't his own. More than that, anyone attached to him developed a really ugly target painted on their chest, courtesy of his uncle. He pinned Galen with a look until his friend dropped his hand. "I know what's at stake."

"Never said you didn't."

His attention drifted back to the crowd, to the flicker of red that drew him like a siren's song. "It won't kill us to have a little fun, Galen. A little distraction is good for the soul."

"I know." Galen stepped back, willing to follow Theo's lead even as he watched his back. He gave a grim smile that was barely more than a quirk of his lips. "She challenged you."

"Fuck yes, she did." And damn if that didn't make his cock ache for her all the more. She'd caught his eye the second she walked through the door earlier, obviously not wanting to be here but determined to enjoy herself all the same. Then she'd boldly met his gaze.

A long time ago, he'd been caught in one of the summer storms that ravaged his country from time to time. Before it hit, the air had a bite to it that snapped at his skin, the only warning before the skies opened up, releasing a deluge, and the thunder had boomed loud enough that he still felt it rattling around in his bones from time to time.

Even as his ten-year-old self had been sure he was going to die, something had risen in him in response. A savagely defiant beast that would not go quietly into the night. A part of Theo that never went to sleep again after that night.

Looking down from the VIP lounge and seeing her raise her chin as she took him in…

It roused the same feeling inside him.

Theo cut through the dance floor with ease, searching for her. She might play at the chase, but she wanted to be caught. There had been no mistaking the interest—the need—written across her face as she moved between him and Galen. Add in the flash of defiance that prompted her to lay this particular gauntlet at his feet, and Theo couldn't have walked away if he'd wanted to.

He sure as fuck didn't want to.

A hand on his arm stopped him. He glanced back at

Galen and followed his friend's gaze to the VIP stairs. The woman in red stood there, that single damn eyebrow raised as if she was disappointed by his response time. He approached slowly, enjoying the view.

She really was something. Her short red dress teased the senses, clinging to her breasts and hips and ass, painting a picture he wanted nothing more than to unwrap at his leisure. She'd left her long dark hair down, and his fingers twitched against the need to tangle there, tilting her head back for better access to her mouth. And what a mouth she possessed. Lips sinfully curved and made for pleasure. Combined with the way she moved and, yeah, she was fucking perfect.

Exactly what he needed to get his mind off the cluster-fuck his life had become.

More importantly, to get *Galen's* mind off it.

He closed the distance between them and held out an imperial hand. If anything, her brow arched higher, but she slipped her hand into his and stepped into him, speaking in his ear. "I got tired of waiting for you."

"Patience, princess."

She pressed her other hand to his chest and flexed her fingers. Unknowing or not, she'd placed her hand in the exact same spot that Galen had earlier. If Theo was one to believe in signs—and he wasn't—then this would only confirm his plans for the night. She leaned back to get a look at his face and, this close, he saw that her eyes weren't the blue he'd expected. They were a strange sort of green that tipped toward hazel in the low light.

She gave a brief smile. "I'd like that drink."

He nodded and touched the small of her back, guiding her up the stairs. The U-shaped booth he and Galen had earlier remained unoccupied, which was just as well. He hadn't been recognized since he arrived in New York several months ago, but there was always the first time. With his increasingly shitty luck, tonight would be the exception to the rule.

She slid into the booth and he followed her in. Galen, being Galen, took the other side and scooted until he could see the entirety of the VIP lounge. Assessing for threats. But Theo didn't miss the way his friend angled his body slightly toward the woman, not quite touching her, but the slightest movement would bring them flush against each other.

He approved.

Theo left a little more space between them. He had what he wanted—she was here and she was interested. He wouldn't fuck things up now by doing something to spook her. That said, he wasn't a fucking saint. He draped his arms over the back of the booth and let his fingers brush her hair. "What's your name?"

"Meg." She answered easily, clearly having nothing to hide. Why would she? Most people didn't move through life with the weight of an entire country on their shoulders.

Neither do I.

Not anymore.

"I'm Theo." He nodded at his friend. "This is Galen." The bartender—a spunky woman who somehow managed to make school bus yellow hair look good—approached with a smile. Theo lifted his voice so she could hear him over the music. "The same for me and my friend. Crown and Coke for the lady."

Meg shook her head. "I don't know if it's sexy as hell or stalkerish that you were watching me long enough to know what I drank before we started dancing."

Theo shrugged a single shoulder. "You can see a lot from the VIP lounge. You caught my eye—both of our eyes."

"I guess I did." She leaned back against the seat more firmly. "What brings you to New York?"

Theo waited for the bartender to deposit their drinks— bourbon for him and Galen, Crown and Coke for Meg— and leaned forward a little. "That isn't the question you want to ask."

She mirrored his move, bringing their faces kissably close. "Pretty sure it's exactly the question I want to ask since I just asked it."

"Mmmm." He twined a lock of her dark hair around his finger, giving it a gentle tug. The desire that flared across her face in response gave away more than she could possibly know. Theo ran his thumb over the hair, enjoying this small connection. A prelude of things to come. "The question you're dying to ask, princess, is if we're really offering what you think we're offering."

She went so still, he suspected she held her breath. "And what do I think you're offering?"

"The answer is yes, you know." He released her and sat back. "Us. You. Tonight."

Meg blinked and gave herself a shake. "Arrogant, aren't you?"

"I know what I want. I don't see a point in pussyfooting around."

She reached for her drink with a shaking hand and tossed the tiny straws aside. Meg took a passably large gulp and set the drink back on the table. She turned to Galen. "He talks a lot and you don't seem to have much to say."

Galen didn't take his attention from the VIP lounge. "In this instance, Theo speaks for me."

Some steel slid back into her spine and the strength reappeared in her tone. "I'd rather have you speak for yourself."

"Doubt you'd like it."

277

"Try me."

Galen gave Theo a look, and Theo nodded. No reason to hold back now. She was interested and, as he told her, he knew what he wanted. What all three of them wanted, even if Meg was understandably hesitant about going for it.

It wasn't every night an opportunity like this came across her path.

Galen twisted to face her fully, his big arms creating half a cage, bracketing her in. The move brought his thigh against hers, and Theo's cock jumped as her dress slid up a little. Another inch and he'd know if she was wearing panties or not.

Fuck, man, focus.

Galen leaned down, though he pitched his voice just high enough for it to reach Theo. "You want to know what I want."

A tremor rode through Meg's body, but she didn't retreat. She nodded slowly. "Yes."

"I want to watch." He met Theo's gaze and then turned his attention fully back to her. "I want to sit here while Theo slips a hand up your dress and plays with your pussy until you're coming and we're the only three people in this entire fucking club who know it. When you're shaking and wondering how it can possibly get any better, I'll have my turn."

"You want…to take turns." Only the slightest breathiness in her voice. Theo's estimation of her rose yet another notch. She was no wilting flower. With the right opportunity, she'd give as good as she got.

Galen gave the slightest shake of his head. "Only to start. Theo and I have known each other a long time, and we're very, very good at sharing."

"Oh." She sat back in the booth and took another big

gulp of her drink. She looked downright shellshocked, and Theo stamped down on his disappointment. He'd misjudged her. Galen was usually subtler than that, but the stress of their current situation affected them both in different ways. He didn't hold it against his friend, but damn it, he'd wanted to taste Meg tonight. She let loose a shuddering breath. "Well, then."

Galen shifted away to refocus on the rest of the club. "Told you that you didn't want to know."

Meg's mouth went tight and her eyes flashed. She suddenly laughed. "God, what a night. You sure you two aren't serial killers or something? Because what you're offering is usually filed under 'too good to be true.'"

Well, shit. He hadn't misjudged her, after all. "It's only one night, princess. We won't be in town much longer."

If anything, that seemed to draw her in further. She gave him a shaky smile. "Want to know something funny?"

Where is this going? He nodded. "Sure."

"It's my birthday. The big two-three."

Twenty-three. Fuck, she was barely more than a baby. Theo started to lean back, but her next words stopped him cold. Meg picked up her drink and looked into the dark depths as if it held the answers to the mysteries of the universe. "I always wondered what it would be like to be with two guys. Kind of one of those filthy fantasies you never speak out loud. I don't do this. I don't even hook up, really, because who has the time or energy for that shit, but damn it, it's my birthday and I'm here and you two are seriously sexy if you're not murderers."

Theo took a moment to pick apart that stream of consciousness she'd just rambled out. "We're not murderers."

"That's something a murderer would say," Meg countered. She jerked her thumb at Galen. "He looks pretty murderous with that expression on his face."

"That expression is just my face," Galen said without looking at her. "And you already decided that you're coming home with us, so there's no point wasting the energy to justify it."

Her jaw dropped and she shook her head. "Wow, at least let a woman have some pride."

Galen moved in that crazy fast way of his. One second he was studying the VIP lounge and the next he tangled his fingers through her hair. He tilted her head back, just like Theo had wanted to do earlier. He nudged her to face Theo and dipped his head to speak in her ear. "Who needs pride when you can be coming inside of five minutes?"

Theo shifted closer, using his body to block her from sight of the rest of the VIP lounge much the same way Galen had done. "Say yes, princess."

She met his gaze steadily. "I'm in."

He touched her knee lightly, exerting the slightest amount of pressure. "Just a teaser for now." He bracketed her knee, letting her feel his strength, and he could see Galen's arm flex as he tightened his grip on her hair. Not enough to hurt—that wasn't their kink—but enough for her to be well and truly present. "Say yes."

Meg tensed and for one eternal moment, it felt like all three of them held their breath while they waited for her answer. If she said no, that would be the end of it. Theo would pay for her drinks, see her to a cab, and he and Galen would head back to the loft they'd rented and work off some of their sexual frustration on each other.

But she didn't say no.

She shot a look over his shoulder. "Anyone can see us."

"No one will see anything we don't want them to." Theo squeezed her knee, waiting.

Finally, she gave a short nod. "Yes."

"You're sure." This from Galen, but the question that wasn't a question wasn't for Meg.

It was for Theo.

He nodded even as she said, "I'm sure."

There was no going back now.

Truth be told, there had been no going back from the moment he laid eyes on her. Theo slid his hand up her thigh, enjoying the way her muscles flexed beneath his grip. *Strong.* Strong enough to take everything they could give her. He stopped at the hem of her dress, checked her expression, and pushed it up that last inch to reveal a pair of red lace panties.

Fuck, I love her in red.

He drew the knuckles of his fingers over the center of her, testing her. Meg gave a shuddering sigh and relaxed back into Galen, trusting him to hold her up. Galen shifted her so she leaned against his shoulder and he reached down to pull her dress higher, exposing more of her, then slowly dragged his finger under the top edge of her panties.

Galen always was a fucking tease.

Theo slid his fingers into her panties from the side, gripping the fragile fabric as he repeated the same move he'd made before, dragging his knuckles through her wetness. And, fuck, she was wet. Wet and shaking as if she might come apart before he had a chance to truly sink into this experience.

That wouldn't do.

That wouldn't do at all.

Theo pushed a finger into her and cursed as she clenched around him. He pumped slowly, his cock jumping at the tightness that stole over Galen's expression as he watched Theo finger fuck Meg. Oh yeah, his friend liked to watch.

Theo withdrew his hand and raised a glistening finger. Meg watched with wide eyes as Galen leaned forward and captured his finger in his mouth and sucked hard. *Fuck.* Sex was always rough and intense with his friend, but the new dynamic of Meg involved ratcheted up his desire for both Meg and Galen.

He wasn't the only one.

Theo felt more than heard his friend's growl of pleasure. *Yeah, you need her tonight. We both do.*

Though his cock groaned in protest, Theo pulled Meg's dress down. No matter what picture Galen had painted for her with his words, tonight wasn't the night when they'd play with her in public. *What are you saying? There won't be a night like that because* this *is the only night you have.* He pushed the thought away and captured Meg's chin. "Come home with us."

"You… You can't just leave me like this."

He leaned down and pressed a painfully gentle kiss to her lips. "I think you'll find, princess, that I can do whatever I damn well please and you'll love every second of it." He set his teeth against her bottom lip as he drew away, tasting her gasp. Theo still didn't release her. "But if you're very, very good, I'll let Galen play with you in the cab back to our place."

Meg blinked, and then blinked again. "When do we leave?"

Galen let loose another of those fuck-me growls. "Right fucking now."

Chapter 3

What am I doing?

Meg didn't have an answer. She couldn't think past the thrumming in her blood and the way every nerve seemed to pulse with desire. Following that need to its inevitable completion was the only thing that mattered right now. The club took on a dreamlike quality, as if nothing was quite real.

Nothing except the men who bookended her between them as they headed toward the door, Galen carving a path toward the door with his big shoulders, while Theo remained a step behind her, his hand a brand across the small of her back. They were almost to the exit when she caught sight of Cara. Meg paused and both men paused with her as if attached to a string wrapped around her middle.

She extracted herself from Theo and crossed to her friend. Cara grinned. "Best birthday ever."

Her cheeks went hot and she managed a nervous laugh. "It's shaping up to be."

"Fill me in on everything tomorrow." Cara pulled her

in for a quick hug. "If you need anything, I'll have my phone on me. Text me later, okay?"

"I will." Some days, she was convinced she and Cara were on different wavelengths, but coming out tonight had been anything but a mistake. "See you tomorrow."

Meg rejoined the men and they headed out the door. It wasn't until they hit the sidewalk that the reality of her situation hit. She was going home with someone. With *two* someones. She missed a step, and Theo caught her under her elbow without hesitation. "You only had the two drinks."

It wasn't a question—he never seemed to ask questions, just make statements—but she answered all the same. "I'm not drunk. I'm nervous."

"Mmmm."

The fever dream dissipated with the cold wind blowing from the north. *What am I doing?* She didn't have an answer now any more than she had five minutes ago. Galen dropped back to walk on the other side of her, his shoulder brushing hers with each step. She looked between the two of them, so at ease in their skin as if they knew their place in life and reveled in it.

As if they'd never gone hungry a day in their lives.

Meg jerked her gaze back to the street. Though cabs clogged the streets, neither man seemed in a hurry to catch one. She cleared her throat. "So...are you two a thing?"

Galen snorted, and Theo laughed aloud. He stroked his hand up her spine and back down again. "Nothing so official. We've been friends a long time. Sometimes we're more. Sometimes we're less."

"That's not an answer."

"She wants to know if I suck your cock, Theo." Galen's gruff voice sounded out of place here in the open air, as if he was more comfortable murmuring in low conversation in crowded rooms than exposed like this. "Or maybe she's asking if I fuck your ass." His dark laugh made her toes curl in her shoes. "Your *princess* has cold feet."

Theo stopped walking and turned her to face him. In there, he hadn't seemed quite as big as Galen, but she realized that was all a front. Even as Meg watched, his posture straightened and he cracked his neck. In truth, he was taller than Galen, though not quite as massive. *This is a man who knows how to hide.*

But what could he possibly have to hide from?

He ran his hands up her arms and over her shoulders. "Do you want me to call you a cab?"

No misunderstanding that. He'd call her a cab, probably pay for it in the bargain, give her a pat on the head, and send her home alone. All she had to do was ask. Even with his mysteries, Theo had the air of a man who took care of the people around him.

He'd take care of her tonight, whether that was seeing her home or following through on all the dark things Galen had promised.

Meg looked up into those blue eyes that were downright electric despite the night shadows. Beautiful. She didn't know many men who could be termed beautiful without it detracting from their masculinity, but Theo managed. Holding her breath, she reached up and touched his mouth, tracing the dip in his upper lip. He stood still, letting her touch him.

Letting her decide.

Really, there was only one option. If she walked away now, she would spend the rest of her life wondering what tonight could have brought if she'd just had the courage to take that first step. Just a tiny leap of faith. It was only one night, after all. She could go home with these devastatingly sexy men and walk away in the morning with a story to hold close to her heart in the years ahead. It didn't have to *mean* anything other than mutual pleasure.

She kissed him.

Theo let her have a second, two, and then he sifted his fingers through her hair and took control. He devoured her, stoking her need with teeth and tongue, banishing the last of her hesitance to dust. She *needed*. He released her as she started to shake and grinned down at her. "You won't regret it." He nodded over her head. "Call a cab, Galen."

The trip passed in a blur. She half expected them to make a move in the backseat, but aside from Theo keeping his arm around her, they both seemed content to stare out the window as if she wasn't three breaths away from coming completely undone.

The cab dropped them at a building a short jaunt from Central Park. Because of course they were rich. They probably had giant cocks, too. *You're going to find out soon enough.* She let Theo take her hands and tug her inside. Meg followed him through the entrance and to the elevator banks, blushing too hard to meet the doorman's gaze.

"Meg."

She startled and pressed her lips together. When it became clear he needed some kind of answer, she reluctantly said, "Yeah?"

Theo held open the elevator doors. He looked at her as if trying to read her mind, to lay out her history, her personality, her everything, for his perusal. "If you change your mind at any time, it's good."

She shivered at the intent in those blue eyes and wrapped her arms around herself. "If I didn't know better, I'd think you were trying to talk me out of it."

"Never that." A sharp shake of his head. "But I'm invested in you having a good time—we both are."

Somehow, she doubted that applied to Galen, no

286

matter what Theo said. The other man might want her—
she had no illusions about *that*—but there was only one
person he was there for tonight. It wasn't Meg.

She nodded. "I'm good, Theo. I promise."

He tugged her into the elevator, his gaze never leaving
her face. "Then up we go."

The elevator went straight to the top and opened into
the penthouse suite, or whatever the stupidly expensive
residence was called. She absently let go of Theo's hand
and wandered to the floor-to-ceiling windows that
stretched the length of the living room. NYC's lights
created a masterpiece on the other side of the glass, a
dark absence marking Central Park in the middle. If the
view was amazing now, it would be spectacular in the
daylight. *Even if money doesn't buy happiness, it buys views
like this.*

She was pretty sure it bought happiness, too, but it
wasn't like Meg would know.

All she could be sure of was that an absence of money
meant stress, anxiety, and the kind of fear that followed her
into her nightmares every night when she closed her eyes.

She turned to find Theo on the couch, watching her.
He was just at ease here as he'd been at the club, and why
not? Even without Galen at his side as a glowering presence, he seemed to own every room he entered. That kind
of ease only came from being born into power. She'd seen
it enough over the years—albeit from afar—to recognize
that, even if she knew nothing else about him.

He crooked a finger. "Come here." The couch was a
monster-sized sectional, situated to face the view and little
else. No television, no other ornamentation. *What more do
you need with that view?*

But the lack of electronics brought home that this was
temporary. Wherever these two men called home, it wasn't

this apartment. This place was set up like a show home, all cold beauty and no heart.

The room was missing something else important. "Where's Galen?" She looked around as if staring into the shadows hard enough would reveal the man in question.

"He'll be back shortly." He motioned her forward again and she closed the distance between them, a magnet to his lodestone. The connection that first appeared when their gazes met over the length of the club pulsed between them like a live thing. If she concentrated, she could almost see it connecting them even before they touched.

Meg slipped her hand into Theo's big one and he maneuvered her to stand between his thighs. He made an appreciative sound. "I don't have to tell you that this dress is a piece of art. You look so fucking sexy in it, I couldn't take my attention off you from the moment I saw you." He ran his hands up her legs, stopping just short of her dress and skating them back down again to her ankles. "Runner."

She nodded and swallowed hard. "Yeah."

"Sit with me." He waited for her to murmur a yes and then he pulled her down to situate her in the corner of the couch, her legs sprawled over his thighs. Theo unbuckled her strappy heels with careful fingers and tossed them away from the couch.

It all felt so…strange.

She'd fully expected for the pair of them to fall on her the second they walked through the door, had even braced for that eventuality. Instead Galen was MIA and Theo was tracing abstract patterns up her legs as if he had all the time in the world. She swallowed hard. "Theo—"

"Not yet." He squeezed her thigh and started working down the other leg. It wasn't until stillness crept over his body that she realized what they'd been waiting for.

Galen.

He stalked into the room from the hallway and tossed a handful of shiny foil packets onto the coffee table. *Condoms.* Galen draped himself on the long leg of the couch, well out of reach. He and Theo shared a charged look that changed the atmosphere in the room in the space of one heartbeat to the next. Meg barely had a chance to process that they were green light, full speed ahead, when Theo shifted closer and kissed her.

He took her mouth as if he had every right to it—as if it had been his all along and he was just now assuming ownership. Meg melted into the contact and tried to turn to face him, but he used a hand on her hip to shift her back to his chest. He kissed down her jaw and set his teeth against her neck. "Open your eyes, princess."

She hadn't even realized she'd closed them. Meg opened her eyes as Theo hitched one of her legs up and over his, spreading her wide. The move bunched her dress up around her hips, leaving her with only her panties covering her. Her gaze landed on Galen, whose languid posture was as relaxed as a tiger about to pounce on its prey. He watched Theo coast a hand down her stomach and pull her dress higher yet and then palm her pussy. His touch was light, teasing, but the hard cock pressing against her bare ass through his jeans was anything but.

"She's so wet, Galen. Wet and…" Theo slid his hand beneath her panties and pushed two fingers into her. "Tight. It's a good thing we're in the mood to play."

Play.

Like she was a toy they'd share between them.

Meg didn't know how she was supposed to react to that, but desire stole her concern and took her pride in the process, leaving only the need for Theo to keep touching her. She rocked her hips to take his fingers deeper, but he gripped her with his free hand, forcing her still. His breath ghosted against the shell of her ear. "Should we show Galen what he's missing?"

With anyone else, the game would be just that—a game. Fun, sure, but ultimately disposable. Meg didn't really know either of them, and they obviously had a history as deep as time itself. She *should* have felt like that.

And yet…

Theo's touch, while authoritative and demanding, was nothing less than reverent. And Galen's gaze was on her as much as it was on Theo. They were here with *her*—not someone else.

Did she want to show Galen what he was missing so he'd get his ass over there and touch her, too?

Fuck yes, she did.

Meg made a noise that must have been enough for Theo, because he tugged her panties to the side, framing her pussy for Galen. The only reaction they got was a tightening in his jaw and his dark eyes going molten. Theo laughed softly. "I'll tell you a secret, princess. I've never met a man with better control than Galen. It's downright supernatural. It'll take a better show than this to get him over here to put his hands all over you." He nipped her earlobe. "If you make it very, very good, I'll even let him use his mouth."

There wasn't enough air in the loft. There couldn't be. Her breath hitched in her lungs, and it took her two tries to force words out. "What if I want his cock?"

This time, Theo's laughter filled the room. He sat up, taking her with him, and positioned her on his lap with her legs on either side of his thighs. "Tell her, Galen."

The other man spread his arms across the back of the couch, his features cold. "You have to earn my cock, princess."

His arrogance should have been a turnoff. It *should* have made her want to put him in his place and make *him* earn access to *her*.

Instead, a part of her that she'd never give voice murmured deep inside her. *I want to earn your cock, Galen. Tell me what I need to do.* Meg slammed her mouth shut hard enough that her teeth clicked to avoid giving those traitorous words voice. She took a breath, and then another. Only when she was sure she wouldn't betray herself did she lean back against Theo more firmly. "Fuck him. I'd rather play with you."

Theo didn't laugh again. He skimmed off her dress and tossed it aside to join her shoes, leaving her in only her panties. A few seconds later, his shirt joined the growing pile. "Lean back."

Meg obeyed immediately. The shock of his bare skin against her own drew a small sound from her lips. There wasn't a soft spot on his body, and he caged her with his chest and arms, holding her open for Galen's perusal.

She twisted to offer him her mouth, needing to taste him again, and Theo didn't hesitate to give in to her unspoken request. His tongue twined with hers, and he cupped her bare breasts and pinched her nipples to aching peaks. Theo spread his thighs, forcing *hers* wider, she felt Galen's gaze all over her.

On the curve of her neck. Following the path of Theo's hands. Centering where her tangled panties left her pussy partially exposed. Her skin sparked as if he'd reached out and touched her. Or maybe Theo's ministrations were responsible for the growing lightning storm inside her. It was too much and not enough and she whimpered against his mouth. "Stop teasing and *touch* me." She grabbed his hand and pressed it between her spread thighs. "Please, Theo. I've been aching since the club."

"Can't have that." He drew her wetness up around her clit with a single finger and circled the sensitive bundle of nerves, easily finding the motion that made her entire body go tight and hot. She opened her eyes and met Galen's gaze as her orgasm spiraled closer and closer. A challenge. *I'll get what I want, and you'll have to watch while it happens, knowing you could have been a part of it.*

Theo, damn him, seemed to know exactly what roads her thoughts traveled. He slowed his pace, dragging it out. "You see how he looks at you. He's seconds away from stalking over here, smacking my hand away, and licking that pretty pussy until he takes your orgasm for himself."

She made that soft whimpering sound again. She couldn't help it. The whole situation was overwhelming her senses, dragging her into a place where every part of her centered around these two men. "Theo, please." Meg didn't know what she was pleading for.

An orgasm. Theo. Galen.

All three.

"I'll make you a deal, princess," he murmured in her ear, his finger never stopping its slow circles that seemed designed to keep her on the edge but never take her over it. "I'll let you choose this time. Who do you want to gift this orgasm to?"

"Both." The answer tore itself from her lips, too true and far too telling.

For the first time since she'd caught sight of him in the club, Galen grinned. His white teeth flashed and his dark eyes lit up with amusement, the whole effect knocking him from attractive to downright dangerous. *Oh God, what have I gotten myself into?*

A night.

It's only for a night.

You can't fall in love with a person—let alone two people—in a single night.

Theo kissed the back of her neck. "Good girl." He slid his hand out of her panties. "Stop playing and get over here, Galen. We've got to take care of our girl."

Chapter 4

Each step that Galen took ratcheted Meg's pulse higher, until spots danced along the edges of her vision.

"I feel like that when I watch him sometimes, too." Theo slid his hands up her arms and caught her elbows, arching her back, and offering her breasts to Galen. He kissed one of her shoulders and then the other. "It helps if you breathe."

But she couldn't draw in air. Not with Galen pulling his shirt over his head in a smooth movement, revealing a chest that would have been at home on a gladiator in ancient times. Muscles roped his frame, not a single inch missing the chance to be its best self. A sprinkling of dark hair dusted his chest, trailing down to disappear beneath the band of his jeans, broken only by a handful of angry scars.

He stopped in front of them and dragged his thumb over her bottom lip. "This mouth was made for one thing."

She caught his thumb between her teeth and bit him, just hard enough to get his attention. To prove that she wasn't helpless, that she wasn't here because they'd steamrolled her into it. She felt off-center and floaty and needy, all wrapped up into a desperate package—but she wasn't *weak*.

Meg lifted her chin and met his dark gaze. "Then do something about it."

There it was again. That thread of amusement that struck her right down to her core. She shifted, but Theo held her caged and spread. She rocked her ass back against his cock, desperate for him to lose control the same way she was on the verge of doing. For *someone* to lose control. But Galen just stood there, staring down at her with his mouth quirked in something that, on any other man, she'd call a smile. He released her mouth and shook his head. "You haven't earned my cock and you damn well know it."

Galen braced his hands on Theo's thighs. His knuckles dragged along her inner thighs, close enough to where she wanted him that she felt the air move against her exposed clit. Galen leaned down, his dark eyes intent, and Meg braced for the experience of being kissed by this intense man.

But he didn't kiss *her*.

He dragged his rough cheek against hers, and she twisted as best she could to watch him take Theo's mouth. Meg stared in shock as they kissed. No, calling it a kiss was too mundane by far. Galen and Theo came together like two titans clashing, like opposing forces of nature, where one had to submit or they would destroy each other.

Theo shifted his grip on her elbows to one hand and used his free hand to tangle his fingers in Galen's hair. He wrenched his head back, and Galen groaned softly. She felt that groan as intensely as if it had come from her throat instead of Galen's. Theo raked his teeth over his bottom lip as they parted. His blue eyes were darker than they'd been before, as if feeding off the lust and need filling every corner of the room. He ran his thumb over Galen's bottom lip, mirroring the move Galen had done to Meg. "You get his cock when I say you do, princess. Not before."

Through some unspoken agreement, they reversed positions. Theo released Meg's arms and Galen caught her wrists in a single hand before she had a chance to fully appreciate her freedom. He dropped onto the couch with Meg sprawled on his lap. She huffed out a breath. "I can move on my own, you know."

"We like moving you." Theo knelt between their spread thighs. "And you like being moved by us." He caught the band of her panties with his thumb. "Are you attached to these?"

Her words caught in her throat like live things, fumbling over themselves to vocalize whatever it took to take this thing with them to the next level. To satisfy the aching desire pulsing through every nerve in her body. She shook her head, mute from the need to say too much.

"Good." He ripped them off in a single move and tossed the ruined fabric aside. "Wider, Galen. I want to see all of her."

Galen responded, spreading his thighs and parting her legs further. Theo ran his thumbs up the dip where her thigh met her pussy, exploring her, his expression intense as if committing every bit of her hidden self to memory. He glanced at Galen, and that was all the other man needed to guide her hands down to the couch on either side of his hips. "Don't move." He spoke softly in her ear, as if too much volume would break through the spell Theo wove around them with his touch.

He wants his hands free, too.

Lust made her head spin. Meg nodded, drunk on their presence. "Okay."

There it was again, that quirk of his lips. "Good girl."

He ran his hands up her stomach and cupped her breasts as Theo dipped his head and dragged his tongue up her center.

Her body went hot and cold, tight and unfurled, all at the same time. She gripped the edge of the couch cushions with everything she had and bit her lip hard. It was only when Galen nudged her back to lean fully against his chest that she realized she was frozen in a half sit-up, waiting for Theo's next move. The man between her thighs chuckled, the sound vibrating across her skin to her clit. "Let Galen watch, princess. He lives for it."

Galen moved her hair to the side with one hand and dragged his mouth along the line of her shoulder up to her neck. His short beard prickled against her skin, which only made the slick slide of Theo's tongue even more of an intoxicating counterpoint.

Her brain couldn't handle the onslaught of sensation. Theo's hands gripping her thighs as his mouth worked her pussy. Galen playing with her nipples as he sucked on the pulse point in her neck. A sound came out of her mouth that she'd never heard before, a keening cry that was more animal than human.

"There you are," Galen murmured.

Theo speared her with two fingers, and then a third, spreading her almost painfully, the sensation completely at odds with the way he sucked her clit. He met her gaze and then looked over her shoulder, and she knew he and Galen were watching each other as Theo ate her pussy.

The realization sent her hurtling into an orgasm that blanked what few thoughts she had left in her head and bowed her back sharply enough that she would have toppled off Galen's lap if both men hadn't held her down. Words penetrated her pleasure, and Meg realized it was *her* speaking. "Oh shit, oh shit, oh my god, oh shit."

Theo brought her down gently. He gave her clit one last thorough suck and shifted to ever-widening circles. He nipped her thigh and sat back on his heels. "We've barely gotten started."

She blinked at him. "I don't know if I can survive more."

"You can take it." This from Galen. He reached down and cupped her pussy, his big fingers squeezing her ass in the process.

Theo snagged one of the condoms from the coffee table and tore it open. "Change your mind, princess?"

"Is that a trick question?" They'd just gotten her off harder than Meg had gotten off in…ever, probably. Like hell was she walking out of this apartment before she discovered the rest they had to give her. It was hard to keep her composure with her breath tearing itself from her lungs with each exhale, but she lifted her chin. "I want this."

"Good." He didn't take his gaze from her face as he unbuttoned his jeans.

Meg had no such self-control. She stared at his cock. *Holy shit.* She'd known he was big—he'd had the damn thing pressed into the curve of her ass like Galen's was right in that moment—but he was *big*. "Oh, fuck."

"That's the idea." Galen lifted her and turned her around as Theo caught her hips. She ended up with her hands braced on either side of Galen's neck on the back of the couch, her legs spread wide on the outside of his thighs, her breasts nearly in his face. Meg looked down the long line of his body to where his cock strained against the front of his jeans, but Galen touched a single finger to her chin and brought her face up. "Not yet."

Theo stroked a hand down her spine and gripped her hip as he guided his cock to her entrance. She tensed, part of her worried—hoping—he would slam his entire length home in a single shot. She should have known better. Theo held her too tightly for her to thrust back and teased her, pumping his cock into her an inch as a time.

Desperate, she writhed against him, her body undulating over Galen's. "More. Theo, *more*."

Galen caught her mouth with his. His tongue tangled with hers as Theo shoved into her to the hilt. Galen broke the kiss before she could fully sink into it, and he sat back with a satisfied smirk as Theo started fucking her.

Oh. My. God.

Theo drove into her again and again, drawing a sob from her lips with every stroke. Pleasure spiraled through her, drawn from his cock, pulled forth by the way Galen watched them both. She was so…so…*so* close.

Everything stopped.

Theo went still, buried as deep inside her as he could go. He kept one hand on her hip, holding her in place, and braced his other on the couch back. The new position pressed his chest to her back, and it should have made her feel caged and claustrophobic but…

Meg didn't feel anything but safe.

Galen moved, sliding down the couch to sit on the floor. *What is he…* "Oh fuck." He captured her hips, his hands partially overlapping where Theo held her, and then his mouth was on her. "Oh *god*.'"

"Not god, princess. Galen." Theo started moving again in long, slow thrusts that annihilated her ability to do anything but take the sensations they dealt her.

Galen never stopped his onslaught. There was nothing cold or restrained in the way his mouth moved over her pussy. He tongued her clit even as Theo fucked her, his fingers clasping her thighs hard enough that she hoped there would be bruises tomorrow. A physical token to prove this had actually happened. That it wasn't all some fever dream she'd wake up from in the morning and laugh about as she went about her normal life.

Meg clung to the back of the couch hard enough that her knuckles went white. The sight of Galen's dark head between her thighs, of knowing exactly how close his mouth was to Theo's cock... Her body went tight and she moaned.

Theo, damn him, seemed to understand perfectly. "Another time, it would be a stroke for your pussy, a stroke for his mouth." His dark chuckle rumbled against her neck. "You'd like that."

"Yes," she gasped. *Like* didn't begin to cover how that image made her feel. The pleasure they dealt her wound tighter and tighter, so acute it almost hurt.

Theo laced his fingers through Galen's hair again, holding his face to her clit. It was too much. What they were doing to her was too much. How could one person survive this much pleasure?

Meg's orgasm buckled her knees and drew a scream from her lips. It was only their hands on her that kept her on her feet, and even then, every bone in her body turned to liquid lightning. They held her in place as Theo kept fucking her, his strokes becoming wilder, less controlled. He came with a curse, and they both melted into a puddle on top of Galen.

She wasn't even sure how it happened. One second she was trying to figure out how to lock her knees to keep from collapsing, and the next her head was in Galen's lap and Theo was stretched out next to her between his friend's thighs. Meg opened her mouth to say...

There was nothing to say. Two orgasms—three if she counted Theo's—and even as a part of her purred in pure satisfaction, there was no mistaking the fact that this wasn't over yet.

That she didn't want it to be.

Theo climbed to his feet and disappeared down the hallway leading deeper into the apartment. A few minutes later, he walked back in, his jeans done up. He pulled her to her feet and pressed a quick kiss to her lips. "Hungry?"

Meg blinked, her mind scrambling to make the jump he obviously had. "Is that an innuendo?"

"I'm starving." He took her hand and pulled her along with him into the kitchen just off the living room. It was situated to maximize the view of the park and city, the bar overlooking the window and everything top of the line.

She stopped in the middle of the kitchen and watched as he dug through the fridge. For what felt like the millionth time that night, she couldn't shake the certainty that she'd tumbled into some alternate dimension. The feeling only became more pronounced as a soft weight settled over her shoulders. Meg looked down to find that Galen had draped a thick robe around her. She pulled it closed out of habit and was halfway through tying it before she registered that it smelled like sandalwood and spice.

Theo.

She shouldn't be able to tell the difference after such a short time, but she knew without a shadow of a doubt that she wore Theo's robe. Galen smelled like clove cigarillos, though there was no smoke in the mix, which made her think he'd just been handling them. *Former smoker.* She was sure of it.

Meg clutched the fabric closer to her throat, irritated at herself for finding comfort in something so meaningless as wearing a man's clothing. Even this man—these men.

Galen sat on the corner of the counter near the stove, where he could see the entire room—and the door—

without moving. He seemed to do that in every room, which reminded her of the special forces guys who came into her bar sometimes. She could always tell which of them were still enlisted and which had been out for long enough to successfully settle into civilian life. The ones still in the military moved the same way Galen did—as if expecting an attack at any moment. Even when they drank, there was an air of something about them that had even the most idiotic drunks keeping their distance.

He turned his head and met her gaze, as if daring her to speak what was on her mind. Meg crossed her arms over her chest. "Maybe…I should go."

"You don't actually want to go, so no point in playing the reluctant virgin card." Theo pulled a stack of Chinese takeout containers from the fridge and set them on the counter to inspect them. The words weren't harsh, exactly, but they stung all the same. He glanced at her, blue eyes devoid of the amusement she'd come to expect there.

The truth snaked through her to take up residence in her stomach. *It was all an act.* When she'd first met them, she'd assumed Galen was the ringleader. He was so intense and, even if he let Theo do the talking, his presence overwhelmed her with proximity alone. Theo had seemed safe by comparison. Normal, even, if she didn't think too hard about the fact they were obviously some kind of item.

Meg had been so, so wrong.

There was only one man in charge here, and it was the one currently holding out a container of fried rice as if in a dare. She licked her lips and took the container, because there was nothing else to do. She had no business being intrigued by these two beyond what they could give her physically, but being around them was like holding one of those Russian hatching dolls in her hand. Every time she thought she had their number down, a new layer would be revealed.

It's only been an hour or so. How many layers can they possibly reveal tonight?

There was no telling.

She stared at the food and finally set the white box aside. "What is this?"

"Chicken fried rice. Seemed a safe enough bet. Everyone likes chicken fried rice."

She rolled her eyes. "That's not what I meant, and you know it."

Galen hadn't bothered to put his shirt back on and every breath seemed to send a ripple through his muscles. "Theo is trying to give you a chance to process, princess." He snorted and leaned back against the cabinets. "We barely tested the waters and you were on the cusp of hyperventilating."

"It's called an orgasm, Galen. You should learn to recognize it," she snapped back. If there was one thing Meg couldn't stand, it was being handled. She'd dealt with that bullshit from the time she was a child, first after her father left, and then later whenever the subject of the unending bills arose with her mother. With her teachers sending pointed notes home about being properly fed and clothed, she'd learned to recognize what a furrowed brow or nervous hands meant.

Bad news was coming.

These men weren't delivering bad news, but they were treating her as if she was some idiot who didn't know what she'd signed up for when she left the club with them. She'd just come harder than she ever had before and, damn it, she wanted more.

She wanted what they'd promised her.

Meg took them in, from the guarded way Galen held

himself, able to spring into motion as the slightest provocation, to the carefully casual way Theo leaned against the counter as if he really was the least dangerous person in the room.

She took a step backward, and then another. Meg kept her expression contained, but she almost laughed at the disappointment that flickered through Theo's blue eyes. *Don't have my number down quite yet, do you?* She twisted to look behind her, taking in the single hallway that undoubtedly led to a bedroom—or more. The front door was in the same direction, which seemed to be where they expected her to go from the tension filtering into their bodies.

To leave.

"Theo. Galen." She waited for them to look at her and dropped the robe. Meg crooked her finger at them and tried to act like she was cool and collected and not about to bolt at the sheer hunger that flashed through their expressions. "Come and get me."

Chapter 5

Damn it, Galen liked her.

He slid off the counter and glanced over to find Theo watching him. They'd known each other so damn long, had gone through so much shit, he didn't have to hear his friend's words aloud to know what that look meant. "Shut up."

"Told you so."

"You didn't tell me shit." He started across the living room, heading in the direction he could hear Meg's footsteps as she fled. A quick touch to the front door confirmed it was still locked and secure. He hesitated, even though every instinct he had shouted for him to chase Meg, to bear her down to the floor, to fuck that sexy smirk right off her face.

It didn't matter what *he* wanted, though.

Not entirely.

"Go." Theo didn't raise his voice, but he didn't have to. Even without his public speaking training, Galen was so fucking attuned to him, he could pick up a whisper across the room if he concentrated. A necessary skill he'd developed over the years. Theo had a nasty habit of biting off more than he could chew because his eye was so focused on the game that he didn't acknowledge the threats rising up against him. He saw the big picture, and he was brilliant at putting all the pieces into place to get the end result he wanted.

If Galen had one skill set, it was keeping Theo safe.

Even from himself.

He turned and walked backward, pointing a finger in his friend's direction. "This is only for tonight."

"Mmmm." Theo smiled. "Guess we'll see, won't we?"

He could stand around and argue, but what was the point? They had tonight, and Galen would make damn sure it was enough. They'd left the club early enough that no one had paid them much attention, which meant no one should be able to connect them to Meg. She would wake up tomorrow with some good memories and he and Theo would move on. They'd got what they came to New York for, and it was just happy coincidence that they found Meg before they left.

It couldn't last.

For anyone's sake.

They were safe enough for now, and that was all that mattered. Theo had it right when he accused Galen of being too tightly wound. If he didn't let off some steam soon, he was going to start making mistakes.

The price of his mistakes was already too high.

He shoved the thought from his mind and turned to pick up his pace. Meg had reached the bedroom by now, and she'd have realized there was no escape. Against his better judgment, his heartbeat kicked up a notch and his adrenaline surged.

It was just a game, after all. Tonight was the only thing

in the last six months that didn't have deadly stakes and he'd be a fool not to enjoy it as much as he was able.

He stalked into the room and barely had time to brace before Meg threw herself at him. Galen caught her as she wrapped her legs around his waist and gave him a smug look. "I caught you."

"I was the one meant to catch you." He let his gaze drip over her full lips and down to her flushed chest, her full breasts tipped with pink nipples gone dark from both his and Theo's touch.

"Spoiler alert—you did." She tightened her thighs around him and tangled her fingers in his hair, the feeling twin to when Theo had done it earlier. And, damn her, she knew it. Meg leaned in and kissed his neck, his jaw, the sensitive spot beneath his ear. "The question is what you're going to do with me."

Fuck him, who *was* this woman?

Galen turned them and backed to the bed. He sat down and disentangled her. "That's not the question."

Meg seemed to sense the direction of his thoughts. She slipped to her knees, as graceful as a queen. He'd know. He'd seen more than one in his time. Galen pushed the thought away—just like he always did when memories of home threatened to intrude on his new reality. Meg brought him back with an open-mouthed kiss to his chest, working her way down his stomach. She paused just above the line of his jeans, her breath ghosting over the skin she'd just licked. It sent goosebumps rising in waves across his entire body and his cock hardened impossibly in response.

She looked up, her eyes an intoxicating green in the light of the bedroom. With her lipstick smeared from their mouths and her eye makeup smudged, she looked exactly like what she was—a sexy as hell woman who'd just been well-fucked.

Night's not over yet.

As if she could hear his thought, she licked her lips. "What's the question, Galen?"

Did Meg know the power of his name whispered in that throaty voice? If she didn't, he sure as fuck wasn't going to tell her. Galen braced on hand back on the bed and lifted his brows. "The question is what *you're* going to do to *me?*"

Meg unbuttoned his jeans with shaking hands, but there were no nerves in evidence on her face. Only eagerness. As if she couldn't control herself well enough to get his cock out because she could already taste him on her lips.

It was so sexy, he could barely stand it.

It only got better when Galen looked up to find Theo leaning against the bedroom door, watching them with the possessive look of a king surveying his kingdom. Galen gave his head a small shake. *No, Theo. This isn't for keeps.* It didn't matter what Theo thought, because they were leaving tomorrow. End of story. There was no space in their new life for any woman, let alone *this* woman. Even knowing her a few short hours, Galen knew that Meg would offer nothing but complications.

Pleasure beyond imagining, maybe, but it wasn't worth the trouble her presence would bring.

She stroked his cock, slamming him back into the present. Galen tore his gaze away from his friend as Meg licked him experimentally, as if savoring his taste. Her satisfied smile might as well have been a mule kick to the chest. Then there was no time for thinking because she sucked him deep, until he bumped the back of her throat.

And then she took him deeper yet.

His growl drew Theo. Galen sensed his approach even as he kept his attention on Meg. She closed her eyes as if the feeling of his cock in her mouth had her blissed out. That made two of them. He looped her long dark hair around his fist to keep it clear from her face and create an unobstructed view of his cock disappearing through her red, red lips.

"You're a vision, princess."

Galen glared at Theo. His friend knew damn well what he was doing with that nickname. From anyone else, it would be a charming endearment. From Theo, it was a declaration of intent. *Don't you fucking dare*, he mouthed.

Theo leaned down and took Galen's mouth. His kiss drowned out all Galen's common sense, just like it always did. It didn't matter how many mistakes they made or what bullshit landed in their lap from circumstances beyond their control. They always had *this*.

Theo broke the kiss and rested his forehead against Galen's. "Oh, I fucking dare, Galen."

That's what he was afraid of.

Meg barely had a chance to sink into her enjoyment of sucking Galen's cock before she felt Theo behind her. She tensed, waiting for him to slide inside her, but he just grabbed her around the hips and hauled her off Galen's cock and onto the massive bed. It was like landing on a cloud. She sat up, her protest dying on her lips at the sight of both men stripping out of their jeans.

Oh.

Oh.

Galen's scars descended down his hips and over his thighs, breaking up the dark hair dusting there. His cock glistened from her mouth, and her whole body went tight at the sight of him fully revealed.

Theo slid off his jeans in the same casual way he seemed to do everything. A man sure of his place in the world, and at ease as a result. His body was leaner than Galen's, more a slicing sword than a blunt war hammer, but no less carved from muscle. Even having had his cock inside her, she still shivered at the sight. He was freaking massive.

They were both freaking massive.

They moved toward her as one, climbing onto the bed, and she let loose a nervous laugh. "It's like being in a candy shop and having to choose my favorite flavor."

"That's the beauty, princess." Theo stopped in front of her on his knees and urged her up to kiss him. "You get two favorites tonight," he murmured against her lips. He kissed her as Galen moved up to her back, mirroring the position they'd held while dancing.

Except nothing stood between them now.

There were no witnesses to watch Galen cup her ass and slide his big hand down to spear her from behind with two fingers. Or to see Theo use his tangled hold on her hair to guide her to kiss first him and then Galen. Or to view her take each man's cock in her hand and stroke them.

Meg was a lifeboat caught between a raging sea and a hurricane. On their own, Galen and Theo were larger than life. Together... Together, she didn't have words. They overwhelmed her even as they kept her grounded. Her entire existence narrowed down to their hands on her body and their mouths taking turns claiming hers. To the orgasm even now threatening.

Not yet.

I'm not ready for this to end.

Theo guided her to her hands and knees in front of him, her ass pressing against Galen. She reached for his cock, but he held her still with his grip on her hair. "Not yet."

Galen's weight behind her disappeared, and she heard the sound of a condom ripping open. Meg's heart thundered in her chest, her breath sawing through her throat with anticipation. It was happening. She looked up Theo's body, momentarily stunned by the possessive way he watched her. As if he owned her, body and soul.

In that moment, it might even have been the truth.

He used his free hand to stroke a thumb over her cheekbone and down to her lips. "Another night, I'd take your ass while he took your pussy. And the next time we'd switch. We'd both claim you in every way possible."

She shivered. "Why not tonight?"

He didn't answer, and she didn't get a chance to ask again. Galen returned to his position behind her and urged her legs further apart. She had to brace both hands on the bed to keep from tumbling face-first into the mattress. Theo wrapped a fist around his cock and gave it a rough stroke. "Open."

As if there was any other option.

There had only been one outcome from the second she agreed to come home with them, and every moment of the night since had been leading to this moment, to having both of them inside her.

She took Theo's cock into her mouth as Galen's slid into her pussy. Both men moved slowly, testing her, and she could do nothing but take what they chose to give. With Galen's rough hands on her hips and his cock filling her impossibly full, and Theo damn near cutting off her ability to breathe…

Panic flared.

Theo's grip was harsh in her hair even as he stroked

her face gently with his free hand. "Relax, princess. Take what we have to give."

They held perfectly still as she fought to obey. Meg took in a long inhale through her nose, and then another. She could do this. She *wanted* to do this. On her next exhale, she gave herself over to them. Her body relaxed inch by inch and a slow, glorious languor spread through her. Pleasure overtook her need to be in control, and she gave Theo's cock a hard suck to convey that she was ready.

"Good girl." He withdrew and thrust slowly into her mouth, Galen mirroring his movements between her legs. Letting her get accustomed to being overwhelmed so completely.

Then Galen slid his hand from her hip to her clit. He stroked her with his fingers the same way he'd done with his tongue. Her body flashed white hot and she moaned around Theo's cock. They picked up their pace, fucking her closer and closer to the edge of the abyss. She reached up and gripped Theo's thighs to steady herself. His muscles flexed beneath her grip and Galen's hands spasmed on her hip and clit, and she knew without a shadow of a doubt that they were kissing above her back while buried deep inside her.

As she pictured that, pictured herself between them as if watching it from across the room… it was too much.

Meg came screaming around Theo and Galen's cocks.

Just like that, whatever little control they'd displayed snapped. Galen drove into her again and again, his curses filling the room. Theo was more careful, but only barely. He fucked her mouth even as he wiped the tears from her eyes with his thumbs. The blend of harsh and caring, rough and gentle, shoved Meg under again. She sobbed as she orgasmed. She wasn't sure she believed in a god, but she tasted heaven in Theo and Galen's touch.

The men came within seconds of each other, each one half of a coordinated dance that had been going on long before they met Meg tonight.

Theo pulled out of her mouth and urged her up to claim a kiss. He stroked her hair away from her face. "If you could see yourself right now, princess." He kissed her again and flopped onto his back, tugging her and Galen down with him.

They ended up in something resembling a pile. Galen's breath was harsh on the back of her neck, his big thigh pressing against her throbbing pussy, his arm draped over Theo's stomach just below where hers was. She lay with her head on Theo's shoulder, her leg hitched up and over his hip.

Perfection.

Meg let her eyes close and concentrated on relearning how to breathe. That had been… She didn't know how to put it into words. *It's good it's only tonight. I couldn't experience this more than once without losing myself completely.* That was one thing she could never do. It felt too wonderful to give herself over to them. Too good to submit.

Meg didn't submit to *anyone*. Not indefinitely.

She shivered, and both men shifted closer, eliminating what little space there had been between them. It felt wonderful. Even more terrifying, it felt *right*.

"I'd like to see you again."

Meg tensed, distantly aware that Galen also went rigid behind her. She didn't open her eyes—to do so was to break the spell they'd created in this room. "You said you're leaving town."

"We are," Galen growled.

"Yeah, we are." Theo stroked a hand down her arm and back up Galen's. "But we'll be back in a few weeks. Let us take you out on a proper date, Meg."

The use of her real name, rather than the pet name he'd lavished on her all night, let her know exactly how serious Theo was. Just like she knew exactly how unhappy Galen was with this unexpected twist from the way he didn't seem to breathe behind her. Not from anticipation. No, nothing so simple as that would turn him from the languid man who'd just enjoyed a good time back into a predator. He might as well have put up a neon sign screaming "No!"

Reluctantly, she opened her eyes and lifted her head. "It would never work."

"It's dinner." Theo didn't smile, his blue eyes serious. "No harm ever came from dinner."

"I can list half a dozen examples that prove that *plenty* of harm can come from dinner." She should move, should put some distance between them so she could think clearly, but Meg wasn't willing to come back down to earth yet.

Galen growled against the back of her neck. "It won't work. Once Theo has his mind set on something, he'll see it through and to hell with the consequences."

"Taking me out to dinner is hardly the end of the world." She cursed herself as soon as the words were out of her mouth. Damn it, she was supposed to be putting a solid stop sign at the end of this night and leaving it as a fond memory—not letting Galen bait her into agreeing to it.

But he only laughed harshly. "It might be for you."

"Galen, enough."

"One night, Theo. You promised *one night*. Don't go back on your word now."

They aren't talking about me. Or they are, *but this has nothing to do with me.*

Meg eyed the door, but there was no getting out of this bed with any mount of stealth or grace. "It's a moot point what Theo does or does not want. *You* couldn't be clearer that you're not interested in dinner, and *I* already said no." She poked Theo's chest. "You're outvoted."

"That's not how it works."

"That's exactly how it works." She shifted, but they made no move to back away. Meg sighed. "Now, either you can hold off arguing until morning or you can keep fighting while I get dressed and catch a cab home." She lifted her head to look around, but there didn't seem to be a clock in the room. "What time is it, anyways?"

"Don't worry about it." This from Galen. Apparently he'd decided to shelve his fury for the moment, too, because instead of curses against her skin, he pressed a thorough open-mouthed kiss against the sensitive spot at the top of her spine. "It's not morning yet."

Her eyes slid shut without her brain giving the command. It took Meg two tries to get the words out. "I… You can't possibly be ready again."

"One night is all we have. You can be damn sure we're going to get our fill." It sounded more like a threat than a reassurance, but she couldn't bring herself to care. Meg relaxed back into his body, bending her head forward to give him better access to her neck.

Theo sighed. "Make no mistake—we *will* be revisiting the topic in the morning."

Meg grabbed the hand Galen had on her hip and guided it between her thighs. "What did he say?" she murmured, a small smile on her lips. What he was doing felt good, but it felt even better to put Theo in his place. He might think he could steamroll right over her—over them—but he *was* outvoted, and she had no intention of letting him have his way.

"No idea." Galen nipped her neck and then soothed the spot with his tongue. "I was too busy taking full advantage of having you in my bed to worry about his grand plans."

Theo growled. "Point taken." He shoved Galen's hand from her pussy and slid down to settle between her thighs. "You two win—this time."

Chapter 6

Meg woke up alone. She stretched, enjoying the way the expensive sheets felt against her naked body and smiled. *Holy crap, that really happened.* Even if she wasn't waking up in a strange bed, her memories of the night were played out in delicious aches and pains on her body. She sat up and pushed her hair back from her face. A quick look around the room found her dress, her shoes, and her purse laid out on a chair across from the bed. After a quick detour to the massive bathroom off the bedroom, she pulled the dress on.

The apartment was eerily quiet, and Meg smothered the disappointment threatening to sour her stomach. She signed on for one night. Better that neither Theo or Galen had stuck around for awkward morning-after conversations. Obviously Theo had reconsidered his determination to take her out to dinner, which was just as well.

Meg didn't have time to date, let alone to enter into a complicated relationship already in existence. If Theo and Galen weren't *together*-together, they were still more than friends. Being third to anyone, let alone these two, was out of the question. Fun for a night? Hell yes. Fun for weeks or months or, god forbid, *years?* No way.

The only thing she could handle right now—in between school and her job—was to focus on getting the money she needed to pay for her last year of college to finish out her degree. That was it. As things stood now, she was going to have to try to get another job this summer— or two—just to close the gap between her current bank account and the money the school needed to keep her enrolled. Nowhere in her insane schedule was there time for anyone else.

Really, she barely had time for *herself.*

She checked her phone—it was noon, which gave her plenty of time to get home, heat up some ramen, and get to work on time—and slipped her purse over her shoulder. After a quick consideration, she hooked her fingers through her shoes instead of putting them on.

Meg reached the bedroom door and paused. Was she really going to sneak out like a thief after last night? Awkward morning-after conversations or not, she should at least say goodbye to the guys. Last night had been beyond fun, and souring it with her cowardice was a shitty thing to do.

She headed back to the nightstand and pulled the top drawer open. There were the usual knickknacks and random shit in it, but nestled near the bottom was a small pad of paper and a marker. Before she could talk herself out of it, Meg scrawled her number across the first page and ripped it out. She folded it in half and set it on top of the pillow.

If they call—and that's a big if—it doesn't mean I have to answer.

Satisfied she'd left things on the right note, so to speak, she slipped out of the bedroom and padded down the hallway. Voices stopped her before she made it halfway to the door. Theo and Galen spoke softly, but the volume didn't detract from the intensity of the conversation.

She should just leave.

Nothing good ever came from eavesdropping.

Meg shifted her shoes to her other hand and crept closer to the mostly-closed door. Through the crack, she could see a desk and computer. *The office.* She frowned and focused on what the men were arguing about.

"I swear I will knock you fucking senseless and throw you in a trunk before I let you endanger yourself because you're thinking with your cock instead of your head."

Movement through the small slice of the room she could see. Theo dropped into the office chair, putting his profile in her view. Unlike last night when he'd been dressed casually, this morning he wore a suit that fit as if it had been made for him. *Expensive. Really expensive.*

Meg knew they had money, of course. Someone didn't live in an apartment overlooking Central Park without some serious heft to their bank account. But that suit drove reality right through her post-coital bliss.

They were from different worlds.

Whatever issues he and Galen had—were currently having—he wasn't going without. He wasn't hungry and worried about where his next meal would come from. He wasn't working sixty hours a week and going to school another twenty just to get by.

Theo crossed his arms over his chest. "No one is coming for us, Galen. If they were, it would have happened months ago, before I left Thalania in the first place. Phillip's grip might be absolute in our country, but it's sure as fuck not as far-reaching as you seem to think."

"I'm not worried about his *reach*." Galen cursed long and hard, sounded like he wanted nothing more than to throttle his friend. "As long as you're alive, you're a threat. You know that, so stop acting like you don't. He might be willing to play nice until Edward gets on the throne, but the second they put the crown on your brother's head, it's over. He'll send one of his people to dispose of you quietly and you'll become just another unsolved legend. The missing prince of Thalania."

The missing prince of Thalania.

Meg sagged against the wall, her mouth moving as she tried to draw in breath. She knew about Thalania. *Everyone* knew about Thalania—even people who didn't spend their entire life filling a world map with pins for the places they wanted to escape to.

The tiny little kingdom was nestled in eastern Europe and had the good fortune of never having been conquered by its powerhouse neighbors. From the way the media talked about it when it came up, one would think it was a land of milk and honey. A paradise that supported itself from within and kept strict trading alliances with a handful of other countries. One still ruled by a royal family that could trace its lineage back to the country's founding.

Theo…

Meg rubbed her chest. *Oh my god*. If Theo was the man Galen seemed to be indicating, he was none other than Theodore Fitzcharles III. Former crown prince of Thalania.

I have to get out of here.

It was one thing to play at the idea of having an affair with a pair of rich men who seemed to come and go from the city as they pleased. It was entirely another to dabble with royalty—even former royalty. It was sheer dumb luck that there hadn't been a horde of press haunting the club last night to see her leave with them. The *last* thing she needed was her name attached that kind of dumpster fire.

The party boy prince who had somehow managed to lose his throne and devastate his country in the process.

Meg didn't have the details—Thalania was on her list of places she wanted to go someday, but it wasn't *high* on the list—but even she knew that he'd been banished in disgrace. Knowing what she did about the atrocities committed by people with that kind of power and money, she wasn't interested in finding out what Theo had done to earn his punishment.

She had to leave, and she had to leave now.

She hesitated, casting a look back at the bedroom where her number lay on the pillow, about as innocent as a bomb ready to go off on her haphazardly balanced life. *I'll change my number if he can't take a hint. That's easier than walking back into that bedroom.*

With one last peek through the gap in the door, she traced Theo's profile with her gaze. He really was beautiful in the way of fallen angels. But a fallen angel was just a prettier name for a demon, and Meg had more than her fair share of demons in her life already. She couldn't afford another one—another *two.*

No matter how wonderful it felt when they made her come.

She touched the door, a silent goodbye, and walked down the hallway and out the front door. It hurt. Even though she knew it was the right call, her chest felt tight and her stomach twisted itself in knots. Meg slipped her heels on and took the elevator down to the main floor. By the time the doors opened, she had herself together. Whatever path Theo and Galen were on, she wished them the best—but they would damn well continue on without her. One night was all that was promised, and one night had been more than fulfilled.

She'd miss them, though.

After spending a night in bed with a prince and his bodyguard, how could a normal guy compare?

⎯⎯

Theo exhaled the second he heard the front door shut softly behind Meg. "She's gone. Are you fucking happy?"

Galen stalked to the computer and pulled up the security cameras of the building. They had access by virtue of owning the penthouse suite. They watched in silence as she took the elevator down and walked out through the lobby with her head held high. Theo didn't relax until she hailed a cab and slipped into the backseat.

For all his attempting to convince Galen that the danger wasn't actively pointed in their direction, Theo had no intention of playing fast and loose with the lives of people around him. Just because he was more or less untouchable for the next year didn't mean his monster of an uncle wouldn't paint a target on anyone Phillip decided had come to matter too much to Theo.

One night shouldn't be enough to gain his uncle's attention.

More most definitely would, no matter how careful they were.

"You're right." He cursed. "Is that what you wanted to hear? You're fucking right."

Galen watched him with an unreadable look on his face. At least, it would be unreadable to anyone else. His displeasure was there in the tightness of his jaw and the steely expression in his dark eyes. "I liked her, too, Theo."

That admission deflated the last of his anger. He wasn't really pissed at Galen. The entire situation was beyond fucked, and it wasn't unfucking itself anytime soon. Right now, his options numbered at two—run or hide. Neither sat well with Theo. He preferred to meet his problems head-on and deal with them permanently.

It wasn't in the cards this time.

Not with his two younger half-siblings in the mix. Their uncle wouldn't hurt Edward. He needed an heir to sit on the throne and, even if he could dispose of Theo easily enough, taking out all three of the Fitzcharles siblings would raise suspicion.

But their little sister Camilla didn't have the same protection.

And in a year, neither would Theo.

He pinched the bridge of his nose. Last night had been a revelation in a way he wasn't prepared to deal with. He and Galen had shared women before, but that was *before*. Before their lives were turned upside-down and shaken until they were unrecognizable. Back then, it had been all fun and games and bullshit.

Meg hadn't known who he and Galen were. She hadn't recognized him, hadn't made the connection between Theo and Theodore Fitzcharles III.

It felt good to just be Theo.

It felt like maybe he might be able to make a life with the ashes of everything he'd ever known burning down around him.

Galen was right, though. To indulge himself—to indulge both of them—with Meg was to endanger her. Theo might be a bastard, but he wouldn't drag an innocent woman under with him just because she made him feel good. Whatever problems Meg faced were of a much more mundane nature than princes and crowns and assassins in the night. He wouldn't change that, not for anything.

He let his hand drop. "We need to get moving."

"Yeah." Galen pushed away from the computer and

headed for the door. "I'll get the bags." He hesitated in the doorway. "We'll find a way through this, Theo. I won't let the bastard win. Not again."

Theo nodded. There was nothing else to do. They had an impossible battle in front of them, and there was no way to get through it without casualties. Meg wouldn't be one of them, and that had to be enough for him.

He didn't want it to be.

Theo headed back into the bedroom. He stopped just inside the door and stared at the bed, memories from last night imposing themselves over the white sheets. Meg's moans, her cocky smile, her laughter.

Damn it, Galen, I like her, too.

Even if his didn't have a country-load of baggage he was carting around, Meg had made her preferences pretty damn clear when she snuck out without saying goodbye. Maybe he'd pushed too hard about having dinner, but Theo didn't believe in playing games when he saw something he wanted.

He wanted Meg.

They both did.

He started to turn for the door and paused at the sight of a folded piece of paper on the pillow. He crossed the distance in two large steps and picked it up. A number scrawled across the paper, written in the pen he kept in the nightstand.

An invitation.

A slow smile drew his lips up. So she hadn't wanted to leave the door fully closed on a possible future dinner… and more. Theo slipped the paper into his pocket and took one last look around the room. Regardless of what he wanted when it came to Meg, they had to leave the city for a few weeks while they ran down one of Galen's seemingly endless leads. One of them would carve a path home. It had to.

But when they got back to the city…

Theo ran his thumb over the folds of the paper. An honorable man would leave Meg alone. He'd take last night for what it was and move on with his life. He wouldn't call her, and he sure as fuck wouldn't see her again.

Theo turned for the door. Maybe he really *was* that much of a bastard after all, because he had no intention of leaving Meg alone. He'd handle the danger for both of them—for all three of them.

"Game on, princess."

Coming Soon!

Want a looking into what happens now that Theo has taken the crown and named both Meg and Galen as his Consorts?

THEIRS EVER AFTER will be available Winter 2018!

Afterword

Thank you so much for reading FOREVER THEIRS. This book is particularly close to my heart because it was so damn fun to write. I hope you enjoyed the ride!

If you loved the book, please consider leaving a review on your site of choice. Every review makes a difference!

Acknowledgments

Thank you forever and always to my readers. This series wouldn't have been possibly without your enthusiasm and your willingness to go on this journey with me.

Thank you to Eagle at Aquila Editing. Your notes and insight helped make this book it's best version, and it was a joy to work with you.

Special thanks to Andie J. Christopher for being my first reader on this book. I'm sorry (not in the least sorry) that you lost sleep!

All my love and thanks to Tim for being my pillar during a particularly interesting year, and for not giving me *too* much side-eye about all the threesome photos on my phone. It's RESEARCH, babe. Kisses!

About the Author

New York Times and USA TODAY bestselling author Katee Robert learned to tell her stories at her grandpa's knee. Her 2015 title, The Marriage Contract, was a RITA finalist, and RT Book Reviews named it 'a compulsively readable book with just the right amount of suspense and tension." When not writing sexy contemporary and romantic suspense, she spends her time playing imaginary games with her children, driving her husband batty with what-if questions, and planning for the inevitable zombie apocalypse.

Website: www.kateerobert.com

The Marriage Contract

New York Times and USA Today bestselling author Katee Robert begins a smoking-hot new series about the O'Malley family—wealthy, powerful, dangerous, and seething with scandal.

Teague O'Malley hates pretty much everything associated with his family's name. And when his father orders him to marry Callista Sheridan to create a "business" alliance, Teague's ready to tell his dad exactly where he can stuff his millions. But then Teague actually meets his new fiancée, sees the bruises on her neck and the fight still left in her big blue eyes, and he decides he will do everything in his power to protect her.

Everyone knows the O'Malleys have a dangerous reputation. But Callie wasn't aware of just what that meant until she saw Teague, the embodiment of lethal grace and coiled power. His slightest touch sizzles through her. The closer they get, though, the more trouble they're in. Because Callie's keeping a dark secret—and what Teague doesn't know could get him killed.

Available Now!

9 780998 840291